DEVIL EYE

A Penny Larkin Thriller

Rebecca Jean Downey

Devil Eye

Copyright © 2025 by Rebecca Jean Downey. All rights reserved.

Published in the United States of America
1. Fiction / General
2. Fiction / Thrillers / General 13.12.04

ISBN: 979-8-9926031-3-2-5

Imprint: ISBN: 979-8-9926031-2-5

DEDICATION

This work of fiction is dedicated to the people of Mexico, whose reality sometimes means facing a day of uncertainty. Their courage and love of family are tremendous sources of encouragement in times of terror inflicted by the *devil eye*.

ACKNOWLEDGMENTS

I would like to express my appreciation to author Nancy Hamilton for her proofreading and editorial assistance. And I would also like to thank my cousin David Collings and his friend, Mari Bottom in Miami, for their editorial expertise and their encouragement and enthusiasm for this project. My knowledge of guns comes from the help of Steve Vines and my husband, Mike Downey. And it goes without saying that once again Frank Muňoz and his wife, Timi, were so helpful in Spanish translations and grammar.

INTRODUCTION

The first documented era of gun smuggling along the US-Mexico border occurred in 1915, when President Woodrow Wilson refused to sell any more weapons and ammunition to Mexican rebel Pancho Villa. The people of Mexico were emerging from the thirty-one-year dictatorship of Porfirio Diaz and confronting the growing dominance of wealthy hacienda owners who were buying as much land as they could from smaller farmers in order to control the price of sugar cane for rum and rice. Historians estimate that two million people may have died in Mexico from 1910 to 1917 as rival rebels and warlords fought each other. In response to the victimization of the Mexican people, José Doroteo Arango Arámbula—nicknamed Pancho Villa—seized land for redistribution to peasants and soldiers. He quickly gained the allegiance of the Mexican people. Villa lost President Wilson's favor after the massacre of fourteen thousand of Villa's soldiers in the Battle of Celaya, in the Mexican state of Guanajuato, against warring rebel Venustiano Carranza. President Wilson shifted his support to Carranza and forced Pancho Villa to rely on contraband and corrupt gun dealers in the United States for his supplies. Wilson's decision to secretly send guns and ammunition to Pancho Villa and then to Carranza could be construed by some as the forerunner of modern-day government sanctioned gunrunning operations.

In retaliation for President Wilson's decision and for other reasons still unclear to historians, Villa and five hundred of his soldiers attacked the town of Columbus, New Mexico, on March 9, 1916. When the gun smoke cleared, half of Villa's men were killed or wounded and eighteen Americans were dead. Enraged by Villa's audacity, President Wilson ordered General John J. "Black Jack" Pershing to Columbus with ten thousand soldiers in order to pursue Villa into Mexico. Pershing's eleven-month hunt for Villa failed, but Camp Furlong in Columbus became the staging area for our nation's first mechanized and armored vehicles. Soldiers rode motorcycles mounted with machine guns and flew airplanes equipped with grenades. In fact the entire United States eight-plane squadron was stationed at Camp Furlong for a time. In total, more than twenty thousand soldiers gained invaluable experience in combat conditions in Columbus, helping to prepare the US military for World War I.

Today the population of Columbus, New Mexico, has dwindled to about 1,700 people, but the movement of drugs, weapons, and ammunition still continues to impact the town. In 2011, the mayor, the police chief, and a village trustee were arrested for gun trafficking, bringing an unwanted national spotlight on this small community.

The two-thousand-mile southern border of the United States remains a red zone of dispute in American political spheres, and on more than two hundred occasions since Villa's raid, the Mexican Army or the Mexican Navy have crossed into the United States, either to allegedly protect drug or gun traffickers entering or exiting the United States or to undertake reconnaissance missions for reasons that still remain unknown.

Devil Eye is loosely based on real events about gun trafficking but in no way insinuates that anyone in Columbus, New Mexico, or Luna County and currently serving in an official capacity as a law officer or city leader is involved in gun trafficking or illegal activities of any kind.

PROLOGUE

At the turn of the twentieth century, Columbus, New Mexico, just a mile north of the Mexican border, was a speck of dust in the eyes of pioneers looking for a place to set down roots. Most wagon trains headed for greener pastures, but a handful of hearty souls stayed and carved out a living as ranchers, cowboys, and storekeepers. Today the town has become a haven for campers, hikers, birders, photographers, and artists who want to experience the northern Chihuahua Desert without distraction. The sun's lens is full open most days, focused on the unending dome of blue sky and the escapades of the red-tailed hawk, whose *devil eye* is always on the hunt for the unsuspecting rabbit, squirrel, or prairie dog.

What other dungeon is so dark as one's own heart?
What jailer so inexorable as one's self?
—Nathaniel Hawthorne

CHAPTER 1

Penny Larkin shoved her way through the overgrowth of pigweed whose brittle stems were jutting out of the desert floor like knives. They snapped in pieces as she passed them, piercing her jeans and cutting into her skin. It was almost noon, and wearing blue jeans in the New Mexico desert had been a bad idea. Her entire body felt like it was in a sweat lodge, and she was sure her legs were bleeding. Perspiration congregated in the band of her wide-brim hat and under her arms and kneecaps. The sweat was also trickling down her calves and into her leather boots, making her feet itch. The relentless rays were defeating her sunglasses too—all but blinding her.

She had to keep moving. Penny had been given an urgent assignment by the US Marshals Service to locate Juan Rico, a suspected gun trafficker, before he did any more business with a Mexican drug cartel. A mole inside the cartel reported the exchange of cash for guns was imminent. Since federal agents had completely lost track of Rico and time was running out, Marshal Eugene Lujan, the head of the Western District in El Paso, Texas, had asked Penny to join his team of expert trackers.

It was just six months ago that Penny had garnered acclaim as a remote viewer working with the El Paso County Sheriff's Office. Together with Sheriff Leo Tellez, she had helped discover and dismantle an international child-trafficking ring. Since then Penny had received two job offers from federal law enforcement agencies, US Immigration and Customs Enforcement and the US Marshals Service. The choice was easy—the marshal paid more money.

Remote viewers study targets such as photographs, videos, maps, and even clothing to generate a mental picture of where a missing person might be. Penny had retrieved a photograph of Juan from Rico's wife, Alicia, who lived fifty miles away in Lordsburg with her parents and two daughters, Nancy and Paula. Luckily, the photo had been good enough to set her viewing skills into action. In her mind, Penny had seen the ranch, where she now stood, and had asked Juan's wife to give her the location. This information led her to this eighty-acre property near Columbus, New Mexico. Juan's wife insisted it would yield no clues to her husband's whereabouts, and Penny was starting to agree with her. The land was probably only inhabited by coyotes and an occasional rattlesnake. The more she thought about it, she had been foolish to go here alone.

Penny was disgusted with what looked like a dead end. She would return to her car and consider where to go next. She made a U-turn and hurried toward the refrigerated air of her new red Mustang. About fifty yards from the road, she caught the toe of her boot in the spokes of an old tractor wheel—hidden in the underbrush—and tumbled onto the ground. The spines of a *jumping cholla* snagged her bottom lip, burrowing into her face like tiny, unrelenting fish hooks. The jumping cholla cactus, the jellyfish of the Southwestern desert, felt like match sticks bursting into flames. Penny's fingers grasped the prickly ball and yanked it out, spilling blood onto her hands. The cactus now clung to her fingers. Her lips were still on fire, but they didn't hurt as much as her pride. *How in the world did I do something so stupid?*

She spit the sand out of her mouth and shook her hand until the piece of cactus fell to the ground. Penny tried to stand but could not. Her right foot was trapped between two of the wheel's steel rods. She could not pull free without removing her boot, which reached halfway up her calf. Her predicament did nothing for her foul mood. It was Penny's fifth assignment for the marshal, and things had yet to go well, at least in Penny's eyes. She had located the last two suspects easily enough, but while calling for backup, they had ganged up on her, and she had to run for her life. Two US drug enforcement agents, who had been on a stakeout nearby, came to her rescue. This was an embarrassing fiasco, and it certainly didn't earn her any points with the federal agencies she wanted to impress. She had high hopes of locating Rico and redeeming herself, but it didn't look good.

Even though he was a small fish in the big pond of sharks, the marshals service wanted to bring Juan Rico in and use the gift of immunity to convince him to give up his cartel contacts. All Penny had to do was locate him and call one of her teammates to move in for an arrest. It sounded easy enough, but Penny was learning that tracking federal fugitives was never a simple job. And now she was a victim of her own carelessness. She wiped her sweaty forehead with her shirtsleeve.

The noonday sun pressed against her shoulders like a flat iron. In a matter of minutes, her fair complexion would burn without protection, and within the hour, she would feel the effects of dehydration. She remembered her car's thermometer had registered well over one hundred degrees before she had ventured out onto this desolate piece of land. Why had she thought she could find clues to Rico's whereabouts here? The ranch looked abandoned except for scattered pieces of trash and old clothing, which Penny guessed had been discarded by people crossing the border from Mexico, just a mile to the south.

Penny longed for the bottle of water in the console. She swallowed hard. The back of her throat ached. She found her broad-rim hat crumpled under her legs and managed to pull it free and jerk it down over her ears. She looked around and realized no one was going to come along any time soon. There hadn't been a car up or down the gravel road since she arrived fifteen minutes ago. Penny exhaled and sucked in a breath of hot air, which stung the insides of her nose. Perspiration trickled down her face and into her ears. She had no choice but to remove her boot, which would not be easy. She hoped she didn't ruin her brand-new pair of ropers in the process. She stuffed her left hand inside the back of her boot and cupped the palm of her right around the ankle of her sock and tugged. No luck!

She took another scorching breath, and this time, it left a burning sensation in her chest. She coughed and wiped her hand on her jeans. Penny reached for the boot heel but could touch it only with her fingertips. She was able to get a better grip by using her other hand to grab the welt, along the back of the roper.

All the commotion had stirred the interest of a wheat-colored scorpion. It scampered onto the vamp of her boot, and Penny jerked her hands back, waiting for him to move on. He did not. She grabbed a small stick lying nearby and knocked him off her boot. He was not alone! There were little babies squirming beneath Penny's legs. This was not a *he* but a *she*.

"I have all the luck!"

Penny forgot about the searing sun. She recognized the scorpion as a venomous and often deadly bark scorpion. She pulled as hard as she could on the backside of her boot and finally yanked her white stockinged foot free.

Liberated from the metal rods and the scorpions, she limped as fast as she could through the sand and rocks toward her car, watching carefully where she placed her right foot, protected only by her sock. She did not stop, even when a thorn pierced the skin of her big toe. Upon arriving at her car, Penny drank from the bottle of lukewarm water, but it gagged her, and she spit the water on to the ground. She would have to stop somewhere on her way home to El Paso for something cold—something with lots of ice.

In the trunk, Penny found a pair of running shoes. She removed the thorn from her toe and pulled the shoes on without even unlacing them. She also retrieved a narrow aluminum rod she had just purchased at the hardware store to stake her tomato plants and walked back to the old wheel. She forced the end of the rod through the loop of her boot and began yanking as hard as she could. The boot flew out from between the spokes and whacked her on the forehead. She fell backward, this time bruising her right hand on a rock while trying to break her fall.

Penny drove a gust of hot air out of her lungs. She wanted nothing more than to get in her car and blow the dust off on the way back to El Paso, but gut instinct told her not to leave just yet. Besides, Marshal Lujan had begged her not to come back to El Paso without a real lead. He was that worried. Penny wanted to keep her lucrative new job, so she decided to move further into the property, searching for a clue to Rico's location.

According to Lujan, Juan Rico had not been seen for two months even though there were rumblings across the border that he was actively gathering firearms through straw sales. When gun storeowners in the region reported these suspected straw sales, agents from Alcohol Tobacco and Firearms had told the storeowners to go ahead and make the sales. ATF promised it would follow up and return their guns once the suspect was apprehended. There had also been a burglary at the gun store in Lordsburg, which the marshal's office figured was Rico's doing, but nothing was for sure.

Lujan had received a tip that Rico might have sold guns to the Chihuahua drug cartel before. This information had been enough to convince a Federal Grand Jury to issue a warrant for his arrest. Tip or not, Penny just followed orders.

Penny ran her fingers over the photograph again. The snapshot Rico's wife had given her showed Rico standing in a kitchen holding a small child in his arms. His smile belied any cares he might have or thoughts of a life of crime. He didn't look like a gun trafficker. He looked like an innocent twenty-year-old who was much too young to be a father. His dark hair was wet and matted against his head, as if he had just taken off his hat.

She flicked on her phone to confirm her fears: she had no service. She searched the horizon for a cell tower. Nothing! If Penny did find Rico way out here, she would not be able to call for help. She would have to reel him in by herself. Penny did have a gun in her car that Leo had given her, but she had only used it once, six months ago, with terrible consequences. A bad man was dead, but it gave her no solace. Killing is killing.

A red-tailed hawk circled overhead, making Penny uneasy. His flashy orange and brown feathers flared like the rays of the sun as he beat his wings against the blue sky. In a split second, the hawk made a sharp right turn and dove straight at her. Penny knelt down and covered her face with her arms. The predator released an agonizing scream as he landed a few feet away. His perilous claws impaled a jackrabbit hiding in the brush. He shook the animal, perhaps to break his neck. Then the hawk spread his wings. They were almost five feet wide!

Penny's entire body shook as she waited for the bird to leave. She lifted her head to see why he was still hanging around. The hawk was staring at her! His eyes were as red as the devil's, and they were locked on her face like the laser beam on a gun site. She inhaled the musky scent of the raptor's wings as they pounded the ground. His shrill voice shrieked out a warning. Don't touch this! *It is all mine!*

Penny jumped to her feet and ran as fast as she could, deeper into the property and away from the angry hawk. She was breathless and woefully out of shape as she trudged up a hill. She looked back to see if he had followed. But there was no sign of the bird or the rabbit.

At the crest, she was surprised to find a crumbling adobe ranch house, which had been hidden from the view of the road. No one had lived there for years, it seemed. Every window was shattered and the front door was off its hinges. To the left of the house was a corral, whose rails looked as if they had been eaten by the sun. Penny caught her breath, dabbed the sweat from her eyes with a tissue, and moved toward the right side of the house, where she found a garden with a few onion plants popping up in neat rows. She dug the toe of her tennis shoe into the sand on the chance there was something or someone buried there. To her surprise, she did find a body—that of a small plastic doll, about three inches long—poking up through the soil. *What is it doing here?* Penny picked it up, rubbed the dirt off, and shoved the doll in her pocket.

Convinced there was nothing else to see at Rico's ranch, Penny returned to the car and climbed inside. She pulled the tiny doll out of her pocket and threw it on the passenger seat. The doll's tiny brown eyes met hers. Penny blinked. She searched for the photo of Juan Rico, which she had shoved deep into her blue jeans pocket. The snapshot was now badly creased from folding it so many times, but she could still see the little girl's hands. The child in Rico's arms was holding that same doll!

Penny was hot and tired and desperate to get home, or she would have returned to Lordsburg and confronted Juan's wife. Maybe holding the doll in front of the little girl might loosen somebody's lips. But she just couldn't bring herself to make the forty-mile trip in the opposite direction from El Paso. She was exhausted and dying of thirst. It was time to head home.

XXX

Penny drove the few miles into the tiny town of Columbus where she found a Gas N Go market. She would load up on water and fill a thirty-two-ounce cup with soda and lots of ice and then call her colleagues and tell them she had nothing. She made a beeline for the soda station where she ran into Federico Castañón, the Columbus mayor. He was well over six feet tall, and his black, curly hair kept falling over his dark eyes, giving him a mischievous appearance. Penny had known Castañón from other visits to town when she worked as a freelance reporter. He took the occasion to drone on about how the Mexican drug wars had killed tourism.

"I'm not going to write about that, Mayor. I gave up writing."
"But you were so good at it!"
"Tell that to the bank that holds my mortgage. It was hard to find enough work to pay my bills."
"What are you doing?" "I'm a private investigator."

The mayor squinted his eyes and inhaled deeply and then sighed, apparently trying to take this all in and not believing it to be true. "For whom?"

"Whoever will hire me!" Penny laughed and secured the plastic lid on her drink and poked the straw through the slits. Her throat felt like parchment. She was dying for a sip, but she hesitated as the mayor kept up the small talk. He was leaning very close to her, as if he were about to reveal a secret. It was hard to concentrate on the conversation with him so near. She kept imagining the tingle of the cold drink on her tongue and wished he would go away.

Castañón droned on about the lack of tourists and then turned the conversation back to her new line of work. He shifted his stance and leaned on the counter and looked straight at her. Penny could read his mind. His brown eyes showed his skepticism. He was wondering how a five-foot four-inch blonde could take on such a dangerous job. The mayor didn't know that Penny had a special advantage. She could see things that others could not, and her remote viewing skills usually gave her advanced warning of immediate danger, allowing her time to take cover. A blast of cold air passed by them as the store's air conditioner kicked on. The mood between them had grown cold too. Goose bumps popped up on Penny's arms, and she shivered.

Castañón slapped Penny on the shoulder and turned to leave. "Well, good luck with that!" She rocked forward and dropped her drink on the floor, splashing it all over her tennis shoes. He didn't seem to notice. The mayor was so anxious to exit that he walked out of the store without taking his drink to the counter to pay for it. Penny started to shout at him but thought better of it. She had struck a nerve. And besides, she had to clean up the mess on the floor and hoped the soda hadn't soaked into her shoes. She would hate to pull on her boots again. There still might be a baby scorpion tucked inside.

Penny headed to the restroom to clean up her shoes and returned to the soda station with paper towels to mop up the floor. This took even more precious time from her urgent desire to get home and take a shower. Penny finally paid for his drink and hers and jumped in her car and headed for El Paso.

CHAPTER 2

It was twelve minutes after 2:00 p.m. when Penny reached Deming and gained access to Interstate 10. If she didn't have any more delays she would be home in two hours. She had checked in a second time with her team crisscrossing Luna County and told them she was returning to El Paso without any leads for the marshal. They weren't having any luck either. The marshal would not be pleased.

Penny hated driving on this particular stretch of interstate in the late afternoon because of dust storms, but she had to get home and regroup. She put her car on cruise control at 75 mph, sat back in the leather bucket seat, and blew out a long breath. Everything would be okay. They would find Rico somehow and go on to the next case. She looked to her left and saw a Burlington Northern train barreling east. She pushed her foot on the accelerator and tried to outrace it.

The memory of her ill-fated visit to Juan Rico's ranch was slipping away as she belted out one of her favorite songs on the radio. Life was good, and Penny had a well-paying job! Ten months ago, her house was nearing foreclosure, and she was a month behind on her electric bill. Things had really changed for the better, and she was grateful.

At this rate, Penny would be home in plenty of time to tend to her own garden and stake up her tomatoes before the sun went down. She glanced out the passenger window, and the song died in her throat. She saw a dust devil spiraling northward into the path of her car. Major car pileups were common when the dust obliterated driver visibility. It was August; the grass was dry, and the surrounding desert was a tinderbox. She looked out the passenger window again and noticed the cloud of dust was gathering in density. Penny slammed her right hand against the steering wheel. "I've got to get out of here!" She pressed her foot even harder on the accelerator, disengaging her cruise control.

The first gust over the bough of her car blew her into the path of a semi, whose driver was hell-bent on getting somewhere safe. He sounded his horn. Penny whipped back into her lane just as he barreled by her, flinging the grit from his wheels into the side of her new car. She checked her rearview mirror and saw a long string of vehicles behind her. Her grey-green eyes looked tired. She drew her fingers through her short, cropped hair and frowned. Her cheeks and nose were sunburned, and she had used a little bit too much hair gel this morning, giving her a frenzied look.

Reaching 85 mph, Penny knew she was still not moving fast enough to escape the storm's wrath. She watched the wind scooping up the sand from the desert floor and tossing it under her wheels. She turned off her air conditioner, hoping to keep the dust from spoiling the Mustang's leather interior, which still smelled new. She would have to find a safe harbor soon.

When she could no longer see more than one hundred feet ahead, Penny signaled her intention of pulling off the road. She chose a wide spot where the ground was relatively free of low- lying brush and thorny plants and where the sand was firm. Other cars blew by her, still determined to dodge the inevitable. She parked parallel to a drainage ditch and turned off her engine and headlights. Penny knew the rule: In a dust storm, turn off your lights as soon as you are parked so that other drivers won't think you are still on the highway.

Without the air conditioner, the car's interior was growing stuffy and making it hard to breathe. A powdery substance was settling on her dashboard, and Penny was certain she could feel it penetrating her lungs too. She ran her fingers through the dust and wiped them on her jeans. She coughed, cleared her throat, and placed her hands over her nose and face. She tried not to think about what might happen if the storm lasted too long. She took quick, short breaths, which only made her chest tighten more. Maybe she was hyperventilating. She retrieved a fast-food bag from the passenger seat and blew in and out of it. This helped some, but her hands were sweaty, and her mouth felt sour. She reached for her drink, which was now warm. *Yuk!*

Why did I let the mayor keep talking? Her good manners had placed her smack dab in the face of this brutal dust storm, and it could be the stuff of nightmares. Just two weeks before, a California mother and her baby son were killed when their car was rear-ended by a semi during a storm on this very road. Penny was off the highway, but this was of little comfort. Anyone could plow into her car if they lost their way.

The wind picked up velocity and rocked her car back and forth like a baby in a cradle. She was certain her Ford Mustang would hold its ground, but it still made her anxious. Penny saw a couple of cars and a large truck proceeding cautiously on the highway, and that could only mean they were looking for a place to pull off too.

Within ten minutes, the whirling dust blurred Penny's view from her windows. It reminded her of a television station that had gone off the air. She stared at the nothingness for several minutes, but the waiting and wondering were unsettling. To distract herself from the uncertainty, she decided to use the time constructively. She took out a notepad and reviewed the Rico case and considered her next move. Marshal Lujan suspected Rico might be hiding out across the border until the sale. His ranch was walking distance from the village of Palomas, Mexico. Palomas was known for keeping its secrets, serving as a haven for cartel enforcers and lower level drug traffickers. In fact, just last week, Penny read about how Mexican nationals had boarded a crowded school bus in Palomas and had ridden with the children across the US border. This little caper was a tremendous embarrassment to the US border patrol. No Federal agency likes to be made to look like fools, but this incident, Penny thought, certainly pointed out the gaps in border security.

She added her notes about Rico's ranch and closed the portfolio. She was tired of looking at it, and her head was aching. She wished she could talk this puzzle over with Leo, but the marshal suspected that someone in law enforcement was involved, and she had to remain guarded. This time, she was on her own.

Six months ago, there had been two major shifts in her life. She had given up her corporate writing career to help law enforcement agencies solve crimes, and given up her long time love affair with Porter Jenkins, to form a closer relationship with Leo. She was thirty-five and eager to settle down. Leo, forty-two, had lost his wife five years earlier, and Penny knew he had not completely recovered. She had concluded, however, that Leo Tellez was worth the wait.

She checked her watched and realized forty minutes had passed, and still the wind showed no sign of letting up. She packed her files back into her brief case, threw them in the back seat, and drummed her fingers on the steering wheel. Penny was restless, and her legs were tingly. She moved her feet in a marching motion and then grabbed the wheel and pulled her rear end off the seat, trying to stretch her legs. The heat of the car made her whole body sticky, and she could feel the perspiration running down her face and onto her neck. She could hardly wait to get home and jump in the shower.

Penny found it ironic that she was a prisoner in the very car she loved. She tried to imagine how she would react to solitary confinement. Apparently, not so well! She was growing claustrophobic at the thought of not being able to get out of the vehicle. And she was feeling disoriented, even though she knew darn well where she was. Penny was surprised to find her hands shaking. She wiped her fingers across her damp face and cleaned off the grime that had accumulated there. *Why is there so much dirt in the car?* She checked her air vents and, to her disgust, found them wide open. *I am so stupid.*

She shut the vents and threw her head back against the headrest and let out a long breath. *Calm down!* She was feeling a bit foolish for overreacting to her circumstances. The storm would end soon, and she would be back on the road. She accepted her situation as eventually solvable and shook the tension out of her shoulders. Once the vents had been closed, the dust accumulation slowed, and Penny relaxed. She closed her eyes and fell asleep.

XXX

The sudden impact of something crashing into her car brought her fully awake. A man's body slammed against the windshield, causing a hairline crack to race across the breadth of the glass. Penny bolted forward and grabbed the steering wheel. Had another car plowed into hers and thrown the driver out of his car? His face was bleeding and swollen. His eyes pierced hers, and his hands clawed at the windshield as he called to her for help, "¡Audi! ¡Por favor! Ayudame!"

Penny was confused. *Is this man really crying for help, or is this a dream?* She was prone to dreams in her work as a remote viewer.

Maybe she would wake up, and he would be gone. Before she could sort things out, he disappeared off the hood of her car. She swore she could still hear him calling for her—or was it just the howling of the wind? There was no way she could get out and check on him anyway. The dust obliterated anything beyond an arm's length. Besides, something didn't feel right. Penny checked to make sure her doors were locked.

The Mustang began to rock violently. She jerked her head left and right trying to determine the cause. Her mind was in overdrive. She was breathing heavily, and she could not keep back the tears. Crying blurred her vision, and she strained to make out the foreboding shapes pressing against her windows. She wiped her eyes with her sleeve. Penny could see them clearly now. There were a half a dozen men encircling her car—maybe more! She could hear them laughing and shouting in Spanish. What sounded like a glass bottle shattered against the side of her vehicle.

Are they trying to hijack my Mustang?

"Get out of the car!" a man yelled in broken English and hammered his fist on the driver's window. He was holding a jagged piece of a bottle in his left hand. Penny clenched her teeth and reinforced her grip on the wheel. The car inched forward. *They are pushing it!* She had to stop them; she was parked within a few feet of the ditch. If the car's wheel got hung up in the ditch, she would never be able to escape. She tried to turn the wheel away from the embankment but could not with the engine off. Penny jammed her foot on the brake, and when this didn't help, she yanked on the emergency brake. This stalled them for a moment. She considered starting the car and backing over them, but she couldn't see where she was and figured it would only make things worse. Her heart was pounding so hard that she swore she could feel the veins bulging in her arms.

"*Ugh!*" Penny let out an agonizing scream, one that expressed her fear and her determination not to let them have her car. She released her right hand from the wheel and fumbled around in the console for her .38 revolver. The men were shoving the car forward again, this time by pure brute strength, even with the emergency brake engaged. She wrapped her fingers around the gun, lifted it out of the storage compartment, and laid it in her lap. She wasn't sure she could even pull the trigger. Penny palmed the revolver. It felt slick and foreign in her sweaty hands. She ran the tips of her fingers over the initials carved in the butt of the revolver and remembered why she possessed it in the first place. "Leo!" Penny cried to him for help, even though she knew it was a stupid thing to do. The car tilted to the right. *I'm rolling into the ditch!*

The man pounded harder on the driver's window, and this time, his fist made a spider crack in the glass. Penny turned on the ignition and braced herself with one foot on the floor and one on the console. She opened the sunroof. The sand poured in, showering her face and shoulders. She could feel the grit on her tongue. Penny cocked the gun with both thumbs. She carefully moved the index finger of her right hand into the cradle of the trigger and shoved the gun through the opening of the sunroof. She readied herself for the blast, which she knew would reverberate throughout the confines of the car. She squeezed the trigger, and the bullet blew a hole into the hazy sky. The rancid odor of gunpowder stung her nose and eyes. Her ears were ringing, but the rocking stopped.

CHAPTER 3

Penny's head fell forward into the steering wheel where she watched tears drop onto her jeans. She was drained of energy, but had managed to close the sunroof, even though her wrist ached from the gun's recoil. The right front end of her Mustang was in the ditch, and she could only keep her body upright by hanging onto the wheel.

There had been no sign of the men for several minutes, but she kept the gun wedged between her legs. They might be waiting for the storm to pass before attacking her again. She rubbed her wrist and then rummaged around in her bag for her cell phone. She doubted there would be cell phone service, but she had to try and call for help. Her eyes were clouded with tears, making it tough to see the numbers on the phone. Before she could punch in Leo's number, the phone slipped out of her sweaty fingers and fell in between the seat and the console. She tried to force her hand into the small crevice. Her fingertips could touch the phone but could not pick it up. Then she remembered she had voice command in her new car. She turned on the ignition to activate it. "Call Leo!" Penny shouted his name into the air.

She was relieved to hear Leo's voice on the other end. "Leo, I need help!"

There was silence. "Leo, can you hear me? If you can, I am in a ditch somewhere between Deming and Akela Flats. Please send someone." Penny was probably too far away from any cell tower to get anyone to help her. She could only hope that Leo had at least been able to hear her, even though she could no longer hear him. She hated feeling this vulnerable. Penny knew that when the storm ended, if the men were still around, they would see that she could not escape with her car hung up in the ditch. She took a chance and called out 911, hoping that the emergency call would go through.

"911 operator. Do you have an emergency?"

"Yes. Please help me. I am stranded on the side of I-10 east of Deming."

"That road is closed. Can you wait until the storm clears up?"

"No, I need help now! A gang tried to hijack my red Mustang. I'm afraid they will come back." She sobbed into the receiver. Clearly, she was losing her grip. She was asking the dispatcher for the impossible. How could help come when there was no visibility? Penny waited for the operator to give her instructions, but the line had gone dead. She shivered. The storm had blown in a front, and the temperature was falling. The desert could be hot one minute and freezing the next. She slipped on her jacket, which she had thrown in the backseat. Pulling it close to her chest, much like a security blanket, she propped her feet against the dashboard and slouched in the car's bucket seat. She would wait—for what, she wasn't sure.

Finally, Penny looked at her watch. It had been an hour and a half since she parked her car on the side of the interstate. She watched as a few cars passed by her on the highway. The storm was lifting. Maybe someone would see she was in trouble and call for help. But then again, they probably didn't have cell phone service either. She looked around for the men who had attacked her and caused her to fire her gun. There was no sign of them.

Thank God! She turned on the engine, cranked up the heat, and flipped on her emergency signal.

When she saw the red and blue flashing lights in her rearview mirror, Penny at first felt thankful and then a little embarrassed. The danger had passed, and her attackers were gone. She would ask the police to call a wrecker service to pull her car out of the ditch, and she would be on her way home.

CHAPTER 4

Penny saw the name beneath the badge of the New Mexico State Trooper before she saw his face. He towered well above the roof of her car, which sloped down to the right. Captain Johnny Trejo knocked on her shattered window and bent down to look at her through the cracks in the glass. She opened the door cautiously, not certain if the Mustang's window could be lowered without breaking it. The wind was buffeting the trooper's hat, and his dark, wavy hair was literally dancing across his forehead. His brown eyes were moist from the sting of the sand, which still hung in the air.

"Miss, would you mind stepping out of your vehicle?" "Thank God, you're here!" The officer helped her climb out of her car but refused to let go of her arm as she stood beside him. Her legs were wobbly. "Thank you." It was difficult to look at him with the sand whipping around them, and she wasn't sure he had heard her. "I'm fine now. Thanks." She tried to pull away from his grasp, but he held her firm.

"I'm responding to a report that there is a body lying in front of a red Mustang. Do you know anything about that?"

Penny was stunned, but she tried to appear nonplussed. She wasn't sure how to answer the question without implicating herself. She took a few steps forward trying to see for herself. "Hold it right there. May I see your driver's license and registration?"

"It's in my bag—in the car."

He released her so she could climb back in her car and retrieve her wallet from her purse, which sat on the passenger seat. She felt secure the officer would never find her marshal's badge, which was pinned inside the lining at the bottom of her bag. But he would find her revolver! Would he notice if she hid it under the seat? She thought better of it and threw her bag over the gun and fumbled in the glove compartment for her registration and insurance card for safe measure. Then she climbed back out, handing everything, including her wallet to the officer.

Captain Trejo studied her papers for several minutes. Penny began to shiver from the bracing wind, which was peppering her with debris. She hoped he would hurry so she could get out of the cold. "Ms. Larkin, where are you headed?"

"I've been in Columbus visiting friends and was heading back to El Paso when the storm—" She didn't finish her sentence. She hated to lie to the officer, but it couldn't be helped. Marshal Lujan had explained to her that an informant with ties to the drug cartels had reported that someone in law enforcement was helping to smuggle large shipments of automatic weapons across the border. "And it could be anybody," he had warned.

"I'm going to ask you to sit in my car while I investigate this report." The officer gripped her arm again.

Penny didn't like where this was going. "Is this really necessary? Are you arresting me?"

"No, I am not. I am asking you politely to sit in my car while I check out the area. It is safer for you." He was probably right, Penny thought. Interstate traffic had now resumed. Drivers were anxious to get to their destinations and were driving perilously close to them as they walked along the edge of the highway. A semi sounded its horn; Penny jumped, and the trooper steadied her. Her windbreaker was not designed for the chill, and she tried to keep from shaking so hard. It would look like an admission of guilt. Penny shoved both hands in her pockets, smothering her anger, and moved obediently to the officer's Dodge Charger, which was still running. Trejo placed her in the backseat. It was warm, and it felt good. "Please believe me. I've done nothing wrong."

The trooper ignored her and slammed the door. She heard the automatic locks click shut. She was alarmed. Maybe this wasn't a real policeman. Maybe this was a trap! Penny pounded on the window. The officer turned around and walked back to her and opened the door. Penny lunged toward to open space between the officer and freedom. He pushed her back into the seat.

"You've got to hear me out, sir. I've just been sitting in my car waiting for the storm to pass."

"And as I told you, we have received a call that a man is lying on the side of the road near a red Mustang. Yours is the only one I can find. Wait here while I check it out." Penny was horrified. Instead of helping the man who had landed on her windshield, had she killed him with her gun? A pang of guilt shoved against her chest. She began to bawl. She knew crying would only make her look guilty, but the tears fell anyway. She guessed what would come next. The trooper would find her revolver and realize that it had recently been fired. Would she be arrested? She looked down at her hands. They looked innocent enough. They were small, and her fingers were slender. Her nails were neatly trimmed and polished. Penny Larkin prayed she hadn't killed again.

CHAPTER 5

Johnny Trejo had received the call at 3:00 p.m. about the body of a man lying in front of a late model red Mustang on the edge of the eastbound lane of Interstate 10 between Deming and Akela Flats. The New Mexico State Trooper's southeastern office in Las Cruces, which handled the southern third of the state, was an expansive mix of desert, rolling foothills, and pine tree–covered mountain ranges. It wasn't uncommon for state troopers, who were sadly understaffed, to investigate crimes alone in remote locations. Sometimes these calls turned deadly. Johnny had seen enough dead bodies of late and hated to see another one so soon after his father's funeral. His father, Johnny Trejo Sr., the deputy chief of the New Mexico State Troopers, had been gunned down last week in the historic town of Three Rivers.

His father had managed to take out four of the five members of the Barrio Norteño gang with his AR-15 before he died at the hands of the second man he shot, who, according to the gang's lone survivor, remained alive long enough to fill his father with enough bullets to stock an armory. This survivor, who had taken a bullet to his thigh, decided to cooperate because he realized he would not live long in a New Mexico prison without protection. It was common knowledge that the dreaded Betas drug cartel controlled the New Mexico prison system. The Betas hated the Norteño gang, which had long served as guns for hire for the Chihuahua cartel. You needed a cheat sheet to sort out the players in the drug war.

Johnny's father had been following up on a tip that the Norteños were hiding in an abandoned Three Rivers storefront. The gang was supposed to be working as relay agents for a shipment of cocaine by the Chihuahua drug cartel to Denver, where they would exchange the load for semiautomatic rifles and the accompanying ammo. The drugs were being moved north to Denver on Highway 54, which ran right through town.

Three Rivers attracts hundreds of tourists in the summer, but it had been the second Monday in August, and the antique shops, art galleries, bead makers, and potters were closed. According to the police report, one of the gang members had stepped out onto the shop's front porch for a smoke, taking Johnny's father by surprise. This must have been around the time Johnny received a desperate call from his father. "Sonny, I'm in deep water in Three Rivers. Call for backup. I've killed one, and I'll try to keep these losers inside until help comes to haul them to jail." Johnny could hear gunfire in the background.

"Dad, don't do anything stupid!" He had yelled into the receiver, but his dad had disconnected the phone. Johnny jumped into his car and headed to Three Rivers, while relaying his father's request for backup to headquarters.

His dad had done something stupid, and now he was dead.

So was the man lying face down on the right side of the highway, a few feet in front of the young woman's Mustang. Johnny rolled him over and saw that he had been hit by a single gunshot wound to the chest. Daylight was fading, so it was difficult to even hazard a guess as to the caliber of the bullet, but Johnny could see that the damage was so on the money that his assailant had no reason to waste any more ammunition. His jacket looked like it was part of a uniform. Johnny checked his sleeves and noticed a patch from the Luna County Department of Corrections. Sheriff Jack Pritchard ran that DOC like a gulag, and most lawbreakers hated to be sent there. Johnny opened the man's jacket and saw that his shirt was torn, as if his identification badge had been ripped off his chest.

Johnny went to his vehicle and retrieved a blanket from the trunk. He covered the dead officer and called for an ambulance to transport him to the morgue in Albuquerque. It was the only forensic unit in New Mexico—a mere two hundred miles to the north. Then he checked out Penny Larkin's car. It was clear someone had tried to put a fist through the driver's window. That much agreed with her story that she had been attacked. His earlier check with the 911 dispatcher in Deming confirmed that a woman had called for help at 2:40 p.m., but contact with her had been lost. The dispatcher relayed the woman's request to the Luna County Sheriff's Department, who in turn called the New Mexico State Police. The sheriff's office was the nearest law enforcement agency, and that was protocol on Interstate 10, but the bad weather had kept them diverted with other emergencies, so they had asked the state troopers to handle it.

Johnny opened the door to the Mustang and poked his head inside. A faint smell of nitro hung in the air. "Lady, you're lying to me! You fired a gun in here."

Johnny took out his flashlight and moved its shaft of light throughout the Mustang, checking even into the deepest crevices. He found Penny's cell phone in between the seats, and on the passenger side, he noticed Penny's purse. He retrieved the phone, and when he lifted her bag to put the phone inside, he discovered the .38 caliber revolver. "Bingo!" He recognized the gun as an old-time police issue from the 1950s. His dad had one like it that he called the chief.

"Where did she get that relic?" He murmured under his breath and shook his head in disgust. He would have to run a registration check to see who owned it.

Johnny got out a pair of latex gloves he kept in a pouch on his belt and slipped them on. The Mustang was now a crime scene and needed to be treated accordingly. He picked up the revolver and pulled a white cleaning patch from a packet and ran it down the barrel, retrieving a gray line of gunpowder. Johnny shook his head. He placed the revolver in a plastic zip lock bag, along with the cleaning patch.

Next, Johnny climbed into the ditch where the Mustang's front end was resting in the depths of the sand and rocks. There was a broad indentation in the hood and a streak of what looked like blood was smeared across the front of the car. Had the woman struck the man with her car first? Johnny would have to wait until he saw the car back at the garage and, of course, heard from forensics and ballistics in Albuquerque before drawing any conclusions.

By the time he finished his examination of the crime scene, the sun had finally dropped behind the mountain range. Johnny was satisfied that he had enough evidence to arrest Penny Larkin. He left her emergency lights flashing and he walked back to his patrol car to use his radio to call for a wrecker to place the Mustang on a hook and haul it to the garage at the New Mexico State Police headquarters in Las

Cruces. Then he revved the engine and looked through the cage at the woman in his custody. He could tell she had been crying but too bad. She had, in all likelihood, killed an officer of the law, and this was a capital offense in New Mexico.

The ambulance and the wrecker both made the trip in less than thirty minutes, for which Johnny was grateful. Now he could take his suspect to his headquarters in Las Cruces for more questioning.

Johnny wouldn't know much more about the kind of gun that killed the officer until he received a report by midday tomorrow. In the meantime, he would hold Larkin in the Doña Ana County Jail. He got out of the car, opened the back door, and handcuffed his number 1 suspect in the killing of the Luna County corrections officer. "Penny Larkin, you have the right to remain silent…"

CHAPTER 6

Sheriff Leo Tellez was having lunch in the village of Old Mesilla, New Mexico, on the outskirts of Las Cruces when he got Penny's call. He could hear some of what she said; she was stranded on I-10, but even when he shouted into the phone, it was obvious she could not hear him. He knew Penny had planned to travel to Columbus on an assignment from the US Marshals Service, and in all likelihood, she was calling from a place on Interstate 10 that had little cell phone reception. There was a real dead cell zone near Akela Flats.

"It's Penny! She's in need of help on I-10." He looked over at his lunch companions, Doña Ana County Sheriff Ted Rodriguez and Adriana Martinez, the twin sister of his dead wife, Alejandra. "I heard the road is closed. Damn dust storm!" Ted said. He had only returned to work halftime, after his near-fatal gunshot wound six months before but had agreed to meet Leo at La Posta, a historic Mexican restaurant that first opened its doors in the 1840s. Leo surprised Ted by bringing Adriana along. She had just moved back to El Paso from Los Angeles. Leo knew Ted would enjoy seeing her again. Ten years ago, Leo and Ted and Adriana and Alejandra had been classmates at the University of Texas at El Paso. There had been a period where Ted and Adriana dated, and Leo hoped that they would marry, like he and Alejandra had done a few years after graduation. But Adriana had gone on to law school at UT Austin and then headed to Los Angeles, where she had practiced for the past ten years. A few weeks ago, she moved back to El Paso to keep an eye on her mother, who was having a difficult time living alone.

Of course, Ted was now happily married to Isa and had three children. Still it was fun to see his reaction. The table conversation became a spirited event, with the three of them recalling the good times at UTEP. Leo could tell that the decision to bring Adriana had been a good one. Other than walking with a cane, Ted seemed like his old fearless self.

Adriana had changed very little, and Leo couldn't help but stare at her. As he did, his heart skipped a beat or two. She had the same long, silky black hair and the wide smile he had found so appealing in his wife. The pain of losing Alejandra and his infant daughter, Marta, in childbirth was still an open wound that five years had not healed, even though his relationship with Penny had done a great deal to lift his spirits. Just for a few moments, Leo let himself remember life as it was. He pretended that Adriana was Alejandra and that all the laughter and back slapping at the table was a time warp and a salve for his grieving soul. This was, of course, a foolish thing to do. He shook his head and picked up his cell phone. His call to Penny went straight to her voice mail.

Ted was on his cell too, checking with his office for a status report on the storm.

"Thank you, Donna. That is good news. See you shortly." "What's up?" Leo asked.

"It looks like the road is now open."

"We need to get going. Penny sounded desperate, which isn't like her." Leo stood and pulled out Adriana's chair so that she could join him.

Ted grabbed the check and waved Adriana and Leo away from the table.

"You go on now and save that young lady. She's one special woman, and I don't want you to keep her waiting!"

Leo turned to Adriana. "I hope you don't mind heading to Deming?"

"Of course not. I am looking forward to meeting Penny. You can't say more than a few words without mentioning her name." Leo helped Adriana into his Chevy Tahoe and jumped in the driver's seat. "It'll take us about thirty minutes to get to Akela Flats."

They entered I-10 from Old Mesilla Highway and headed northwest. Leo wished he had his patrol car. They could make better time. But he was soon booking it at 85 mph anyway and was able to relax a little. He loved to drive and felt totally at home behind the wheel. Leo assumed that Penny was just panicking over being stalled on the highway. Surely, it was nothing more serious than that. He fiddled with the radio and found a blues station that reminded both him and Adriana of good times and sat back for the thirty-minute drive.

Leo saw his phone light up on the console, even though he never heard it ring. Adriana handed Leo his phone and turned off the radio.

"Penny, are you okay? Take it easy! I'm just fifteen minutes away." Leo looked at Adriana, whose face was full of questions. "Sorry, we've got to turn around. Penny is in Las Cruces at the New Mexico State Police station. She's being held on suspicion of murder.

CHAPTER 7

Juan Rico turned over in his cot, which held a jumble of fraying quilts. He pounded his lumpy pillow, trying to find a softer place to lay his head. It was freezing in the tiny cabin, which was nothing more than an afterthought on the sixty-thousand-acre Rosemary Ranch, called the Double-R by locals and owned by Juan's uncle, Martín Romero. The cabin was squeezed in between two outcroppings of volcanic boulders and had been all but abandoned since Romero's cattle no longer roamed the land that surrounded it. His uncle grew tired of losing money and putting down calves that were continually breaking their legs in the rocky terrain. Romero fenced it off and forgot about it.

Juan knew he could hide here and do his business undisturbed. This section of the Double R was located near the City of Rocks State Park north of Deming, and unless you knew where to look, the cabin was difficult to see from the scenic drive dissecting the park. His uncle had given him a key to the cabin years ago, and Juan doubted that Uncle Martín would remember that Juan still had it on his key chain.

The wind-up clock on the bedside table read 5:30 p.m. He had two more hours to wait before the gunrunners from Mexico arrived to pick up the load of firearms Juan had hidden in a mineshaft near the road. Juan was excited about his latest haul.

He had been able to fill the cartel's order of one hundred vest buster handguns, but not without some creative efforts on his part. Most came through straw sales, but the final batch had to be stolen from a gunsmith in Lordsburg. He had to steal them because the gunsmith had been quick to catch on when Juan sent in his friends to keep buying guns on his behalf. The manager had just plain turned them down.

Juan was impressed with how easy it was to break in and take what he needed from the shop, but nothing more. He owed the guy that much. What he learned, too late, was that the man didn't own the store. The firearm inventory belonged to the Betas cartel, the deadly enemies of the Chihuahua cartel, his gun buyers. If the Betas ever found him, they would spare no amount of firepower to cut him to ribbons.

At the thought of this, Juan broke into a sweat under the pile of blankets. He sat up and exposed his damp body to the cold air moving through the poorly insulated cabin. He pulled one of the quilts off his cot and wrapped it around his shoulders. On the kitchen table, he saw one of the stolen guns he planned to use for his own protection. It was an FN Herstal Five-seveN pistol, and it was fully loaded. He stood, dragging the blanket behind him, and picked up the gun. Who knew when it might come in handy? Juan returned to the cot and tucked the pistol under his mattress. Of course, all the guns in the world were of little use to a cartel without ammunition. He also had scored ten thousand rounds of 9 mm shells. His contact had even thrown in a few grenades for good measure. He wouldn't pilfer any of this ammo for his newly acquired pistol. He had purchased his own box from Walmart. If the cartel saw that a box was missing from their crate, they would assume he was trying to trick them. He couldn't be too careful. They frowned on being stiffed for any reason, even the appearance of being cheated. He needed to stay alive. His family was counting on him.

Taking such a big chance would be worth it once he got paid the $25,000 he figured to clear from this deal. He would send most of it for safekeeping to his wife. Their two children, Nancy and Paula, were five and three, and the lights of his life. He missed them terribly, but for now, he had to stay out of sight. The last thing he needed was to drag his family or his wife's parents into this mess.

Having to lie low was making it harder to fill the second half of the cartel's order—twenty-five Colt AR-15.223 caliber assault rifles or AK 47 7.62 caliber assault rifles or a mixture of both. He had a good lead and was really hoping what he heard was true— that the mayor of Columbus had connections. Juan planned to have everything settled within a week or so. He would call on the mayor tomorrow.

The cartel's final payment of $50,000, combined with this $25,000, would be enough to begin building his family's dream home on the small ranch his mother had left him after her death two years ago. He had tried without much success to start a vegetable garden there and had spent a number of hours, with the help of his older daughter, Nancy, hoeing a small patch of soil. They had planted corn, tomatoes, beans and zucchini, and winter onions. He could hardly wait to get back and see if anything had come up. But in the meantime, he had to stay far away from his family, which was plenty hard when he heard his children crying for him as he talked with his wife on the cell phone.

Juan walked over to the dusty wooden window that was so small it only held four panes. The setting sun was casting slivers of gold across the stones in the field. At any other time, he would have relished the sunset, but tonight, he had more to think about than the end of the day. He had to prepare himself for tonight and the exchange of firearms for cash. Rio, the cartel boss, could easily kill him and take both, but Juan was pretty sure his ability to provide a steady stream of weapons for Mexico would make him more valuable alive than dead.

From where he stood, he had a pretty good view of anyone approaching the cabin. The cartel gunrunners, who would arrive around 8:00 p.m., would have to climb over the boulders and walk a hundred feet or more in clear view of the cabin's solitary window. They would probably bring a flashlight to make their way to the cabin. Juan would clearly see them coming. And there would be no place for the Betas to sneak up on the cabin either. If they came to kill him, it would be like shooting ducks at the Luna County Fair arcade. He was an expert marksman, and his daughters had a bedroom full of stuffed animals to prove it. In fact, in high school, he had won the New Mexico Men's Rifle Championship. A lot of good the trophy did him now. It was gathering dust at home and wouldn't buy food for the table. Juan turned back to the warmth of his cot and covered his head, still shivering from the cold. As his body warmed up, he fell asleep.

CHAPTER 8

Juan felt the front door of the cabin blow open and the cold night air rush across the small room with a vengeance. In the blackness, his body stiffened, and before he could respond, someone rammed the butt of a gun against his chest. Juan yanked off the quilt, regretting that his new pistol was still under the mattress. A bolt of light burned into his retinas, and he brought his right hand up to his eyes.

"Get up, and show yourself," the man demanded.

As he sat up in bed, Juan recognized his Uncle Martín staring at him down the barrel of his rifle, his black eyes full of rage. Juan knew how angry his uncle could get when he was riled up. He had never quite recovered from Desert Storm. The weight of his uncle's .50-caliber sniper rifle was forcing the air out of his lungs. "It's me—Juan!" He sputtered and coughed, trying to push the rifle out of his ribcage.

His uncle reared back in surprise and lowered his weapon. "Damn it, Juan, I could have killed you! I thought you were some poacher looking to take my cattle. Why didn't you tell me you were here?"

"Sorry, I need to hole up here for a few days. I didn't want to bother you."

"Your old lady, throw you out? Come and sleep at the house."

"No, it's not that. I've just run into a bit of trouble and need to lay low."

"I don't want any trouble following you onto my ranch."

"I just need to stay here for a few days." Juan glanced at the window. The sun had dropped behind the mountains and Rio or his gunrunners would arrive soon, and he needed to be ready. He rubbed his hands together. They were cold and dry, and his arms were itching from washing them in the cabin's well water. He longed for the warmth of his bed and the love of his wife. "Please, Martín. I promise no trouble will come your way."

"All right. All right. I'll give you a week, and then I need you to hightail it out of here. It isn't safe anyway. You never know when a border crosser might try to break in and steal food or water. I've had to repair the lock on the door several times this year."

Juan was nervous. The ticking of the clock seemed louder than usual. It was almost time. Beads of sweat popped up on his forehead. Things could go real bad if his uncle stayed any longer. Juan stood up and moved to the door. He didn't want his uncle to sit down. He was quite a talker, and Juan loved his stories but not tonight. It was almost dark, and even though his sixty-five- year-old uncle knew the ranch like the back of his hand, the rocks were sharp, and he might fall.

His uncle must have sensed that Juan was anxious for him to leave. He opened the door and walked out on to the porch. "Okay, Juan. The place is yours for seven days. At the end of that, I'll be back to see that you are gone."

Juan nodded and shut the door. He let out a breath of air and grabbed the keys to his truck from the bedside table. He decided to change his plans. Realizing that the cabin was more of a trap than a refuge, Juan would head off the gunrunners and meet them closer to the road. Having them come to the cabin had been a bad idea.

The crack of a rifle sliced through the walls of the cabin and drove Juan to the window. He could see nothing except the lingering shadows of sundown. A secondblast rattled the window and door, and this time he recognized the sound of his uncle's rifle. Martín Romero served as a sniper in the army and just had to have the same kind of weapon when he returned home from deployment. Juan and his uncle had taken the gun on hunting trips. For Juan, there was no mistaking the blistering bounce back of a .50-caliber bullet being forced into the night air. It would take no prisoners.

Had his uncle seen the cartel members and shot at them? Or did the cartel sneak up on him and kill him with his own gun? Juan had no choice but wait for the answer. His hands shook as he reached under his mattress and pulled out the Herstel. It was a heavy sucker. It had been loaded when he stole it, which was good, because he might have to kill anyone who took down his Uncle Martín.

CHAPTER 9

Penny's right arm ached from being handcuffed to the metal table in the squad room. She had to go to the bathroom, but there was not much chance of that happening any time soon. She and Captain Trejo were the only people in the State Trooper's headquarters in Las Cruces. She was afraid to tell him she had to go for fear he would follow her into the rest room. That would really be humiliating! He had been in his office on the phone since they arrived, and through the room's glass windows, the trooper appeared to be in an intense discussion over her, no doubt. His eyes bounced between her and the heavy wire cage at the back of the room, which Penny feared was used as a temporary lockup for suspects. Her only solution for her discomfort was to shut her eyes and try to imagine that she was somewhere other than in a heap of trouble.

Penny reviewed the nightmare of the dust storm, the injured man on her hood, and the gun—the gun that seems to kill each time she pulled the trigger. She had aimed the revolver toward the sky, and not at any one of the men hovering around her car. Had the bullet actually found that poor, troubled man who needed her help?

His swollen, fearful face appeared in her mind. Who was he? Why was he with these other men who were trying to steal her car? In order to find out, she would have to use her remote viewing skills. Did she have the strength to do that right now? Penny was so agitated that she worried her mind would go blank if she tried to see anything beyond the squad room, but she had to do whatever she could to save herself.

There were protocols she had to employ in hopes of determining the circumstances behind the broken man's face. The first step required that she relax and clear her mind. Good luck with that! But she shook her head trying to loosen the bad thoughts and then imagined herself sitting on a mountaintop looking over a long range of snow-capped peaks. Her breathing slowed, and she smiled at the thought of being somewhere so beautiful.

The second step required that she abandon all personal desires and wants in relation to the target. Penny felt terrible to think she might have killed the man, but in order to break free of his emotional hold on her, she had to dispel those fears too.

The third step was to place her spirit in harmony with the universe. She had to exclude any conflicting thoughts that might be creeping in, like being afraid she was going to be charged with murder.

On step 4, she let her higher power, which she knew as God, take the lead. She was always amazed at the influence of these protocols on time and space. She moved effortlessly from the mountaintop into a world free of clocks and calendars. This suspension of time lay as a protective field of energy between her and Captain Trejo. Now Penny was free to take a closer look at the dead man.

Through the eyes of a remote viewer, Penny could see that the man was in his fifties and had small, dark eyes and brown skin that was wrinkled around his eyes and mouth. There were splotches on his cheeks, where blood bubbled up, giving him the look of a drunkard. But something told Penny the man had not been drinking. He had suffered some kind of injury with a weapon that created triangular marks on his face. She couldn't imagine what that might be. She looked down below his neck and thought she saw a forest green shirt, although she couldn't be sure because it was soaked with blood. As she stared intently at him, she was transported to a low slung, stucco building with bars on the windows.

A jail? Was this where she was headed?

When she opened the door and entered a waiting room, she saw an abandoned reception desk behind bulletproof glass. She moved right through a locked steel door and on down a hall lined with cell doors. Each cell held four men and two sets of bunk beds. Some prisoners were reading. Some were sleeping. Penny could smell the sweat and a faint odor of cigarettes. Oddly, she could see right through the men as if they were ghosts!

An image of the dead man appeared again, but this time, he was leaning against the bars of a cell door—gripping the flat metal strips of steel with both hands. How did this man get out of jail and onto the interstate? And from what jail? She was puzzled about this viewing. Nothing about it made any sense.

"There she is!" A familiar voice broke Penny's concentration. She opened her eyes, feeling dizzy and sick to her stomach. When she finally was able to focus, Penny saw Leo and a beautiful woman with long black hair standing near the entrance to the squad room. A wave of warmth embraced her. Everything would be okay now. She tried to stand but remembered she was shackled by one hand to the table, which was bolted to the floor. She was both happy and embarrassed that Leo had come. She hated for him to see her like this. *And who is the woman with him? She looks so familiar.*

Captain Trejo came out of his office and intercepted the visitors. "Sheriff Tellez, what are you doing here?"

"I've come to get Penny Larkin."

"Oh, so you were her one call." The captain looked at Leo and then at Penny, perhaps a little confused over the relationship.

"Yes, Penny and I are—" Leo stopped in midsentence.

"A number of things have to be cleared up before I can release her," the captain said. "I found a dead man lying in front of her Mustang on I-10 with a bullet in his chest."

"There is no way Penny could have killed him. She hates guns." Captain Trejo went into his office and retrieved the .38 he had bagged from Penny's car. "She fired this." He showed Leo the plastic bag with the gun.

Penny waited for Leo to react at seeing his father's gun.

"I gave this revolver to Penny six months ago, and it is now registered under her name." He rushed over to Penny and leaned down to hug her. Penny noticed that the other woman trailed behind him but remained a few feet away. The woman's large, brown eyes mesmerized Penny. *Who in the world is this?* As if reading her mind, Leo released her and turned to the other woman "Penny, I would like you to meet Alejandra's sister, Adriana."

Immediately, Penny realized where she had seen her. It was Alejandra brought back from the dead! She knew Alejandra had a sister, but Leo failed to mention that Adriana and Alejandra were identical twins. Penny leaned back into her chair. Why had Leo not told her this important detail? Penny's heart banged against her ribs. It hurt to even take a breath. Her stomach felt like it was full of bailing wire. She had to get out of here and protect her territory!

Captain Trejo brought out the keys to Penny's handcuffs and released her. A red line encircled her wrist where the cuff had rubbed it raw. "Why don't we all go into my office? I have a conference table where we can all talk."

CHAPTER 10

The pounding on the cabin door sent shivers up and down Juan's arms. He hadn't acted fast enough! Juan dropped the blanket from his shoulders and shoved the Herstel into a waistband holster behind his back. His heart hammered against his throat, choking him. Without his quilt, he began to shake. There was only one window and one door. He had nowhere to run. His only chance of getting out of this alive was to act normal, but there was nothing normal about doing business with a cartel. Juan took a long, drawn out breath and wiped his nose on his blue jeans jacket. Someone was pounding again. He didn't know if in the next moment, he would be dead or alive, but he had to open it, or whomever it was would probably break in and shoot him anyway. His frigid, shaking fingers twisted the knob.

Sheriff Jack Pritchard stood there holding a large flashlight, the beams of which struck the front porch like a dagger. Juan took a few steps back. It was a shock seeing the sheriff. His gun was not drawn, but had he come to arrest him? Guilt swarmed all over Juan like a mess of flies on cow dung. He held his hands out in surrender. Juan knew the sheriff, not as a friend but from serving time in his jail as a juvey. The Luna County Jail was a notoriously bad place to wind up. The guards were mean, and the food tasted like cardboard. He braced himself for the cuffs.

"Son, there has been an accident. We had a tip that the Chihuahua cartel was making a gun buy in the state park, and we mistook your uncle for one of them. He's been wounded. He wants you to ride into the hospital with him. The ambulance is on its way!"

Juan pushed past Sheriff Pritchard and ran out the door. "Uncle Martín! Are you okay?" It was now dark as a bucket of tar. Juan stumbled and fell into a pile of rocks, skinning his knees and tearing a hole in his jeans.

The sheriff caught up with Juan and pulled him to his feet. A shaft of the sheriff's flashlight was enough to help them make their way to the edge of the boulders. Uncle Martín's rifle lay a few feet away. A deputy was tending to his bloody shoulder. "I think the blast of my rifle broke his arm too." The sheriff leaned over to get a better look at Martín, who was growling under his breath. Sheriff Pritchard's flashlight revealed a sizable wound and a face full of fury.

"Damn it, Jack. You shot me on my own land. What were you thinking?"

CHAPTER 11

Leo waited for Penny to come out of the rest room and then helped her walk into the conference room. She was unsteady on her feet, and her mind was jammed with conflicting images— the wounded man on her windshield, the beautiful Adriana, and the ugly jail she had seen in her viewing ten minutes before. She smelled bad, she was sure. She had taken off her coat, and carried it under her arm. Her jeans were covered with dust, and for one of the few times in her life, she had generated bands of sweat under her arms. She noticed that Adriana had a scent of vanilla and strawberries.

Penny sat down between Leo and Adriana. Captain Trejo pulled out a chair opposite them and slapped a file on the walnut table. The table was scratched and filled with white rings left from numerous cups of hot beverages. Penny wondered who else had sat at this table and worried whether or not they would wind up in jail.

"The John Doe has just arrived in Albuquerque at the state morgue. It will be late tonight at the earliest before we know the caliber of the bullet in the dead man's chest." Johnny began.

"What are you saying? You can't release Penny because you don't know if she shot this man? I can assure you, she did not!" Leo leaned over and grabbed Penny's hand. Leo's hand was warm. His positive energy moved up her arms and into her heart.

"I am pretty sure that my ballistics expert will agree with my on-site tests that Penny's .38 revolver has been recently fired. I smelled the residue in her car."

Penny cleared her throat and pulled her hand away from Leo and thumped it on the table. "I don't know what happened to that man! He landed on my hood and called to me for help. The next thing I know, a bunch of men were rocking my car and trying to get me to open my door. One guy had a broken bottle and threatened me."

"Did you fire your gun?" Leo asked.

"When they started pushing my car forward, I knew I was going to roll into the ditch, and then I would be stuck there and have no chance of getting away from them. I fired my gun out of the sunroof trying to scare them off. It worked! They left."

"It looks like the man was killed at close range with a straight shot to the heart," Captain Trejo explained. "A stray bullet would have entered his chest on an angle." The captain rubbed his chin, as if considering Penny's innocence.

"Until you have more information, I would like you to extend professional courtesy and let me take Penny home. I'll be responsible for her," Leo said.

The phone rang in the squad room, and Captain Trejo went to answer it.

"Penny, don't say anything else," Leo told her. "Let's wait until ballistics and the coroner have something tangible. If it looks bad then, I'll get you a lawyer."

Realizing that she was facing the possibility of hiring a lawyer, Penny put her hands over her face. She didn't want Adriana to see her this way. And knowing Leo might be driving back to El Paso with Adriana brought out her claws. "Leo, you know I am telling you the truth. I didn't get out of my car and shoot him. And how would it be possible for me to kill the man by firing out of my sunroof?"

"It is unlikely. I am sure this will be cleared up by morning."

"Please convince the captain to let you take me home. I'm innocent!"

Captain Trejo returned to the conference room. "I've got bad news. As I suspected, the man who was killed was a correctional officer from the Luna County Jail. His badge number identified him as Harold Moreno, and a photo confirmation has arrived from Sheriff Pritchard. His gun is missing, which means we will have to do a search of the location where Ms. Larkin was parked on I-10. And it also means, there is no way that I can let you take Ms. Larkin home. The death of a police officer requires that we take every precaution. It is a capital offense."

"Are you charging me with murder?" Penny's voice was shrill, reflecting her frustration and fear. She tried to stand, but Leo pulled her back into her chair.

"We will have to hold you on suspicion in the wrongful death of an officer of the law. I regret I am going to have to transport you to the Doña AnaCounty jail for booking this evening."

CHAPTER 12

The ambulance was hot, and Juan found it hard to breathe. His whole body was sopping with sweat, and he rubbed the palms of his hands against his jeans. His uncle was receiving an IV of something, and the EMT explained that he would be more comfortable with oxygen. Juan had numbly nodded his head, agreeing to any treatment that would make Uncle Martín okay. His Aunt Leona had died years ago, and there was no one but Juan to make such choices.

Uncle Martín's eyes were shut.

Is he asleep or avoiding me? Juan wondered.

The siren made it impossible to ask his uncle the questions he was dying to have answered. Certainly, he could figure out that Juan had something to do with the gun sale gone badly. Would he rat on him when the Sheriff met them at the hospital?

I deserve what I get!

Uncle Martín was the only father Juan had ever known. His mother, Donna, who died two years ago, had given birth to Juan twenty years ago at the hospital in Deming, but she never mentioned who his father was, suggesting only that he lived in Mexico.

If Uncle Martín dies because I made a big mistake, I will never forgive myself!

"Is he okay?" Juan directed his question to the EMT who was repacking some equipment into a large duffle bag.

The EMT held his hand up to his ear, indicating that he could not hear. That was a good thing, really. Juan needed time to think how he would respond when his uncle did confront him. Juan decided to act completely surprised and to admit to some lame reason why he was at the cabin, other than selling guns. His stash was safe. No one would look in the abandoned mine. It was a danger to all, and the yellow sign with the skull and cross bones near the entrance warned people to stay away. Juan knew the mine well. When he was small, men were still working it and paid his Uncle Martín for the privilege of pulling bits of copper from its belly. There were rumors of gold in there, too, but no one ever claimed to have found any. When the price of copper fell, the mine closed, and from the looks of it, no one had been near it for years. Desert grasses grew across the entrance, and a prickly pear cactus was entrenched at the face of the mine, as if to ward off any would-be intruders.

XXX

The ambulance roared into the emergency entrance of the hospital. There was no one to greet them. A single bulb, on some sort of automatic signal, lighted the driveway as the ambulance backed into the emergency room bay. Juan watched the driver hop out of the ambulance and ring the bell. Juan had read in the newspaper that extra security was now installed at the Luna County Medical Center to protect hospital staff. American citizens who had been shot in Mexico and who were lucky enough to get back across the border were transported to the medical center with a police escort. Whenever this happened, the Deming City Police Department had to guard the wounded patients, for fear a gunman would break in and finish the job. It had never happened, but who wanted to take that chance?

The double doors to the emergency room swung open, and the driver and the EMT lifted Uncle Martín onto a gurney and rolled him into the building. Juan saw the flashing lights of the sheriff's car, which pulled into the parking lot behind them. Juan was hesitant to join him. He waited until the sheriff went inside the hospital, and then he jumped out of the back of the vehicle. The lights in the hospital hallway were old and intermittent. They gave off a yellowish pall that made Juan shiver. The linoleum was also old but so well polished he could see his reflection in the floor. Behind him, the emergency room doors slammed shut, and Juan heard the bolt on the door engage. Why did he feel like he was caught again? He could always exit out the front of the hospital, couldn't he? He began to breathe hard, and his throat felt like it did when he used to smoke. His wife had asked him to give up cigs, and he did. He was a good husband and a good nephew.

He just didn't know how to make enough money to support his family. He never learned how to ride a horse or wield a pickaxe. He graduated from high school and fell into the world of the occasionally employed. How much of a chance did he have to make it?

Juan buttoned his jacket to hide his pistol and walked down the hall, peering into each room. He heard the sheriff's voice and followed the sound. His uncle was lying on a bed in a large room, crowded with several other beds, all of which were empty. His uncle, who had always been the strongest man Juan knew, appeared small and frail under the white sheets.

The sheriff saw Juan approaching. "Your uncle is going into surgery."

Juan walked alongside the gurney as an aide rolled it toward the operating room. "Uncle Martín, I am so sorry!" His uncle, who had his nose and mouth covered with the oxygen mask, looked up at Juan. His eyes were surprisingly kind. He bent his right arm at the elbow and moved his index finger back and forth in front of his face, perhaps, Juan thought, as a signal to say "nothing." Juan was only too happy to keep quiet. The only talking he planned to do was to God. He would pray Uncle Martín would not only be all right but that he would also find it in his heart to forgive him.

CHAPTER 13

Johnny Trejo was uncomfortable hauling Penny Larkin off to jail with Sheriff Tellez and his friend, Adriana, following them closely in their SUV. The Tahoe's headlights were like stilettos slicing through the metal cage that held his prime suspect. The high beams intermingled with his red emergency lights, spilling like blood onto the highway in front of him. He could well appreciate the sheriff's concern for Penny. He would do the same if he had someone he loved who was in trouble. And he could tell Leo cared deeply about Penny.

Johnny had a great deal of respect for the sheriff. He was admired all over the southwest. Johnny would like to appease Leo and let Penny go home in his care, but the dead jail guard put him in a difficult situation. Penny was his only suspect, and very soon the whole state would know about it. Besides, who else could have killed the correctional officer? She never mentioned that the men trying to hijack her car had any firearms. They were only rocking her car. And Penny had told him that one man had a broken bottle for a weapon. That doesn't sound like someone who had access to a gun. And yet with all of this circumstantial evidence before him, Johnny found himself hoping that the ballistics report would show that another gun had killed the man—not the .38. He was surprised at his hope that Penny was not a killer. He swallowed hard and shoved this thought out of his mind.

When Johnny pulled up in front of the Doña Ana County Detention Center, two uniformed officers were on the front steps anticipating his arrival. Johnny waited until they escorted Penny into the building for booking before he walked over to the SUV and spoke to Sheriff Tellez. "It will take about thirty minutes for them to process and fingerprint her. Do you want to wait in the visitor's lounge?"

Leo and Adriana followed Johnny into the facility. This particular center was different than anything El Paso County had, and it made

Johnny a bit proud. There were no bars separating the officers and inmates, only glass walls designed to ensure that the more than eight hundred residents were constantly aware they were under observation.

Johnny showed Leo and Adriana to the visitors' area, which was lined with sleek-looking sofas and chairs. He offered to get them both coffee and then took off before he had even asked if they needed cream or sugar. Considering the circumstances, he was sure any hot liquid would do. When he returned with two paper cups of steaming coffee, he saw that Leo was leaning forward with his head in his hands, and Adriana's fingers were gripping his shoulder. This surprised Johnny a little. It appeared that Adriana and Leo knew each other very well. This was strange indeed. *Who is she, and why is she here?*

"Penny is ready for visitors," Johnny said.

With that, Leo's hands dropped into his lap, and he jumped to his feet.

"Wait here, Adriana, I'll be back as soon as I am sure Penny is okay."

Johnny showed Leo the entrance to the center's detainment area. He pushed a buzzer, and a guard opened the door for the sheriff and motioned for him to enter. Johnny could see Penny dressed in the customary orange jumpsuit, sitting quietly, her cuffed hands resting on the interview table. Johnny thought it best to leave Leo alone with her. They undoubtedly had a lot to say to one another, and he didn't want to hear it. When the heavy door slammed shut and the electric bolt secured the interview room, Johnny walked out of the detention center and down the steps to the driveway. His car was still warm inside, which he greatly appreciated because his heart felt so cold.

CHAPTER 14

It had been more than an hour since Uncle Martín had gone into surgery. Juan had hidden in a small alcove off the main waiting room, sipping a cold soda. He kept looking around for the sheriff, but he was nowhere around. Maybe he had gone on to fight other crimes.

Juan could only hope.

He pulled his cell phone out of his pocket and pressed his wife's number on speed dial. Did he dare call her when things had gone so wrong? He had to hear her voice. She and the kids were the only reason to stay alive, and he was risking even that by doing business with one cartel and stealing from another.

His mother-in-law, Rhonda, answered the house phone. Juan could hear her calling for Alicia. "Cia, the phone. It's for you! It's Juan."

The echo of Alicia's footsteps running down the tiled hallway to the telephone in the kitchen gave Juan chills of anticipation. He missed her so much. When she said hello, Juan's entire body relaxed. He had not realized how tense he had become.

"Juan, where are you? Please come home. Nancy has a fever!" He couldn't bear to think about his firstborn, his precious little Nancy, being ill. Had he caused it by making her worry about what he was doing? He was filled with remorse for taking such big chances with his family's future.

"I don't have my truck. I am at the hospital. Uncle Martín has been shot, and he is in surgery."

"Oh my God. What happened?"

"We were on the ranch. It was dark, and Sheriff Pritchard shot him by accident."

"Doesn't the sheriff have real criminals to shoot?"

The siren of an ambulance pulling into the emergency room entrance drowned out their conversation. "I gotta go. I'll call you later and check on Nancy."

The doors to the emergency room banged against the wall, and two Deming police officers and an EMT charged down the hall, escorting a gurney that held a hulk of a man, who was bleeding so badly, it was dripping onto the hospital floor. The EMT moved to the front of the cart, helping to balance the IV pole, which rattled in the stark hallway. A doctor, in green scrubs followed them, shouting instructions, "Take him to surgical unit 2!"

Juan heard the doors to the emergency room lock once again. He slipped into the hall and peered out the double doors. An ambulance was pulling away. Two police officers were standing at the entrance. One was smoking a cigarette, even though a No Smoking sign hung just above his head. The light outside the emergency room went off, leaving only the ember of the officer's cigarette in the darkness. Juan turned around with every intention of moving back to the alcove so that he could check back with Alicia about Nancy, but the sound of gunfire outside the hospital caused him to dive on the floor. He crawled as far away as he could from the glass doors.

Two Deming police officers, who had been down the hall, ran toward the entrance. Juan watched them trying to assess the situation outside, but it was too dark to see anything. They pushed the old steel receptionist's desk near the doors and dropped behind it, guns drawn. Juan recognized the automatic rifle that one officer was aiming at the door. It was a Colt AR-15 A3 Tactical Carbine, a duplicate of the kind he was trying to locate for the Chihuahua cartel. Seeing that rifle in use made Juan very uncomfortable. Up until now, he had just considered the supply of guns to a cartel as a simple business deal. He never once considered who might die because he sent these guns south. The officer brandishing the automatic rifle appeared to be hiding behind his firearm. It looked almost too big for him to handle. Beads of sweat dripped down the officer's cheeks. He wasn't much older than Juan. When the policeman coughed and wiped his face with his handkerchief, Juan noticed that sweat had soaked his chest and his underarms. The officer was putting his life on the line for someone he did not know—someone who had been gunned down in Mexico and sought refuge and medical care back in the United States. This officer had the bad luck of being on duty when the attack had occurred, and fear showed on his face. He turned and looked at Juan and shook his head in warning. "You need to move further back into the hospital, sir. I can't guarantee your safety if you remain in the lobby."

A bullet shattered the window of one of the emergency room doors and hit the officer holding a 9 mm handgun. The cop remained standing and tried to return fire. He was shot again and fell forward, landing on the floor in front of the desk.

The security alarm reverberated throughout the confines of the small waiting room. The policeman holding his AR 15 released a barrage of ammo into the night air. Then he leaned over to check to see if his fellow officer was breathing. A man in a black ski mask, brandishing a handgun, appeared at the door and aimed through the broken glass at the officer, who still had his head down. Without even thinking about the consequences, Juan yanked his pistol out of his waistband and blasted the man with a barrage of bullets. The perpetrator fell through the broken window and landed on the vacated receptionist desk and slowly sank to the floor, a ribbon of blood dropping down the sides of the desk. Juan ran to the shattered window where he saw what appeared to be two dead officers just outside the entrance to the emergency room. A smoking cigarette lay at the one officer's side, burning a hole in his uniform. Juan went to check on the man in the ski mask and thought he heard more gunfire coming from somewhere outside the hospital. Were more shooters trying to gain entrance through the front door?

Juan sprinted down the hall to the operating room where his uncle was still in surgery. He decided to guard the door to his uncle's operating room, just in case the other shooters had entered from the front door. The surgeon did not object to Juan's presence when he came through the swinging double doors and showed him his firearm. The doctor said nothing and simply shook his head in the affirmative and resumed his work on Uncle Martín.

Three armed men, also in black ski masks, blew past Uncle Martín's operating room as if they knew where they were going. A salvo of bullets could be heard over the rhythm of the ventilator and the beeping of Uncle Martín's heart monitor. Just as swiftly as they had flown by, Juan could hear the shooters returning down the hall. Their boots sounded like automatic weapons tapping on the linoleum floor. The leader of the pack, visible only by his black eyes, looked in the windows of the operating room door. He held his AR-15 up where Juan could see part of it through one of the small square windows. Juan held his breath. His chest ached with fear. His hands were shaking as he shoved his own gun back in his waistband in an effort to appear unarmed. As he waited for the gunman to make a move, Juan realized how cold the operating room was. He was freezing in his own sweat.

To Juan's amazement, and great relief, the shooter saluted him and ran on down the hall yelling, "¡Vámonos a la chingada!" Let's get the hell out of here!

CHAPTER 15

Leo held Penny's hand as they both leaned toward each other, their elbows resting on the aluminum table, a picnic-style structure, bolted into the cement floor. There was no privacy. The room was full of windows, and Leo noticed there were two guards sitting in observation rooms directly across from one another. What one missed, the other would undoubtedly catch, if anything unseemly occurred between the prisoner and her guest.

"Leo, what will happen next?" Penny asked.

Leo didn't want to make her any false promises. She would read right through a lie. "I feel pretty sure that the gun tests will prove that you did not kill the deputy, but Captain Trejo must follow the regulations that state law requires. He would receive a great deal of criticism if he released you, even to my custody, with the death of a sheriff's deputy yet unsolved. Word will soon spread, and every law enforcement officer in New Mexico will be on alert by later tonight, and no one will rest until the killer is apprehended."

Penny placed her hands over her eyes and groaned.

"I know this sucks, but the fact that the dead man is law enforcement could be a good thing, because the forensics and ballistics will be rushed to find answers." Leo massaged Penny's hands, which were cold. The cuffs accentuated the slight bone structure of her wrists and her slender fingers. They made her look vulnerable, but he knew she was quite capable of taking care of herself. The desire to protect Penny at all costs erupted in his throat. He choked back his words because he loved Penny and didn't want to alarm her. Prosecuting attorneys are generally in a hurry to find cop killers, and Penny wouldn't be the first person falsely accused. To save her from this ordeal, Leo wanted to go find the killer himself, but this crime was out of his jurisdiction. Plus the fact that he was a county sheriff in Texas, even just forty miles away, made reciprocity even more unlikely, but he would try. A sliding steel door to the visiting room opened, and a correctional officer walked over to Leo and Penny. "Sheriff, it's time for Ms. Larkin to head to her cell."

Leo squeezed Penny's hands and rubbed her arm before standing. "Penny, I'll return as soon as I can with an attorney."

"Penny moved quickly around the table and leaned into him, her cuffed hands dangling in front of her. The correctional officer didn't budge, for which Leo was grateful. Leo hugged her and released her to the officer's care.

"I didn't do anything wrong, so I know it will work out." Penny looked right in Leo's eyes, and although they were moist, she managed a smile, a gesture he knew was meant to reassure him.

"I know, Penny. This will be worked out very soon." He turned to leave and then looked back at Penny. "I love you!"

"I love you too, Leo!"

Leo walked out of the visitor's area and did not look back. He felt partly responsible for this situation because he had given Penny his dad's old police issue firearm. He thought he was doing something good. Her job was dangerous and she needed protection. Now it appeared she also needed the protection of an attorney. He felt his own sidearm, which was strapped to his waist. It was then that he realized that Captain Trejo had spared him the disrespect of asking him to remove it before seeing Penny.

He walked down the dark hall toward the bright lights of the waiting room. When Adriana saw Leo coming into the room, she jumped up and rushed to his side. "Leo, I'll do what I can to help. I don't have a New Mexico law license, but I can help you find a good attorney."

"Thanks. I appreciate it."

Leo placed his arm around Adriana's shoulders, and they walked out the door of the Doňa Ana Jail and into the darkness of the late summer evening. The wind had stalled, but there was still a chill in the air, and it made Leo shiver.

CHAPTER 16

The contract killers were gone, but Juan was still shaking. He looked back across the operating room where the surgeon and his nurse were washing up at the sink. He was amazed at their calm demeanor. If they had been scared to death, they didn't show it. It was just like another day at the office to them.

An attendant unlocked the wheels of Uncle Martín's bed and shoved it toward the swinging doors, which opened automatically. Juan stepped aside and watched the aide push his uncle down the hall.

Juan followed him, carefully stepping as best he could around the blood, which was now turning into long streaks of black thanks to the cart's wheels rolling toward the recovery room. A Deming City police officer met them at the end of the hall. "We have a dead officer in the lobby. I would appreciate someone's help."

The attendant, whose name "Sam Short" was printed on his plastic ID, directed the officer back down the hall where the surgeon and the nurse were apparently still cleaning up the unit. Another attendant named Cito Castillo appeared out of nowhere, and Juan walked alongside him until they reached the recovery room. A nurse greeted them both and took the necessary steps to hook up Uncle Martín to a heart monitor and another IV. The room was hot, and rings of sweat encircled the Cito's underarms.

The aide thanked the nurse and then turned to Juan and asked, "You this man's son?"

Juan shook his head. "He is my uncle, but he's always been like a father to me. Is he going to be okay?"

"You'll have to ask the doc. Sorry."

As if on cue, the surgeon popped his head in the recovery room and yelled at the attendant. "Cito, we need you in surgery" "Sure, Doctor. I'll be right there."

Juan admired Cito and Sam. They had careers that helped people. Unlike Juan's own wasted life, Sam and Cito had some training. He wished he had time to ask Cito what it took to work in the hospital, but Cito had followed orders and hurried out of the room.

Juan looked at his hands. They were filthy from crawling on the floor and bloody from touching the dead cop lying in the lobby. He left the recovery room and looked for the bathroom. He would wash his hands before spending any time with his uncle.

Juan wasn't sure which way to go but guessed the restroom was near the emergency room lobby. He saw the lighted globe above the door on the right that read Men. He pushed the door open just as the barrel chest of the sheriff met him head on. The officer was wiping his hands on his uniform. "No towels!" The sheriff laughed.

Juan backed up and gave the sheriff the room he needed to move around him. He must be 250 pounds, he guessed, and no match for Juan, who tipped the scales at a buck fifty.

"Is your uncle out of surgery?"

Juan stammered. He was afraid of looking in the sheriff's eyes. "Yes. Yes, sir. He just arrived in the recovery room down the hall, on your left." He waved his arm in the general direction of the room with his eyes staring at the floor.

"Thanks, son." The sheriff patted Juan on the shoulder and walked past him. Juan was puzzled about why the sheriff was being so nice to him. Certainly it wasn't his normal behavior.

Didn't the sheriff wonder what he was doing at the cabin when a gun sale was going down? The sheriff was a notorious badass, who usually snubbed his nose at jailbirds like Juan. He had done time in Luna County as a teenager for shoplifting, and the experience was so bad, Juan wanted to avoid a return trip at all costs. The jail's guards were mean and it looked to Juan like the sheriff encouraged it. Juan had even seen the sheriff walk by his cell and spit on the floor.

To Juan, the sheriff's goody-goody behavior didn't add up. Maybe he was being so nice because he felt guilty for shooting Uncle Martín. Regardless, the chance encounter with the sheriff at the door of the restroom cut into his belly like barbed wire. He was going to be sick. Juan stumbled into the bathroom stall where he gagged and poured his fear and the contents of his stomach into the toilet bowl. He wiped his mouth with the sleeve of his jacket and headed to the washstand. He used plenty of soap and hot water to get rid of the grime and blood and then threw water on his face. Being cleaner made him feel a bit better, but he still had to avoid any further contact with the sheriff. Where could he hide until Pritchard left the hospital?

Before Juan could figure that out, the bathroom door opened, and two police officers walked in. "Lieutenant, here is the guy who saved my life." The police sergeant held out his hand to Juan, and Juan responded by wiping his fingers on his jeans and shaking the officer's hand. "Ed Jackman's my name. Thank you for stepping up and killing that guy."

Lieutenant Tom Strident was standing behind Jackman and was the next to shake Juan's hand. "You did a very brave thing, young man. Sergeant Jackman is the only officer that made it out, and I thank you for saving him."

Juan stood in stunned silence. If the lieutenant wondered whether or not Juan's firearm was registered, he never asked. Both officers turned and left him alone in the bathroom. Juan went back into the stall and threw up again.

CHAPTER 17

Penny watched the female correctional officer slide the heavy steel bars closed. She heard the automatic locks engage, and the reality of her circumstances crashed in on her. It had been humiliating enough to have her fingers scanned for prints and her photo taken like a common criminal, but now the locks had moved into place, and she was indeed in jail.

"This is just a holding cell," the officer told Penny. You will be moved to a more permanent cell in the morning."

This was not what Penny wanted to hear. The word *permanent* stung. She wanted to be out of jail by morning, and she was praying the gun tests proved she could not have killed the Luna County correctional officer. Penny sat on the cot that jutted out of the wall, hanging by large steel bolts that could hold even the heaviest prisoner. Her feet, donning paper footies, dangled from the bed. There was a pillow with no pillowcase, and a ticking- style mattress that was reminiscent of Penny's days at summer camp in Wisconsin.

She had to use the bathroom, but the stainless steel toilet in the corner of the cell had no seat and no privacy. Penny watched correctional officers escorting handcuffed prisoners in and out of cells. It was a regular circus without the peanuts. She would hold off until the lights went out.

They go out at night, don't they?

Several hours passed before Penny realized the lights did not go off in the holding cell area. She saw the large clock on the wall in the guardroom. It was 2:00 a.m. She had no choice but to use the restroom as discreetly as she could. But in spite of her careful planning, a guard and an unruly prisoner walked by just as she sat down on the toilet. The prisoner lashed out at the guard, who responded by knocking the man into the window of Penny's cell. He was drunk but not drunk enough that he didn't notice Penny, who was literally caught with her pants down. Her orange jumpsuit had to be dropped to the floor to use the bathroom, and there she sat in all of her glory.

"Well, lookee there! I like this place, officer." The man protested loudly as the guard pulled him back to his feet and shoved him forward without a word. "But, officer, I want to go in there with the pretty lady."

It was then that Penny saw the prisoner in the cell opposite to hers leaning on the glass and smiling at her. She ignored his wave and jumped up, pulled on her jumpsuit, and fell into the bed. There was no blanket, so she lay there fully exposed to the cold, cruel world of crime. Her neck was aching from the chill in the air, and her stomach growled. She remembered she had not eaten since she left El Paso many hours ago. She thought of Leo, and this brought her some comfort. But then the face of the beautiful Adriana interrupted her solace. She was clearly jealous of someone she did not know, and she wished she could see what they might be up to on their way home. She trusted Leo, but she did not trust Adriana. To attempt a viewing right now would be too painful to endure. She was better off not knowing. Besides, the jail was as noisy as a nightclub, making it impossible to concentrate on anything as difficult as that. Doors clanked open and shut. Men were yelling obscenities. Penny thought she heard a woman crying.

If she ever got out of here, she promised to give up this job. Nothing was worth this aggravation. Just being confined for a few hours was making her physically ill and full of regret. She would have to find another line of work, and right now, even waiting tables looked very appealing.

CHAPTER 18

It took Leo forty-five minutes to drive back to El Paso from Las Cruces and another fifteen minutes to arrive at Adriana's townhouse in the central part of town. They sat in silence for several minutes in front of her house. He dared not look at her. Leo had not planned on being alone with Adriana at night in his SUV. It felt awkward and uncomfortable. He adjusted his seat belt, trying to kill time until she opened the door and said her good-byes. But she didn't make any move to exit the car. Instead, Leo could feel Adriana's eyes drilling into his cheekbones. He kept his neck riveted to his shoulders and breathed deeply, counting back from 30. He would give her half a minute, and then he'd look directly into her brown-black eyes and tell her he had to get going.

He looked out the windshield at the streetlights, and his pupils began to be pixilated. The painful memory of Alejandra's death and the death of his infant daughter, Marta, lodged squarely in his throat, making it impossible to speak. He would remain strong. He did not want Adriana to see that after five years, his heart had still not healed.

Leo could hear Adriana's breathing, steady and secure, unlike his own lungs, which were now tapping in his chest like a snare drum on a battlefield. He felt her fingers on his arm. And then she effortlessly found his right hand, which was gripping the steering wheel. He looked down at her slender fingers, her nails long and painted bright red. She pulled his hand free and began to massage his fingers and the palm of his hand, which was surprisingly sensitive to her touch. A chill shot up his back and through his shoulder blades with the heat of her hand building in his. The rhythmic movement of her fingers caused his affirmation of silence to collapse. Leo's other hand dropped from the wheel, and he reached for Adriana and held her tightly using her body to absorb his grief. She smelled sweetly of strawberries and vanilla, the same perfume that Alejandra had always worn.

"Why don't you come in for a while, Leo? You are in no shape to drive home." She pushed his hair away out of his eyes, but he pulled away.

"I can't do that. And besides, Penny needs me."

"There's nothing you can do tonight. I will help find her an attorney in the morning. I just remembered that I know an awesome defense attorney in Las Cruces. Not to worry. And besides, she's not going anywhere. She's safe. Captain Trejo promised he would keep her isolated from other prisoners until the forensics came through."

"I could use some hot tea," Leo said. His arms relaxed and dropped to his sides.

"Good. Tea is just what the doctor ordered!" Adriana laughed, and even Leo let out a sigh of relief. What harm would it do to spend time with his wife's sister? She hadn't lived in El Paso for more than ten years, and he had to confess he really didn't know her.

Leo locked his Tahoe, and they walked up the steps to the front door of the townhome, which bore the architectural details of a Spanish hacienda. The formidable arched, oak door held steel studs driven into the door in the shape of a shield. It was a cautionary tale for burglars to stay away. *Good luck breaking down this door*, Leo thought.

He had not been inside Adriana's new place, and it was much of what he expected. He immediately felt at home with the polished oak floors, the Native American rugs, and the tasteful mixture of Mexican antiquities and Asian artifacts that Adriana had apparently acquired on her worldly travels.

"Have a seat on the sofa while I fix us some tea."

Leo hesitated. "Don't you want some help? I imagine you are exhausted too."

"I'll just put on the tea kettle and get out the tea and be right back."

Leo sank into the leather sofa. He laid his head against an equally cushy throw pillow. He was happy just to sit there and wait for Adriana to bring him a cup of tea. It had been a long and confusing day, and he was too tired to sort it out right now. His eyelids were irritated, as if laden with sand. He could barely see across the faintly lit room. Leo lifted his hand to rub his eyes and was surprised to find his fingers trembling. What in the world was happening to him? His body and mind were mush. He doubted he could hold his own in a fistfight right now. When he tried to get his hands to stop shaking, he could barely flex his fingers. Was seeing Adriana paralyzing him? Or was it the guilt of leaving Penny alone in jail? He looked around the room and thought he saw a photo of Adriana and Alejandra on the fireplace mantle. Leo tried to stand to take a closer look, but he could not move.

Adriana walked back into the living room and plopped down next to him. She leaned into his shoulder, and when Leo did not respond, she turned her body completely around and lay across his lap. Leo tried to move her, but Adriana was not budging. She lifted her body upward in a fluid movement and brought her face close to his. He could smell her breath. Had she just brushed her teeth?

Adriana took her index finger and moved it back and forth across Leo's lips. His mouth quivered. He was fearful of what his response might be if he didn't leave her house immediately.

But how could he?

Her fingertips moved to his cheekbones and then dropped to a hollow place in his neck. Leo swallowed in a natural reflex to her touch. He knew this was all a very big mistake, but he was paralyzed. He was being stripped of his willpower by the agony of seeing Alejandra's eyes in those of Adriana's. His arms felt like lead bars, and his fingers were fused together like he was wearing mittens. *But I must move!* Leo loved Penny, and she had tried everything to get him past his grief. This was not anyway to repay her loyalty.

"Adriana, I can't do this!" He tried to stand, but the weight of her body pressing firmly into his made it impossible to get up without throwing her to the floor.

"We're doing nothing wrong. Why can't we help one another get past the loss? Don't think you're the only one who has suffered. Alejandra is my twin, my flesh and blood, and she is in my thoughts every day!"

Leo had been callous not to consider how Adriana felt about losing her twin sister. She was right. They both needed time to heal, and why not do it together? Leo may be sheriff, but he was still a man who needed reassurance that life would go on. He should cut himself a little slack and take life as it comes.

He placed his arms around Adriana's waist and pulled her close. His mouth crushed her lips in a response that surprised him, but Adriana did not seem to notice. She moaned and maneuvered her body closer to his. Her reaction, tied with Leo's eagerness to drive away the pain, blinded him to any other reality in his life. This would be nothing like making love to Penny—an often soft and gentle time, after which they lay for hours in the sheets, just talking and dreaming about tomorrow. Tonight, however, his battery was recharging, and the act would be bold and swift.

Watching Adriana slip off her blouse, Leo could think of nothing but sparking a union that he knew would leave him hanging somewhere between life and death. He unbuckled his belt and felt the hardness in his groin. Once he crossed this line with Adriana, his life with Penny would be finished. He could keep nothing from her—after all, she was psychic. Was she viewing this very encounter? Leo took a moment to ponder that possibility and then shook it off. In newfound strength, he lifted Adriana from the sofa and laid her gently onto the heavy pile rug. She reached for him, and he dropped down beside her. He was breathless, and his whole body ached for relief. She took off her slacks, revealing her long slender legs. When Adriana wrapped them around his waist and locked her ankles in the small of his back, Leo was sure the rug's triangular patterns of red and brown were moving in time with the undulating rhythm of Adriana's hips. But his eyes were playing tricks on him. The rug had not moved. He was the one who was dancing.

The whistling of the teakettle broke the spell. Leo heard it first, having acquired an ear and an eye for things in the periphery of a crime scene. Adriana begrudgingly dropped her legs and rolled on to her knees. "Darn it!" She jumped up and stamped off toward the kitchen. Leo watched her walk away barefooted, in only her bra and panties.

The shrill of the teakettle was a wake-up call for Leo and brought him back to his senses. Had he lost his mind? He had to get out of there, while he still had the willpower to do so. He rolled onto his feet, zipped up his pants, while ignoring the ache between his legs, and drove his cowboy hat on his head like a hammer to a nail. He had made it to the front door when Adriana came running out of the kitchen. "Leo, don't go! We need each other!"

CHAPTER 19

Johnny Trejo drove down the long gravel driveway leading to his parents' house. They had lived in the three-bedroom cottage for forty years, and now that his dad was dead, his mother needed her only child more than ever. Johnny had promised his mother he would be there for dinner, but it was now almost 3:00 a.m.

Knowing his mother, he knew she would still be awake and have his meal waiting in the oven.

Maria Olivia Vásquez Trejo was sixty years old, but she had lived so simply and so frugally that her mind and her looks had not aged at all. She was convinced that buying things you can't afford only weighed you down and caused you to grow old before your time. Johnny figured she was right.

He turned the key in the door and stepped into the foyer. He could smell the enchiladas. When his mother had been cooking all day, the house always paid the price. Mexican cooking, often made with lard, had its way of permeating the walls and draperies, but no one ever seemed to care. Food in Johnny's culture meant comfort and security.

"Mamacita!" Johnny called out to his mother, who was probably in her sewing room trying to keep herself busy so she wouldn't worry about why Johnny was late for dinner. Ollie, as her family called her, walked out of the sewing room and moved quickly to greet her son. When he hugged her, he was reminded again of how small she was. She was barely five feet tall.

"Your dinner is in the oven, mijo!"

Ollie moved into the kitchen and pulled the steaming dish of chicken enchiladas out of the oven. She served Johnny's plate, garnished with rice and beans, and a side of pico de gallo. Johnny inhaled the food and tried to forget the grisly day he had just endured. Ollie sat down across from him in his dad's chair and reached across the table.

"I have something for you, mijo. It is a Saint Christopher's medal. It will protect you. I tried to get your papa to wear his, but he refused, and now…" Ollie broke into tears, and Johnny jumped up and tried to comfort his mother. He took the medal that was hanging on a silver chain and hooked it around his neck. "Of course, Mamá. I'll wear it if it makes you feel better.

But don't worry. I don't take chances like…" He broke off his sentence, realizing that his comment was salt in their wounds. His dad had always taken chances with his job, and that was just one way he disrespected them, the other was drinking himself to sleep at night.

Ollie stood up and threw her arms around him. "Thank you, Johnny. You are my only child. I have no one left, but you."

Johnny knew his mother wasn't into guilt trips, but she was doing her best to keep him alive, and he would do everything he could to take care of himself so he could continue to take care of her. He ate his meal and drank a glass of iced tea in silence. His mother had moved to the kitchen sink and was cleaning up the dish she had kept warm in the oven. When she turned back to him, she was smiling. "I have a treat for you, mijo!"

Ollie pulled a large plate of flan out of the refrigerator and cut two pieces and placed them on plates. She poured each of them a cup of coffee. Their conversation turned to the clever use of desert plants she had seen at her garden club and the high price of coffee at the supermarket. The sweet, caramel custard melted over Johnny's tongue, and he couldn't help but feel happy.

"Thanks, Mamá!"

"Oh, I forgot to tell you. Joanna called today, just to talk. She did ask about you too."

Joanna Muñoz was Johnny's former fiancée. They had broken off their relationship six months ago, at her insistence. She wanted to head to Colorado Springs to attend college, something she had dreamed about for years. He had reluctantly let her go. He was not one to stand in her way of improving her life. She wanted to become a forest ranger, and the best place to learn and gain employment was in Colorado.

"She called about your daddy. She said to tell you how sorry…" Ollie choked on those words. She jumped up and made herself busy again putting plastic wrap over the flan and carrying it to the refrigerator.

"Mamá, do you need me to stay with you tonight?" "Would you mind?"

Johnny's cell phone vibrated on his belt. "Trejo."

"Captain, the forensic is back on Penny Larkin's gun. We just got the report over the fax. I think you should see this in person." "Mom, I've got to go. I'll be back hopefully before sunup, so when you hear me come in, don't panic." "What is so important that it can't wait?"

"A law enforcement officer has been killed, and the whole state is focused on finding his killer."

"You mean another officer has died? That is the second one in two weeks." Ollie brought her fingers up to her eyes and let out a small whimper.

"We've got someone in custody, and I've got to follow up on her."

"A girl has shot a police officer?"

"I don't know that for sure. That's why I've got to go." Johnny leaned in and gave his mom a peck on the cheek. He jumped in his patrol car and headed for the headquarters in downtown Las Cruces.

When Johnny got there, he was surprised to find the squad room filled with troopers. Even Ted Rodríguez, the Doña Ana County Sheriff, was sipping coffee in the corner.

"What's up with the report?" Johnny asked as he walked over to Sergeant Gentry Miller who was reading it intently. His bifocals were lying cockeyed on his face as he focused on the details. The lighting in the squad room was notoriously poor, and Johnny had been trying without success to get it improved.

"Well, Captain, it looks like the young woman in custody could not have killed the deputy. A 9 mm bullet killed Harold Moreno. Ms. Larkin's gun is a .38 caliber. Looks like she was telling you the truth."

Sheriff Rodriguez yelled at Johnny, "I could have told you that Penny Larkin was innocent!"

Johnny turned abruptly, grabbed Penny's windbreaker from his office conference table, and headed for the door.

"Where you going?" Sergeant Miller was looking confused. "You just got here!"

CHAPTER 20

Penny had given up any hope of sleep. Her fingernails had drawn red streaks across her arms and legs where the rough material of the jumpsuit had irritated her skin. She turned back and forth on the mattress. Calling it lumpy would have been a compliment. She was too lazy to get up and check the clock in the guardroom, but she figured it must be almost 4:00 a.m. All she could think about was seeing Leo walk through the door to the holding area and telling her she was free to go.

When she heard the clanking of the main door to the cells slide open, Penny held her breath. She had butterflies in her stomach, just like a child hoping for a reprieve from a timeout on the playground. Could she be getting her wish so soon? Had Leo come to get her after all? She raised her head so she could hear the voices of two men.

"Yes, sir. I'll call Judy to help her get dressed."

Penny sat up in her bed and stared out of her cell door. She could not see who was discussing her future, but she hoped that Leo had arrived to rescue her.

The woman deputy opened Penny's door and brought her clothes to her. She hated to put them on. They were grimy and wrinkled, but she was so excited to get out of jail that she yanked on her jeans and stepped into her tennis shoes, once again without lacing them.

Where is my bra? Judy had not brought it, and she had shut the cell door and was nowhere to be found. Penny threw caution to the wind and pulled on the white T-shirt and shook out her hair, which had matted against the left side of her head. She waited for the jailer to return. When she finally did, which seemed like an eternity, a chill rippled through Penny's body as she took her first steps toward freedom. The temperature had dropped considerably in the drafty hall, and she began to shiver. She must have left her jacket at the state troopers' headquarters. Maybe Leo would stop by there to get it for her. She wasn't sure she could make it home without more protection from the night air.

Penny walked down the dark hall into the waiting room. She was shaking hard now, not just from the temperature but also from the sheer excitement of seeing Leo. It took some time for her eyes to adjust to the lighting. The waiting room was a blur. When they did, she saw her windbreaker and her purse in the arms of Captain Trejo. Penny looked around the room, which was so brightly lit she couldn't help think of all the money being wasted.

She squinted and walked up to Captain Trejo who helped her put on the jacket. Penny wanted to ask where Leo was, but she was afraid to. She was grateful to be free, and that would have to suffice until she got to her car. She searched in her purse for her car keys but came up empty.

"Ms. Larkin, the ballistics report came back, and your gun did not kill Deputy Moreno. I'm sorry you had to endure this, but the death of a police officer is a capital offense, and I had to follow the laws."

"Yes, I know. I'm just glad to be out of there. Can you take me to my car?"

"Your car is still the subject of the investigation, and we can't release it until our CSI finishes their tests. They are running fingerprints we found on the side of the vehicle. Maybe i t will bring us some leads."

"Can you call Leo to come and get me?"

"I wasn't able to reach him on his cell. I'm going to drive you home."

XXX

Captain Trejo's Dodge Charger barreled south on I-10 toward El Paso with Penny in the passenger seat. She thought they were making pretty good time, even though there were several work zones that slowed them down. Penny was happy for the warmth of the car, and she leaned back in her seat and shut her eyes. She had stopped shivering from the cold, but she was still wondering about Leo. Didn't he care enough to stay in touch with the New Mexico State Police for the ballistics report?

The Charger's tires rolling across the pavement lulled Penny to sleep. She found herself dreaming of Leo. She saw him lounging on a leather sofa, his head leaning on a pillow. His eyes were closed. Maybe he had been so tired he had fallen asleep and forgotten to check on her. A flash of long black hair crossed the web of her dreams and brought her wide awake! Was Leo with Adriana? Was that why he hadn't bothered to be there when she got out of jail?

Penny didn't feel like sleeping anymore in spite of how tired she was from lying wide awake in the jail. Any more dreaming might show Leo and Adriana doing something that Penny couldn't bear to watch. She shoved both fists into the bucket seat and tried to contain her anger. Had Leo betrayed her? She wiped away a tear and sat up straight. She noticed Captain Trejo staring at her.

"Are you hungry?" he asked Penny.

She was starving. "Yes, I am." Penny looked at Captain Trejo's eyes. She hadn't noticed the brown and gray flecks and the long lashes before.

"How about some eggs? I know a little place on Highway 80. It won't take us too far out of our way."

XXX

Johnny pulled into the gravel parking lot of Dot's Good N Early Café. He knew Dot opened at 5:00 a.m. and closed by noon. It was now almost 5:00 a.m. Dot only served breakfast—and lots of it. The restaurant was a regular stop for troopers in the Las Cruces area. The food was cheap and delicious. Dot's husband had been killed in the line of duty as a Doña Ana sheriff's deputy fifteen years ago, and she held her own financially by serving a really great plate of biscuits, eggs, and bacon.

Johnny walked around the car and opened Penny's door and helped her out.

"Thanks, Captain Trejo."

"Why don't you call me Johnny? I don't bite. Really!" He laughed and was happy when Penny smiled. He hadn't seen her smile since he met her twelve hours ago on that windy section of I-10.

They stood on the front porch of the restaurant, which was located in an aging clapboard house. Dot's restaurant fronted the Old Spanish Trail where sixteenth century soldiers rode their horses northward with promises of great riches in Santa Fe. Johnny knocked on the front door, and within minutes, Dot appeared. Her apron was as white as the bleach bottle could get it. "Johnny, come on in! I'm just taking the biscuits out of the oven."

Johnny stood back and let Penny go through the door. Dot escorted the two of them to a booth in the corner closest to the kitchen where she was moving at breakneck speed to prepare for her first customers of the day.

"You both want coffee?"

Penny nodded her head and smiled at Dot who poured the hot steaming liquid into their cups. Johnny could tell that Penny was relaxing a little. She placed her elbows on the table and leaned into the cup and brought it to her lips. "I never knew I would be so thrilled to be drinking coffee. I'm usually an iced tea person." "Dot makes the best coffee in southern New Mexico. I'm not sure how she does it in that great big pot, but it's the best. It beats Starbucks!"

Dot slid a plate of steaming biscuits and a pitcher of honey across the table. Johnny watched Penny pick up a biscuit and drown it with a glop of honey. She shoved half of the biscuit in her mouth.

Dot remained standing in front of the booth with her hands resting on her hips. "Johnny, you have been holding back on me," she said. "You gonna introduce me to your girlfriend?"

Johnny saw Penny's eyes widen as she covered her mouth and tried to swallow. He worried she would be annoyed with Dot's intrusiveness, but Penny remained quiet. She was enjoying her biscuit too much, Johnny guessed, to worry about being called somebody's girlfriend.

"Dot, this is Penny. She and I are just friends. We're not dating." Dot frowned and then reloaded. "Well, you could have fooled me, Johnny. She looks like such a nice girl, and it's been too long since Joanna left. How long has it been—six months?"

"Joanna is in college in Colorado," Johnny tried to explain this to Dot without drawing any more attention to Penny.

"I'm Dot, in case you didn't guess." Dot seemed to be ignoring Johnny, and this irritated him further. She looked straight at Penny and waited for her response.

"Hi, Dot. I'm glad to meet you," Penny answered. "Cap... Johnny brought me in because we had been working a case, and I was starving to death. He couldn't stop talking about your bacon and eggs, so I begged him to take me here."

"You a police woman?"

Johnny was embarrassed that Dot kept pressing for information. "Dot, go easy on her, will ya?"

If Penny were annoyed, she didn't show it. "I'm an investigator for the US Marshals Service." Penny rummaged through her black bag and pulled out a Federal marshal's badge. It had been pinned inside a pocket in the black zippered lining of her purse. This news stunned Johnny. How had he missed it? And furthermore, how had the jail's guards missed it? He felt like a fool. He picked up a biscuit and jammed most of it in his mouth. A piece of the biscuit lodged in his throat, and he began to choke. Dot pounded him on his back, which helped some, and then he grabbed a glass of water and gulped it down. When Dot saw that Johnny was going to live, she left the table. Johnny thought he noticed Penny trying to hold back a chuckle.

"Why didn't you tell me you were a Fed?" Johnny was still coughing. He wiped his mouth with his napkin.

"I've been ordered not to tell anyone about the case I'm working on—not even Leo." "So you can't tell me?" "Of course not!"

Johnny thought he would take a wild guess. "Is this about the suspected gun trafficking within law enforcement?" Johnny watched Penny's pupils grow big again.

"Why in the world would you think that?" Penny asked him, with a bit of disgust on her lips.

"I'm working undercover for the US Marshals Service too." Penny said nothing.

Dot was balancing two platters in her right hand and carrying a pot of coffee in the other. Johnny grabbed the pot and poured refills for Penny and him. Dot set the plates on the table and left to greet two more customers who had entered the restaurant.

"The marshal said he had a secret weapon in the search for the gunrunners! Is it you?" Johnny asked.

"I don't know what you're talking about." Penny drove her fork into her scrambled eggs and scooped up a large bite. She never looked up from her meal and kept shoveling it in like a lumberjack.

Johnny had to know what was going on. He had been made a fool of, and it had to stop it right here. He hit speed dial, and Marshal Lujan answered on the first ring. "Hey, Eugene, I'm having breakfast with a Ms. Penny Larkin. Is she your secret weapon? She refuses to talk."

CHAPTER 21

Juan was dreaming about Disneyland. His daughters were screaming with excitement as they waited for their chance to ride the Teacups. He felt someone shaking his shoulder and figured his wife needed money for the concession stand. "Mr. Rico, your uncle is calling for you."

At first, Juan was confused. He had never been to Disneyland, but it certainly didn't look like this! The dingy white walls surrounding him were stained with something he didn't recognize. Yuck! And where was his wife? Instead, a very the large woman, with white hair and glasses so thick it was a wonder she could see at all, was bending over him and shoving her large arms against his left shoulder. She wore medical scrubs decorated with Mickey Mouse and her nametag read, "Molly Peters, RN." He tried to move away from her, but he was straddling three pink plastic chairs as a makeshift bed.

Now Juan remembered that he had decided to rest his eyes until his uncle was out of recovery. He didn't mean to fall asleep. What a stupid and deadly thing to do! He shook his head in disbelief and quickly rolled off the chairs. As he did, one of the chairs slammed against the wall, causing him to lose his balance. He stumbled forward into Nurse Peters. Her massive arms caught him and kept him from landing face first on the floor.

"I'm sorry!" A pain shot up Juan's back and into his neck from the uncomfortable position he had been lying in for God knows how long. He looked at the clock on the wall. Two hours could not have passed that fast!

"Don't you worry, son! I know how hard it is to sleep in a waiting room." The nurse smiled, and Juan thought she looked like she meant it. Then she turned around and headed down the hall.

In a panic, Juan remembered his gun, which he was grateful to find still safely tucked in the back of his waistband and hidden by his jacket. He took a big breath and blew it out in relief. He would have to be more careful. The gun could have easily fallen on the floor while he slept.

Juan managed to straighten up and shuffle toward the recovery room where he had left his Uncle Martín. The person lying there was not his uncle but a young man with a bandaged right eye. The patient appeared be under the influence of medication because he was groaning and tossing from one side of the bed to the other. Juan heard the flushing of a toilet, and Nurse Peters came out of the room's adjoining bathroom. He watched her secure the patient and offer him a sip of water from a straw. Then she turned to Juan who was leaning against the door jamb.

"You lost?" The nurse smiled at him. "Come on, I'll show you where to go."

Uncle Martín had been moved to another wing, which faced the front of the hospital. *Hopefully, Uncle Martín would be safer here*, Juan thought. He was glad to see that the other bed in his room was empty. That would make it easier to talk to his uncle in case he woke up angry. He hoped his uncle wouldn't ask him any questions because Juan couldn't tell him anything for fear of getting him involved in his dirty business.

The red flashing lights of a police car parked in front of the hospital bounced through the room's windows and dropped onto the empty bed like splotches of blood. Juan shivered and rubbed his arms. He moved quickly to the window and closed the blinds, not wanting to upset Uncle Martín any more than he already was, and to also shut out the reminder of the police presence for himself. Juan pulled up a straight chair next to the bed and cleared his throat, letting his uncle know that he was there.

After several minutes, Uncle Martín opened his eyes and blinked.

"You want me to shut off the lights?" Juan asked.

"Nah. It's okay." His uncle glanced at his shoulder, which was wrapped in a bandage, and shut his eyes again. "Doggone it, how am I supposed to get on my horse with my arm strapped to my chest?"

"Uncle Martín, why did the sheriff shoot you?" Juan hoped if he played dumb, his uncle would not figure out just what Juan had been doing in the cabin.

"Juan, listen to me. If you are into something with guns, you've got to drop it right now. Once you're in, there's no way out. I know you need money, but this is no way to earn it. And your wife and kids deserve better."

Juan was speechless. He was afraid to answer for fear he'd give up everything he had been doing for the last year. But his uncle went on. "The sheriff shot me before he knew who I was. He didn't even give me a chance to identify myself. This tells me he's involved in some way and that he had planned to kill you right after he got your guns. And hell, he may come back and kill me since he knows I'm not the dumbest rock in the pile."

Juan took his uncle's hand."I won't let him hurt you. I promise."
"Look, kid, I can take care of myself. I've still got my rifle!

Where is that dang thing?" He acted like he was actually going to get out of bed and search for it.

Nurse Peters walked in the room without knocking. "Mr. Romero, Sheriff Pritchard is asking to see you. Are you up to having more visitors?"

Before Juan or his uncle could answer her, they saw the sheriff standing a few feet behind the nurse. His voice sounded like a clap of thunder. "Ma'am, you're in the way!" He took his arm and nudged the nurse backward so that his wide body could get closer to Martín's bed. Nurse Peters frowned, grunted, and headed back down the hall.

The sheriff starred at Martín, apparently not all that concerned about Juan being there. He patted Martín's arm but not in a caring way. It looked more like when Juan's mother tried to make him leave her alone when he had been bothering her. She would tap him three times on the arm and that was his signal that their time together was over. Juan tried to remain calm, but he was breathing too hard. What was the sheriff up to? Juan's chest tightened until he could hear his breath whistling in his throat.

"Romero, you're a lucky guy. It's a good thing I'm a bad shot!" The sheriff laughed as he shoved his sweat-soaked cowboy hat back off his forehead. It exposed a pair of brown eyes that were too small for his pudgy, round face and his very large ears, which in the harsh light of the hospital room reminded Juan of the cartoon character Moon Pie. His children watched the show on Saturday mornings. Juan wished he could turn the sheriff off with a twist of a knob because it looked like he was trying to scare Uncle Martín. Certainly, the sheriff knew that his uncle didn't scare easily even wrapped up like a mummy.

Juan, however, was another matter.

He moved into the recesses of the room and leaned against the wall, hoping to avoid the same kind of treatment. He felt his pistol digging into his kidneys as he shoved his back against the sheet rock.

The sheriff leaned into Martín, moving his IV pole further from the bed. "What brought you to your cabin at dark, Romero? It's downright dangerous to walk through that minefield of boulders, even during the day."

"It's my land. I can go where I want on it, when I want."

Juan knew what the sheriff's next question would be. What was Juan doing in the cabin that everyone knew had been empty for the last several years? Juan rubbed his damp hands on his jeans and then touched his face. It was hot and probably red, like it always got when he was nervous.

"I was visiting my nephew. He has been living in the cabin since his wife threw him out!" Uncle Martín's answer was not what the sheriff expected because he looked confused. Juan exhaled and rubbed his hands against his jeans again. His face was on fire.

The sheriff shifted his eyes toward Juan, considering this possibility. "Well, all right, then." He glanced at Juan and walked toward him. "Son, I'm sorry to hear about you splittin' up with your wife. I know Alicia and your daughters, Nancy and Paula, are pretty special." He leaned close to Juan, breathing heavily into his face. "It would be a shame to lose all that, now wouldn't it?"

Juan's heart crashed against his chest. He leaned back against the wall again, ignoring the weight of his pistol punching a hole in the small of his back. He tried without success to fill his lungs with air. Instead, he focused his eyes on the linoleum floor, which was scarred from the movement of heavy furniture. How did the sheriff know his wife's name? Did he know where his family lived? Juan had wanted to shout, "Don't touch my family!" But he knew it was too late for that.

The smug look on the sheriff's face made Juan so mad that he instinctively felt for his pistol and yanked it from its hiding place. The sheriff didn't see the gun. He had already turned on his heels and was headed out of the room. The cold night air seeping through the poorly insulated window dropped a heavy blanket of dread over the entire room. Juan looked over at his uncle, who was sleeping or perhaps pretending to be. "That's good, Uncle Martín," Juan whispered.

"You keep your eyes closed because you don't want to see this."

Juan was sweating profusely in spite of the chill he felt in the drafty room. His right hand trembled as he tried to get a better grip on the gun. Drops of sweat rolled down his arms into the palms of his hands, and he was forced to use his left hand to steady his right one. Juan took a few steps forward, the pistol knocking against his thighs. He could hear Uncle Martín snoring, which meant his uncle really was asleep and wouldn't see him leave. If Juan hurried, he could catch the sheriff before he reached his patrol car.

CHAPTER 22

Leo drove to the El Paso County Sheriff's Office to check his office phone for a message from Johnny Trejo. He had stupidly left his cell phone at Adriana's, somewhere on the living room floor when he had unfastened his pants. He didn't dare return for it tonight. He had already made a big enough fool of himself.

The El Paso County Sheriff's night dispatcher nodded to Leo as he passed him in the darkened hall. The dispatcher's desk was encircled in a small halo of light, which was just wide enough for him to see the phone system and take notes. When the administrative staff wasn't on duty, Leo had ordered the lights off as a cost savings to the county. It was more of a political move than anything. He was up for reelection, and he needed all the good press he could get. His opponent, Fortuno Parasea, was a handsome, retired captain from the El Paso City Police Force. Leo considered Parasea more flash than substance, but he was rapidly gaining popularity among young women voters. At forty-two, Leo wasn't exactly over the hill, but according to thirty-five-year-old Captain Parasea, Leo was past his prime.

Leo's office was at the end of the hall, and with only the help of the building's emergency lights, it was tough to find the key on his ring of countless keys. Leo dropped them on the tile floor trying to jam the wrong key in the lock. After scooping them up and fumbling around, Leo finally connected, and the door opened. A flashing red light on his phone indicated that a message was waiting. He was desperate for news of Penny, and yet his hand resisted picking up the receiver. He was surprised to find that his whole body was shaking and the live wires dancing in his gut had returned. When Leo was dealing with the loss of his wife and daughter five years ago, his psychiatrist had said the pain in his stomach was a sign of unresolved guilt. Now an excruciating jolt of pain stung his midsection and forced him to his knees. He smelled the nauseating stench of his own sweat and rested his head on the seat of his desk chair. Would he be sick? Leo wondered whether he could make it to the men's room by crawling and without the dispatcher wondering what was wrong. He deeply regretted leaving Penny alone in the Doña Ana County Jail, but he had to take Adriana home, didn't he? He couldn't expect her to spend the night in the jail drinking cold coffee! Leo pulled out his handkerchief and spit into it—it tasted of bile and the bitterness of regret. He managed to hang onto his desk and pull himself into a standing position. The pain roared on, but he had to get back to Las Cruces. He would deal with his feelings for Adriana later. As his father used to say, "Go home with the one who brought you to the dance." Boy he had really screwed things up.

Leo sat in his chair and rummaged through his desk drawer for a bottle of Maalox. Finding it, he took a long swig and wiped his mouth with his handkerchief. He couldn't put off listening to his messages any longer. He leaned toward the phone and tapped in his code for his voice mail. There were two. The first was from Adriana who told him she had his phone and did he want to return tonight to retrieve it. The second call was from Johnny Trejo. He replayed his message several times, trying to decide what to do next.

"Sheriff, you were right. Penny's gun was not implicated in the death of the correctional officer. I tried your mobile and couldn't reach you, so as a courtesy, I am going to take Penny home. We have to keep her car, of course, because of the blood and the indentation on the hood. I may take her to get some breakfast since it's about 4:30 a.m. right now, so you will probably find her at home sometime after 7."

It was well after 6:00 a.m. Leo dialed Penny's home number, but her voice mail clicked on. He hated trying her cell phone if she were in a restaurant having breakfast with Johnny Trejo. Would he sound desperate or genuinely interested in her welfare? He didn't care how it looked. He pressed Penny's cell phone number and waited for her to pick up. She did not. Maybe the phone's battery had died. Certainly, she wasn't ignoring him?

The early morning light now allowed him safe passage down the hall. Leo ran out the door of his office, waving backhandedly to the dispatcher. When he reached the parking lot, he wrestled with his keys and dropped them onto the pavement. By the time he climbed into his Tahoe and placed his car in gear, Leo's world was in complete chaos. He drove straight to Penny's house and pounded on her door. The house was dark. He stumbled over the pot of pink geraniums he had placed on her porch as a gift and nearly fell off the steps. Leo knew he was in no shape to drive anywhere, but he climbed back in his car and headed north on I-10 toward Las Cruces.

He exited the interstate at one of the larger truck stops that Leo knew served a decent breakfast. He cruised the parking lot, not finding a New Mexico State Trooper's car. He jumped out of this SUV anyway and charged into the truck stop, ignoring a line of truckers buying bags of snacks and bottles of soda for the next legs of their trip. The restaurant was in the back of the building, and Leo figured out why. You had to pass by rows of DVDs, CDs, candy, chips, and a wide assortment of truck accessories, followed by a bank of showers, before getting to the restaurant. He squinted, trying to adjust his eyes to the glaring lights. The staff was just setting up what looked like a breakfast buffet. The smell of the food, instead of drawing him in, made his aching stomach queasy again. Leo scanned the room. A couple tucked inside one of booths saw him and gave Leo a dirty look. Leo realized, not being in uniform, he probably appeared to be invading their space. He immediately turned away, embarrassed to have evoked such a response from ordinary folks. Hopefully, they didn't recognize him. Every vote counted.

Leo returned to the Tahoe and pulled back on the interstate. The traffic was picking up even at such an early hour, so he turned on the red flashing lights he had specially installed for times like these. He went roaring up I-10, his mind buzzing with different scenarios, and none of them were helpful to his state of mind. Maybe it was his guilty conscience for putting himself in a compromising position with Adriana, but Leo now imagined Penny and Johnny laughing and sharing stories over a cup of coffee. *They must be lingering at the restaurant, but what restaurant? Where in the hell are they?*

CHAPTER 23

Penny tried to hear what Johnny was saying to Marshal Lujan on the phone, but she could not. Johnny only nodded his head and smiled at her over the table. Then he did a thumbs-up to Penny and disconnected the phone.

"Well, Ms. Larkin. So you're a psychic spy for the marshal!"

Penny knew it was better not to react. Lujan had warned her that nothing about this case was nailed down, and anyone could be involved in helping Rico, even Mr. Smarty Pants!

Johnny apparently was nonplussed by Penny's failure to acknowledge the reason she was working for the marshal. "Lujan said the gun sale is on for tonight, so it's too late to take you home. We've got to head to Deming and check out the hospital there. I guess a Mexican hit squad took out a patient in surgery, and the marshal thinks this killing may be related to the gunrunners." Johnny had both hands on the table with his palms down as if he was ready to push himself out of the booth and fire up the car. "And this is supposed to make me feel better?" Penny asked, just as Dot came around for refills. Had it gotten colder in the restaurant? Penny shivered. She used the cup of steaming coffee has a hand warmer for her icy fingers. She had only agreed to track down Juan Rico, not mix it up with a drug cartel. She wondered if she could call Leo and have him pick her up. This had not been part of the bargain she had made with the marshal. "Relax! He wants to see if we can find any leads as to where the gun buy might go down. He's not asking us to stop it."

"So you read my mind," Penny said. She didn't want the marshal to think she wasn't flexible, but checking out a shooting at a hospital was not all that appealing. And besides, she didn't have her gun. It was in Albuquerque with the state police CSI, so she couldn't defend herself. Penny looked down at her attire and cringed. How awful to spend another hour in these clothes. She was sure she smelled of perspiration and dust. "There isn't time for me to go home and shower?" She stared at Johnny in disbelief. "It's still early."

"My mother lives a few miles from here. I'm sure she wouldn't mind if you showered there."

"But what would I change into?"

"Let's stop at Star Western Wear on the way there, and you can get a pair of jeans and a shirt. I took your boots out of the trunk before sending it to the lab. Now that is good luck. You'll be all cowboyed up!"

After Penny had relaxed a bit, she told Johnny the crazy story about getting her boot stuck in the spokes of the tractor wheel and her close encounter with the scorpions. Reliving her ordeal from this comfy cottage-style restaurant made the whole thing almost comical. She looked at Johnny, who seemed edgy. He drummed his fingers on the table.

"Okay. I guess I have no choice. We need to get on the road in a couple of hours, and there's no time to get me home and back." Penny decided she wouldn't look all that bad if she could also pick up another pair of socks along with jeans and a shirt and maybe a bra! After bidding good-bye to Dot, who waved and winked simultaneously, they headed to Star Western Wear. Johnny got the owner to open up by pounding on the door and showing his badge. Then they made a side trip to Walgreens so Penny could pick up some facial cleanser, a pair of white socks, and underpants. She even found a car charger for her cell phone in the drugstore, no less. She was now good to go, well almost. There was the case of the missing bra.

Johnny's mother lived at the end of a dirt road. The lane leading up to her house was lined on both sides by towering pecan trees, which created a green canopy over the police car. The leafy branches kept sunlight to a minimum, and the rays that got through gave the road a mottled look. It reminded Penny of country roads she'd seen in France, and she couldn't help but relax a little. She let out a long breath and leaned her head back in the seat. Who would have thought that ten hours ago she was angry that this trooper wasn't taking her word about being innocent?

Johnny's mother was waiting on the front porch of the cottage, her arms crossed and looking a little wary of her new guest. After

Johnny's brief introduction while climbing the steps to the front porch, Ollie immediately opened her arms and gave Penny a welcoming hug.

"Johnny, I'll show Penny where she can freshen up. Why don't you get a Thermos from the cabinet in the mudroom and fill it with hot coffee for your trip? I've got a new pot ready for you."

"Thanks, Mamá. That's a great idea."

Penny followed Johnny's mother down a wood-paneled hall to a small bedroom with twin beds and a cedar chest but little more. The room was Spartan but somehow comforting to Penny. Ollie pointed out the bathroom across the hall and then headed to a linen closet where she pulled out two large bath towels and a washcloth, which she handed to Penny. Then as if remembering something, Penny watched Ollie returned to the closet and pulled out a bar of soap smelling of lavender.

"For special occasions," Ollie said. "I make it myself."

This was a special occasion? Penny was confused but took the soap and gave Ollie a polite smile. She liked the simplicity of this house and the peace that surrounded it. And Ollie was growing on her.

Penny inhaled the lavender scent and immediately relaxed. She had not realized how tight her muscles were. "Thank you so much, Ollie. I really appreciate the chance to clean up." Penny looked down at her clothes, which were filthy. "Oh, I'm a mess!"

She lifted her arm, covered with the long sleeves, and took a sniff. "I hope I don't smell that bad!" Penny swore she could smell the stench of the jail on her clothes.

Ollie patted her on the shoulder. "Johnny tells me you and he have to go to Deming on business. I packed you a picnic lunch, and Johnny is filling a Thermos full of coffee."

Penny didn't know how to react to such kindness coming from someone she had just met, but she could tell Ollie was a loving mother who was thinking about the welfare of her son. Sons needed to eat, didn't they? Ollie was nothing like her own mother, who had died in an alcoholic stupor after Penny's father was killed at the helm of an open-wheel racecar. Penny's eyes filled with tears, which she blinked back, hoping Ollie could not see them. "Thanks again!" Penny rushed into the bathroom carrying her bag, with her boots tucked under her arm.

The hot water crashed over Penny's head and ran like a river over her body. At five-foot-four, the water didn't have far to fall. The shower warmed her inch by inch, and she swore she had never felt anything so good. Why couldn't life be this easy? You have a problem, and you get in the shower and wash it down the drain. Even the challenge of locating Juan Rico no longer seemed unsolvable, especially now that she had help.

Penny dried off and washed her face with cleanser in the pedestal sink. She had no makeup, except lipstick and mascara from her purse, and that would have to do. She dressed in her new underwear, Levis, and light-blue long-sleeved shirt. Then she did the unthinkable. She called to Ollie from down the hall.

"Ollie, I know this sounds awkward, but do you have a bra I could borrow?"

Ollie took a few steps back, sizing Penny up. "Yes, I believe I do."

Johnny's mother returned in a few minutes with a bra that looked just about Penny's size and a bit too big for Ollie. "This belonged to Johnny's fiancée, Joanna. I'm sure she wouldn't mind. She's been in Colorado for several months now, and I don't think she's coming back."

Penny was surprised at the news but relieved that Joanna had left something of herself behind. She took the bra and thanked Ollie profusely.

With her shirt tucked back in her jeans, Penny grabbed a brown leather belt that she had bought at the western store and wrapped it around her waist. From the short mirror over the sink, she figured she looked acceptable. She grabbed her boots and headed across the hall to the bedroom. She could hear Johnny and his mother laughing somewhere in the house. Penny sat down on the double bed, covered with a handmade quilt. It appeared to have been made from a mixture of floral housedresses, the kind her grandmother used to wear. It brought back Penny's yearning for a family that the death of her parents had stolen from her. She pulled on her socks and ropers and stood, breathing in deeply and running her fingers through her damp hair. Even though she would have company, she hated heading back to Deming. The interstate would bring up the bad memories of the hijacking attempt on her car. It had scared her to death. She hoped she would never see those men again. But the face of the man with the broken bottle was still fresh in her mind, and she racked her brain trying to remember why he looked so familiar.

As she stepped into the hall, Penny realized she hadn't even given Leo a thought since she and Johnny left the restaurant. This surprised her. Had Leo tried to call her? Her cell phone battery had died, and her phone was charging in Johnny's car.

The laughter of Johnny and Ollie brought her back to the task at hand. She walked down the hall following their voices into a tiny kitchen where Johnny was packing up a wicker picnic basket that looked like it was right out of Mayberry. The morning light was muted by the white café curtains and gave the room a hopeful feel. Ollie gave Penny one of her big smiles and pointed to the picnic basket.

"I hope you like cold, baked chicken and potato salad. It was the best I could do on short notice."

Penny and Johnny walked out to the trooper's Dodge Charger. Penny had not paid much attention to the car until now. In the light of day, the color was somewhere between muddy brown and gray. The New Mexico state seal in blue and gold was the only bright spot on the car. Penny thought that Leo's official vehicle was much nicer, but she didn't want to insult Johnny. As he helped her into the passenger seat, he seemed to be reading her mind again.

"Yeah, I know this car sucks, but I hate using my own Jeep on agency time. New Mexico is a pretty poor state, and this is the best we can do. When the new issue vehicles come in, I've been giving them to my team."

As they headed through the New Mexico countryside, Penny became drowsy. She fought it realizing she had not had much, if any, sleep for almost forty-eight hours. To stay awake, Penny made conversation.

"Your mother is such a delight!"

"Thanks, I'm glad you think so. She's had it rough lately. We all have."

"Really? What happened?"

"Last week my father was killed in a shootout with gun traffickers in Three Rivers."

Penny was stunned to learn that grief had befallen the Trejo household. She hadn't picked up on it—so much for her viewing skills. She felt guilty about charging in unannounced and imposing on Ollie's hospitality. "I'm so sorry, Johnny."

"Don't apologize. Law enforcement officers know what they face when they sign up. My dad loved being a state trooper, and he died, as they say, with his boots on."

"But still, bothering your mother like that…"

"My mother loved doing this. It made her feel like she was making a difference. And she is. So let's go hunt down this bastard before he gives the cartel more reasons to kill."

CHAPTER 24

Juan exited the hospital by a side door hoping not to draw the attention of the city cops guarding both the front door and the emergency entrance. He surprised Cito, the orderly who had rolled his uncle into the recovery room. At the sight of a firearm, the man quickly dropped his cigarette and stamped it out with his tennis shoe and headed back inside the hospital, with just a nod of recognition to Juan.

Juan held his gun with both hands as he walked toward the parking lot where he was sure the sheriff was headed. He caught the top of his broad-rim hat bobbing up and down through a row of parked cars. Juan had one chance to take control of the situation, and he had to act now. He would not have the sheriff threaten him or his family!

Juan sprinted toward the bobbing hat and was just two rows of cars away when a man in a black ski mask jumped the sheriff from behind and threw him on the ground. Juan ducked for cover behind a silver Ford F250. He could hear the men arguing, so he crawled up alongside a Dodge van and lay flat on the ground, parallel to its front wheels. He could see the two men well enough without them seeing him.

"You aren't going to cheat me this time!" The man in the ski mask punched the sheriff in the face and stole the sheriff's weapon from his holster—a pistol—probably a 9 mm, Juan guessed. He could see the sheriff waving his arms. The man kicked the sheriff to the ground, placed his boot on his neck, and ripped off his ski mask.

"I want you to see my face when I kill you!"

"Please don't do this, Delgado. I promise, I'll make it right." The sheriff's voice was hoarse, like his throat was full of gravel.

The man laughed and mocked the sheriff in a high-pitched voice. "Oh, please don't kill me. I'll be good. I promise."

"Look, I'm beggin' you. What did I do to you?"

"You stole our stash of guns in Lordsburg. We know it was you!" The masked man rubbed the pistol against his cheek and then pointed it at the sheriff's head. "Don't cry, sheriff. It won't hurt a bit."

Juan's whole body began to shake. This guy was accusing the sheriff of Juan's crime. Somehow, knowing that the Betas didn't suspect him wasn't making Juan feel all that great. His shoulders fell forward in relief, but he couldn't relax for long. Unless the gunman planned to head into the woods after killing the sheriff, he would probably have to pass right by Juan to return to his own car, wherever it was in the parking lot.

The sheriff continued to plead for his life. "Delgado, I didn't steal any of your guns. You've got the wrong guy."

"It's too late now, amigo! ¡Tengo mis órdenes!"

Juan watched the gunman stiffen and lower his weapon again, pointing the barrel right at the sheriff's head. "¡Adiós!"

Juan fired his Herstel, hitting the gunman between the shoulder blades, just as he was ready to pull the trigger. He fell forward, bumping his head on the side panel of a black Chevy pickup, before landing on top of the sheriff.

Juan rushed to see if the sheriff was okay and then pushed the dead man off his chest. In his hurry, he had forgotten that he also had plans to kill the sheriff. *Now what?*

"My God, son. Thank you. You've saved me from that son of bitch!"

"Who is he?" Juan was afraid he already knew the answer— the kind of guy who shoots first and then maybe tells you why, as you suck in your last breath of air.

"That's Delgado—*un asesino*—a hit man for the Betas cartel. He's called La Nariz or the nose because he is so good at tracking down people the Betas want to eliminate."

This news rattled Juan. How long would it be before the Betas sent someone else to kill the sheriff or figure out who it really was that stole their firearms? The gunman's eyes were still open, and blood dripped from his nose, which Juan thought was ironic. He would not be sniffing out any more people to kill.

Juan breathed in deeply and let out a quick burst of air from his lungs, just happy to be alive. His fingers were tingling, and his ears were ringing from the blast of the Herstel. Juan fumbled around, trying to keep a grip on his gun, which still felt hot to the touch. Juan was breathing too fast—so fast that his chest felt like he was the one who had been hit by a bullet.

A stabbing pain in his chest forced Juan against the black truck, and he dropped his head between his legs. His world was falling to pieces, but he didn't dare look weak in front of the sheriff, after he had threatened Juan in the hospital. He straightened up the best he could, but the pain still persisted.

Juan watched as the sheriff rolled into a sitting position and pulled his own gun out of the dead man's grip. The sheriff was just as dirty as Delgado. Juan realized that now. What would keep him from killing him too, now that he had his gun back? Juan held his pistol with both hands and pointed toward the sheriff.

To Juan's surprise, the sheriff smiled and waved him away. "You put your gun down and get out of here, son. I'll take care of this. And you can be sure I won't forget you were a good little Boy Scout—always prepared!" The sheriff managed a gurgling chuckle as he pulled himself up, with the help of the truck's bumper. He grunted as he stood and stretched his shoulders, like it hurt to stand straight. "I'm getting too old for this!" The sheriff shoved his felt hat tightly down over his big ears. "Get gone! Now!"

Juan didn't wait for the sheriff to ask three times. He started running. He didn't stop until he found a grassy area near a bank of trees. He dropped to the ground at the top of the hill and rested in the cool grass. His chest was heaving, and his lungs grew heavy and hard. When the vomit came, he couldn't get it to stop. Juan gasped for air, but his throat was full of puke, and his nose was stuffed with snot. He rolled to the bottom of the hill, hoping this would help clear his throat. As he fell, his hands smashed into the roots of a tree, and he thought he heard the bones in his fingers breaking. How long would his body lie here until someone found him? He thought of his little girls, and tears ran down his face.

Juan tried to force his hand into his mouth, but it was so painful he could not straighten his fingers far enough to do any good. He pulled his Herstel up over his chest, inching it toward his lips as fast as he could before he lost consciousness. The barrel of the pistol was no longer warm from being fired, which was a good thing. Juan's hands were shaking as he shoved the pistol in his mouth—a last ditch effort to clear his airway.

CHAPTER 25

Leo contacted the New Mexico State Police Headquarters in Las Cruces and convinced one of the troopers to give him Johnny's cell phone number. It was evident that Penny never made it home because she didn't answer either her home phone or her cell. All the trooper could tell him was that Captain Trejo had left four hours ago to pick up Penny Larkin from the jail. The captain also said he would be out for the rest of the day.

Leo's imagination was getting him in trouble. And maybe his guilt of a near miss with Adriana was also driving the fear that Johnny was enjoying his time with Penny a little too much. Why else had she not returned home or at least attempted to contact him?

Johnny Trejo answered on the third ring. "Trejo."

Leo didn't hear any background noise, like the he might be sitting in a coffee shop chatting up Penny. This relieved his worries somewhat.

"Johnny, this is Leo Tellez. I'm just checking on Penny. I got your message, but I haven't been able to reach her. Do you know where she is?"

"Of course I do! She's right here. Let me put her on the phone." Leo was nervous, waiting to hear Penny's familiar voice. "Hi, Leo. Sorry I haven't been able to call you. My cell phone was dead, and it's just now charging up in the car."

"Are you on your way home?"

Leo could hear Penny clearing her throat. There was a long silence. "I asked if you are on your way home?"

"No, Leo. Johnny—Captain Trejo and I are on a special assignment with the marshal's office. It's related to the case I was working when the guys tried to hijack my car."

"Any chance you'll be home later tonight?"

97

"I'm not sure. This is an emergency. Johnny was included in the orders from the marshal." Leo didn't like the sound of this one bit. Did Johnny finagle an invite? He gripped his cell phone so tightly that his fingers p ushed t he disconnect button, and there was silence on the other end. Leo threw his phone across the front seat of the Tahoe, and it bounced against the window.

The phone rang again, but Leo was driving and couldn't reach his cell. It had fallen on the floor in front of the passenger seat. He pulled off the interstate, but by the time he got to a place where he could stop safely, the phone had quit ringing. He saw a missed call from Johnny's cell number, but Leo was too embarrassed to call them back.

XXX

Leo got to the downtown jail in less than ten minutes. He pulled into the parking lot on the east side of the four-story facility and headed to the front entrance. The jail was built in the early 1980s, and it was woefully inadequate. It was built in a square with long dark halls, making it nearly impossible for his corrections officers to keep an eye on all of the prisoners. Leo was grateful that the county had another jail on the east side of town where most of the gangs were housed. The east side jail had pods built in a circle, with a guard in the center, making it possible to have a constant watch on prisoners through glass windows.

Leo was heading back to the downtown jail to check on the status of a sex offender his deputies had arrested last night. He had promised his deputies that he would follow up on the case and make sure the offender was isolated from the rest of the population. Once the photos of alleged sex offenders appeared on television, they had to be placed in protective custody or their lives were at risk. There is a moral protocol in jails, and sexual perverts are at the bottom of the pile. It was Leo's job to keep the guy from getting whacked, even if he might deserve it.

As Leo walked into the lobby of the jail, he was surprised to see Adriana talking with a correctional officer, who sat behind the glassed-in reception desk. All jail visitors and lawyers must log in and out, and apparently, Adriana was just completing a client meeting.

When she saw Leo, she maintained her professional composure, but took Leo's hand and held it for a long time. Her hand was warm and comforting, and Leo did not resist.

"How about a cup of coffee?" Adriana's voice was soft and non-aggressive—a far cry from her behavior just a few hours before. Leo said nothing. His muscles were compliant as he walked without protest to her car, which was parked near his. "How about the Starbucks near my house, or would you rather come to my house for that cup of tea you missed?" Adriana eyes brightened, and she placed her slender, well-manicured fingers on his shoulder.

"I can't do that." Leo said, trying to remain as nonchalant as possible.

"Can't or won't?" Adriana's eyebrows flared. She opened her car door and threw her briefcase across the console and into the passenger's seat.

"I've got to check on a new arrest."

"I'm sorry I came on too strong." Adriana actually looked sincere, but Leo couldn't take the chance of being alone with her again. He kicked some loose stones away from her tires.

"I've got to go."

"Has something happened with Penny? I know I promised you I'd get her an attorney, but you left me so abruptly last night, I didn't have a chance." Adriana leaned into her car and pulled her briefcase into her arms. "I've got his card here somewhere." Adriana shuffled through a stack of papers in search of the lawyer's name.

"Penny's not going to need an attorney. She's out of jail and back chasing down fugitives."

"That's terrific news. So she's free now? How is she feeling?" "I'm not sure. I haven't seen her since she got out of jail." "You didn't go back to Las Cruces to get her?" Adriana's eyes were really wide open now, and Leo could see that she found it hard to believe that Leo had not been in contact with Penny.

Leo turned away from Adriana's prying questions and headed back to the jail. He felt bad enough about letting Penny down, not to be chastised for it too.

Adriana had apparently figured out why Leo didn't get the news of Penny's release on time. "Hey, wait up. I almost forgot! Here's your phone." She pulled it from her purse and fondled it. "Maybe the next time Ms. Penny needs saving, you'll be able to answer the call." She thrust the phone at Leo who caught it with one hand. It felt warm and smelled faintly of vanilla.

Adriana got in her car, revved the engine, and took the exit a little too fast. Her tires etched a fishtail of rubber in the street, but Leo didn't seem to notice. He was busy searching through the previous calls on his cell when it vibrated in his hands.

CHAPTER 26

Johnny and Penny had been driving west on Interstate 10 for about fifteen minutes when Penny saw the sign for the exit to Akela Flats coming up in two miles. She gripped the edge of the passenger seat with both hands as the Charger closed in on the area where the gang of men had tried to take her car. She was squeezing the seat so tightly that her fingers began to ache.

She shook her hands to get the feeling back and began to rub them vigorously.

"It's coming up on the left." Penny pointed a shaky hand in the general direction of her ordeal. It was difficult to see all that much since the crime scene was across the median, but she was grateful that Johnny was slowing down so both of them could get a better look.

"Could you pull off the road?" Penny asked.

"We don't have time to stop now, but on our way home, hopefully we can check it out."

"We can take time!" Penny insisted.

Johnny rolled to a stop on the opposite side of the highway. "I don't see how this is going to help at all."

"Thanks, Johnny. I just want to check out the place. Maybe something will come to me that your deputies missed."

"They were pretty thorough. The killer's gun was never found."

Penny jumped out of the car and ran across the four lanes of highway. Johnny yelled at her to get back in the car, but she acted like she didn't hear him. She had to examine the site for herself without dust obliterating her view.

Luckily, the traffic was light as she walked along the edge of the highway where her Mustang had been parked. She moved toward the ditch and examined the scars in the gravel. She could see the ruts made by her tires from where the gang of angry men had pushed her car forward. And she found an assorted number of footprints and some stones splattered with blood. A chill went up Penny's spine. What if they had been able to get her out of the car? She trembled at the thought.

Penny could hear Johnny yelling at her again, but she waved him off. She had to act quickly! She took a deep breath and closed her eyes. The sound of the traffic buzzing passed her was not going to halt her attempt to view what had happened here. In fact, Penny found the rhythm of the tires rolling by a big help in calming her down. Within minutes, she had used the remote viewing protocols to transport her mind into a new dimension—a place where good and evil collide. In her mind's eye, she saw the gang of angry men laughing and shaking the Mustang. One man was pounding on the driver's side window.

Watching this, even from a dream's perspective, evoked the same terror, the same feeling of helplessness that Penny felt yesterday. She had to shake it off. When she saw Harold Moreno being dragged by two of the men, Penny reacted in anger. She wanted to shout at them, but she knew it was already history. *Keep it together, Penny.*

Moreno's brown leather boots were badly scarred from the rocks, and his face was swollen. His eyes, black and wide, showed the pure horror of his ordeal. One of the men took his rifle and slammed the butt against Moreno's face, cutting a line of triangles into his cheek. He called out, yelling something Penny could not understand.

She followed his eyes. He kept looking back and driving daggers into the eyes of another man who was walking behind him. Who was following Moreno?

It was Federico Castañón!

Castañón must have been lying in wait for Penny to leave the Gas N Go and followed her. How else had he known where she was on this strip of highway? With all the dust, she wouldn't have seen other cars parking behind or in front of her. Now everything made more sense. The mayor apparently had used his thugs to keep Penny from leaving the scene so he could frame her for the murder of Officer Moreno.

Penny was determined not to let her anger at Castañón deter her from finishing her viewing. She forced herself to stay focused as Moreno climbed on the hood of Penny's Mustang, his hands clawing at the windshield. He looked at her sitting inside the car and begged for help. Memories of seeing his desperation brought tears to Penny's eyes. She shook off the guilt of not being able to save him.

Castañón threw his broken beer bottle into the gravel and yanked Moreno's black pistol out of its holster and jammed a silencer onto the muzzle. That's why Penny hadn't heard the other gunshot! With the aid of one of his thugs, he jerked Moreno off the hood and carried him about twenty feet from the front of Penny's car and fired a single bullet into Moreno's chest. The officer's mutilated body dropped into a growth of tall weeds.

Castañón tossed Moreno's gun into a field of sand dunes and tall grass and then ordered his henchmen to grab the dead man by the arms and carry him toward Penny's Mustang. As they got closer to the front of the car, Penny fired her gun from her sunroof. She watched in amazement as the men scattered like rats from a barn on fire. Now she knew the real story behind her bizarre encounter with the I-10 hijackers.

The blare of a horn jolted Penny out of her viewing. She had wandered into the lane of oncoming traffic and jumped to safety just as a truck driver waved his fist in the air. She was drained of energy and fought the desire to collapse on the side of the road. She watched Johnny cross the highway.

"Penny, are you crazy? That truck could have killed you!" "No, Johnny, I'm not crazy. I've seen what happened here.

Let's search the field for the pistol. It's black. I saw Castañón kill Moreno, yank off the silencer, and throw the deputy's gun somewhere over there." She pointed to a series of dunes several yards off the highway. Penny left Johnny in search of the gun. He shrugged his shoulders and followed her.

It didn't take more than five minutes for Penny to locate the pistol. The muzzle was lodged in the sand and hidden from view by the yellow flowers of a brittlebush. At first glance, the dark gun looked just like a piece of volcanic rock. Penny was on the verge of scooping up the firearm when Johnny caught up with her. "Hold it!" He was pulling on a pair of latex gloves.

"We've got to preserve the gun for evidence and check for fingerprints!" Johnny said. "We don't want the mayor to get away with murder, now do we?"

CHAPTER 27

The Deming exit had signage pointing to the Luna County Medical Center, just five minutes from the interstate. Johnny drove into the hospital parking lot and took note of the sheriff's deputy standing guard at the front door. He pulled around to the emergency room entrance, where the shootout had taken place. Yellow police tape was strung across the pedestrian entrance to the emergency room and another deputy stood guard there, too. Only the ambulance entrance remained unobstructed. In fact, EMTs were unloading a heavy-set woman, her bare feet exposed, and rolling her into the hospital for treatment. Johnny pulled into a parking spot and shut off the engine. "I want you to stay here until I get the lay of the land, and then I'll come back and get you."

"I'm not waiting in the car! Besides, I can be of help if I perceive something that isn't immediately apparent. I'm going with you."

Johnny thought better of having an inexperienced partner at his side, but she was, after all, part of the team of trackers that the marshal had assembled. And Marshal Lujan knew better than Johnny just how helpful Penny could be. But he was not going to have her tag along without being armed. Johnny reached into his boot and pulled out a .38 special Smith & Wesson double-action revolver that he used as a backup to his .357 SIG Sauer pistol. His department had issued all state troopers .40 Smith & Wesson Remington ammunition, but he preferred .357 Sig ammo, which he stored in two additional thirteen-shot clips, attached to his belt. This gave him thirty-nine rounds, which, heaven forbid, he would not have to use anytime soon.

He rolled the .38 revolver over in his hands and considered what instructions he should give Penny. It was a double-action gun, so it wasn't necessary to pull the hammer back first, like the Chief that Leo had given her. This worried him some. He didn't want her to shoot herself in the foot. "Penny, carry this gun in your bag. It holds five rounds. Keep your hand on it at all times as we approach the hospital, and if someone threatens you, you can fire right through your purse."

"Wow, and destroy a Dooney and Bourke bag?" Penny laughed and took the gun and unzipped her purse and placed her right hand inside. "Like this?"

"Yes, that's exactly how to carry it. And it will be most effective at close range, so if someone tries to grab you, it will do the job." "I don't plan on shooting anyone, Johnny. I'll leave that up to you."

"In police work, you always have to be prepared. Never let your guard down. If we get separated, I want you ready to defend yourself."

"Got it. Thanks."

Before getting out of the car, Johnny used his cell phone to call Marshal Lujan. He didn't answer, so he left him a message that he and Penny had arrived at the Luna County hospital an hour ahead of schedule and a New Mexico district judge had granted them a search warrant for it. "We're about to head into the hospital now. We will keep you up-to-date as soon as we have interviewed the folks who witnessed the shooting."

Johnny and Penny headed toward the emergency room entrance. He didn't know what to expect, but something didn't feel right about it. The deputy guarding the emergency room entrance looked way too relaxed. He was leaning against the slump blocks of the hospital wall, smoking a cigarette, even though a sign just to his right said "No Smoking" in big red letters. Johnny felt uneasy. Were they walking into a trap? His hand moved over his pistol strapped to his waist, and rested there, while he took everything in. The last thing he wanted to do was expose Penny to violence, but she was going to have to hold her own. He looked over at her. She was taking long strides, trying to keep up with him. Her hand rested inside her designer bag. He didn't know if he could count on her, but now he had no choice.

XXX

Penny and Johnny identified themselves as law enforcement officers and were allowed to enter through the emergency room door, which normally accepted only ambulances. The pedestrian door had a piece of cardboard covering a hole where the glass had been. Penny could still see shards of glass scattered across the entryway.

As they entered the waiting room, Penny recognized Jack Pritchard, the Luna County sheriff, wagging his finger at one of the orderlies, whose eyes were darting back and forth in what Penny surmised was pure fear. The orderly shook his head and ran down the hall. Flashes of the Luna County jail rushed through Penny's mind as she recalled her vision of the guard who had begged her for help after he slammed into the hood of her car. Was the sheriff somehow involved in his murder? The dead man was after all one of his employees.

Sheriff Pritchard was clearly annoyed by their arrival, but he walked briskly toward them and shook Johnny's hand and nodded hello to Penny. He appeared to be the epitome of politeness, which drew goose bumps on her arms.

"What can I do to help you, Captain?"

"We're investigating last night's gun battle. How many were killed?"

"As you can see, we've got things under control now, but we lost four Deming police officers, one shooter, and the patient, who was undergoing surgery for a gunshot to his belly."

Johnny took a couple of steps back. It appeared to Penny to be an unconscious response to the sheriff's aggressive behavior. "Who's in charge of the investigation?" Johnny pressed on in spite of Pritchard's surliness.

"I've taken control of the situation since the city police department is in shock over the death of their officers."

"But this appears to be a federal case since the perpetrators came over the border in pursuit of an American citizen."

"Oh, I expect the Feds will be here soon enough, but until they get their fat asses out of bed and head to Deming, I'm in charge." Penny's dislike of Sheriff Pritchard grew with every movement of his lips.

"What exactly happened?" Johnny pressed the sheriff for more details.

"Well, Anderson Dean was shot about five or six miles south of Palomas in a tiny village called Vista de Flores. Since he was an American citizen, a Mexican ambulance brought him to the US border, where a Deming ambulance brought him here for treatment. It was about 11:00 p.m., far as I remember. The gunmen pursued the victim across the border, ramming their Chevy Avalanche through one of the cement barriers at the border station and managed to maneuver around two other barriers to get away from the guys at immigration and customs. The border patrol contacted the Deming Police Department, which showed up, and the gun battle ensued. Of course, it wasn't a fair fight. The police had 9 mm pistols against AK-47s. It's a wonder we didn't lose more men."The sheriff shook his head in disgust and then pulled a handkerchief from his pocket and wiped his lips, before going on.

"The hit man sure did have the advantage, but we were lucky that fast action by Officer Jackman took out one of the gunman before the others headed straight for this emergency room.

According to a nurse, they ran straight away into the operating room and found the surgeon who was trying to save the gunshot victim.They put a single bullet in the patient's heart but amazingly left the surgeon and the anesthesiologist alone."

"How did the shooters know where to find the man?" Penny asked.

"Well, that is a puzzle. We had another patient in another operating room at the same time, but they ignored him. They seemed to know how to get in and hit the right target and then get out."

"We'd like to take a look around the hospital," Johnny said. "Like I said. We don't need the state troopers in our town.

We've got this covered."

Apparently, the sheriff was unaware that Penny was with the US Marshals Service, having just assumed she worked for the state of New Mexico. She thought it best to stay under his radar. "Sheriff, I've had enough of your delays." Johnny moved into the sheriff's face and waved a warrant to search the hospital.

Much to Penny's surprise, the sheriff backed off. Pritchard put up his hands, as if he were surrendering.

Penny looked around the emergency room waiting area. The orderly had returned with a heavy cotton mop and a rolling bucket full of what smelled like ammonia. Penny watched him shove the soapy mop back and forth across the linoleum floor, trying without much success to remove a large stain. An image of the dying police officer that had shed that blood hovered over the floor and then was swept away by other thoughts that pushed them aside. But Penny had seen enough to know where and how the dead officer had been killed.

"So one of the dead officers was lying here, beside some large metal barrier?" Penny asked.

Sheriff Pritchard tried to hide his disdain for Penny's question, but she knew she had caught him by surprise. "Who told you about a metal desk the police officers had used to block the gunmen's fire?"

"Seeing the dark spot on the floor, I assumed that the officer was shot near the door. He would have been a fool not to take cover, and the receptionist's desk was the best he could do in an emergency. I also noticed the skid marks on the linoleum where the desk was moved out of place. My guess is, the first bullet grazed him, but he stood anyway and returned fire. The second shot to his stomach was deadly, and he fell over the desk, onto the floor. You can see how the stain has spread across the surface in an amoebic pattern."

"Well, aren't you Ms. Sherlock Holmes!" The sheriff let out a horselaugh that clearly conveyed his disrespect for her.

"It looks like the police officers were trying to keep the gunmen from barging into the hospital," Johnny said. Penny appreciated his coming to her defense and pushing Pritchard for more details. Johnny walked around the metal desk to have a closer look. The desk had been moved back into its regular position and was now occupied by an emergency room receptionist, who was trying to calm down a teenage boy, whose mother had just been transported to the hospital by ambulance.

The receptionist, who was not much older than Penny, had long black hair, which was pulled into a bun. The hairdo accentuated her dangling silver earrings that nearly reached her shoulders. Her eyebrows were drawn on her face with black eyeliner, and from the looks of her enlarged pupils, she would not last much longer without reinforcements.

"I want my mother!" The boy screamed and pounded his fist on the desk, causing the receptionist's papers to rise in the air. A nurse appeared from a room somewhere and took the young man in her arms and ushered him away. Penny could hear him crying all the way down the hall.

Penny returned to the stain on the floor and moved the orderly out of the way. She tucked her bag under her right arm and used the index finger of her left hand to draw an imaginary circle over the smallest part of the discoloration. "The officer's shoulders hit the floor right here." The blood from the officer had permeated the aging floor, which was porous from constant cleanings. "It has soaked the blood up like a sponge."

"When do you expect the ballistics report?" Johnny asked the sheriff.

Pritchard was playing passive aggressive. He ignored Johnny's questions and walked over to check on the work of the orderly. "Go get some bleach. Ammonia isn't getting the job done."

"We'd like a copy of the report when it arrives." Johnny persisted. "No sense looking at it. Officer Jimenez and Officer Jackman were trying to defend the hospital. Jimenez was killed, and Jackman responded by killing the shooter. The second shooter's bullet banged off Jackman's Kevlar, bringing Jackman to his knees. Jackman saw the hit man run down the hall to the operating room. He called 911 on his cell phone and took cover under the desk, waiting for the shooter to leave the way he came in, but Jackman said he never returned. We assume he must have left by another door."

Penny watched the sheriff's eyes. He blinked a lot when he talked, which was a sure sign of a liar, Penny thought. Johnny and Sheriff Pritchard were examining the desk and tracing the blood splatter on its legs. The receptionist said she was heading to the kitchen for some coffee, and she rushed down the hall, wiping her hands on her uniform as she fled the crime scene. Penny doubted she would return, and who could blame her?

Penny moved to the far end of the waiting room and stood against the wall hoping for some insight. Sometimes answers came, and sometimes they did not, when she moved into a viewing mode. From her new vantage point, she was able to scan the entire crime scene instead of standing in the middle of it. She closed her eyes and inhaled, trying to relax. She started counting backward from 399—an old habit she used when trying to fall asleep at night. By the time she reached 300, her mind was leaving her body behind and spiraling into the ether. When her count reach 259, the gunfight was flaring to life and projecting an image of the actors upon the floor of the emergency room in movie screen fashion. The battle went down just like the sheriff said, except there was a third man in the room that he had never mentioned. *Who was this?*

Penny tried to get a better look. She focused her mind on the young man who was dressed in jeans, a blue jeans jacket, and scuffed cowboy boots. He was just exiting the long hall from the hospital's main wing when the shooting began. He crouched down and peered around the corner, watching the killers take down the first officer. Then a gunman in a black knitted mask stepped forward and aimed his automatic rifle at Officer Jackman. Without hesitating, the young man pulled a pistol and took down the killer with one bullet to the head. Officer Jackman never even fired his gun! Instead, he dove behind the desk in fear. Penny was stunned by this young man's expertise with a firearm. And lucky for Jackman, the guy had arrived just in time to save his life. Who was he?

"Just pour that bleach right on the stain!" Penny was jolted out of her viewing by the sheriff's loud voice, demanding the orderly try a bottle of bleach instead. Penny opened her eyes just as the orderly emptied the entire bottle of bleach onto the floor. The scent of ammonia and chlorine gave off a toxic odor that floated through the waiting room. The orderly had endured a direct hit to his throat, and he gagged. He covered his mouth and nose with his sleeve and staggered out of the room. Penny grabbed a tissue from her blue jeans pocket to cover her mouth, and the photo of Juan Rico and his daughter fell to the floor. She had transferred the picture from her old pair of jeans to her new ones, hoping to show Johnny what Juan Rico looked like, but she had yet to do so. She picked up the picture and unfolded it. Juan Rio looked a lot like the hero shooter, but that would be too much of a coincidence if they were one and the same, Penny thought. And why would he be hanging around the hospital? Penny's mind was racing and full of questions, but paramount in her mind was, if this is Juan Rico, where is he now?

CHAPTER 28

When Juan opened his eyes, the sun was up, and he was lying in his vomit at the base of the hill, where he had rolled the night before. His pistol was still in his mouth, and his index finger was wrapped around the butt of the gun. He blinked. The gun must have opened his airway, when his injured fingers could not. The last thing he remembered was thinking that if he were going to choke to death, he would rather end it with a bullet. It was a more dignified way to go than choking on your own puke. A swell of panic swirled through his unsettled stomach, reviving his nausea. Maybe he wasn't alive at all. Maybe this was hell—the place where a guy goes when he can't get his act together. His knuckles were bruised and swollen, and two or three fingers were black and blue on his left hand. The pain was terrible, but he managed to pull the pistol out of his mouth and drag it off his chest and onto the grass. The red dot above the trigger showed Juan that the safety was off, meaning that any wrong move could have blown his head off. He breathed in deeply. The fresh air felt good in his lungs.

As he reached for the safety lever, located right above the trigger, a long shadow fell over his body. At first, he thought the sun had gone under a cloud, but the spit shine on the black cowboy boots caught his eye. He traced the sharp creases of the towering figure's slacks up to his waistline where the morning sun reflected off the silver buckle that secured a black alligator belt. The man wore a pair of aviation sunglasses, so Juan couldn't see his eyes. When he smiled, the visitor showed his perfect white teeth. For a moment, Juan thought maybe he had died after all, and he was meeting the devil for the first time.

"Mr. Rico, you wanted to see me?"

This rattled Juan further. Was the devil there to collect his own? "Who are you?" Juan's voice cracked from the dryness of his throat and lips. He had no idea who in the world was looming over him. His stomach groaned, and a bolt of pain crashed into his chest. He thought he might get sick again. But instead of the devil driving a stake into his heart, the man's tan, slender fingers handed Juan a cold bottle of water. Juan grasped it, and in spite of the pain in his crushed fingers, he lifted it to his lips and drank as much as he could. A lot of it rolled out of his mouth and down his neck.

"I'm Federico Castañón. I heard you were looking for me."

Juan was stunned. He realized the mayor of Columbus was standing there before him. He raised himself up and leaned on one elbow.

The mayor knelt down beside Juan and placed his hand on his shoulder. "What do you need?"

Juan would be taking a big chance telling him anything. And lying on the ground with mangled fingers, he was vulnerable. He could never pull the trigger on his pistol in time, even with the safety off, if the guy was setting him up for a hit. Could he trust Castañón? Who had sent him anyway? The sheriff? Juan decided he had to take a chance. He was out of options.

"Guns! I need guns." When Juan heard his own words rattling around in his throat, he coughed and fought back the tears. His tongue was jammed so hard against his front teeth that he thought they might break. It was too late to take the words back. His future—his very breath—depended on Castañón's response.

He pulled in one last gasp of air, and saliva fell out of his mouth and dribbled down his chin.

Castañón handed Juan a starched white handkerchief with his initials FJC on it. It reminded Juan of the fancy ones he saw at K-Mart at Christmas. Only those were stiff and scratchy while this one felt soft against his skin, and it smelled of sunshine. He wiped his face and mouth and blew his nose. He spoke in a low tone, as if someone else was in earshot. "AR-15 assault rifles or AK 47 7.62 caliber assault rifles…lots of them."

Juan blew his nose again, and this time blood spurted out on to Castañón's handkerchief. Embarrassed, Juan rolled the hanky in a ball and tucked it between his legs. "I have an order from the Chihuahua cartel for twenty-five rifles."

"My god, where am I going to find that many…in an armory?" "I get a bonus if I meet my quota, but the cartel will take whatever I can get them." "How much can you pay?"

"I can give you $500 a rifle and still make some money. Of course, if you can fill the whole order, I'll split my bonus with you."

Castañón took Juan's arm and pulled him to his feet. "You're a mess! You might want to walk over to the hospital emergency room and have a doc check out your hands."

"Sure. Juan winced and took a couple of shaky steps. He would rather avoid the hospital if at all possible, but his Uncle Martín was still there, and he didn't have a ride to his truck. Juan was dizzy and lurched forward, falling against Castañón's side. "Sorry, I still don't feel so good."

The mayor held him steady. "Don't forget your gun." Castañón leaned over and picked up the Herstel with two fingers, noticing the vomit all over it. He held it at arm's length.

Rico took the gun from him, clicked on the safety, and held it close to his chest with his arms. His fingers were purple, cold and stiff, even as the sun warmed the rest of his body.

"I'm leaving now," Castañón said. "I'll be in touch." The mayor took a small slip of paper out of his pocket and handed it to Juan Rico. "My cell phone number."

Juan clutched the paper and shoved it into his pocket. His fingers burned, and the pain shot up his wrists. He mumbled thanks and watched Castañón disappear over the hill, his shiny black boots clipping the grass.

CHAPTER 29

Two hours after learning of Penny's collaboration with Johnny Trejo on some secret assignment, Leo was cooling his heels in the waiting room of Marshal Lujan's office. He had arrived unannounced at the Albert Armendáriz Federal Court House in downtown El Paso, and Lujan was not yet available. He was tied up in a meeting of the Border Enforcement Security Task Force or BEST as it was known in law enforcement circles. BEST, an offshoot of ICE, the US Immigrations and Customs Enforcement agency, analyzed raw data collected by various federal agencies on the trafficking of firearms and munitions across US borders.

This particular BEST group was made up of law enforcement agencies from El Paso to the Houston Seaport. Leo had assigned his good friend and colleague Lieutenant Paco Ontiveros to represent the El Paso County Sheriff's Office whenever he couldn't attend. The El Paso County Sheriff's Department played a key role in BEST's attempt to halt the deadly cocktail of drugs, guns, and human trafficking that was spreading like a poison across the US.

The drug cartels had permeated almost every major city, and law enforcement agencies across the country sometimes called on BEST for help. One of the worst places was Chicago. The news media was blaming the violence on local gang warfare, but Leo knew three different Mexican cartels were also fervently defending their territories on the streets of Chicago's southwest side. It was just a matter of time before other cities would be infected. Firearms, the swizzle sticks of drug use, were being shipped into Mexico from the United States in increasing frequency, and El Paso County was smack-dab in the heart of all that traffic.

XXX

Ten minutes went by, and Leo kept checking his cell phone while he paced the floor in the waiting room. He had not heard anything else from Penny, and it had him worried. He decided to confront Lujan and demand to know about the assignment that was so urgent as to put Penny in harm's way.

Lujan's assistant, Patsy Renner, walked into the waiting room. "Something tells me you would rather not have to socialize with the task force members when they come out of the meeting. You look pretty upset."

Leo nodded and followed Patsy into the marshal's office, where she seated him in a substantial leather chair opposite a large mahogany desk. Patsy was a sixty-something legal aid, who had given up her private practice with a local lawyer to work for the marshal. A tall, slender brunette, Patsy had lost her twenty- five-year-old son to a drug overdose six years ago, and she had come to work with the marshal because he had been relentless in helping the drug enforcement agency shut down stash houses and clear the perimeters of high schools from dopers selling drugs. She was passionate, and Leo had always appreciated her work in the community.

With 50 percent of all cocaine and marijuana moving from South America and interior Mexico to Ciudad Juárez and on through El Paso into the rest of the United States, some of the contraband usually found its way into the hands of local teens and adults, like Patsy's son, Robbie, with deadly consequences. Leo knew it was an uphill fight, but the town needed more people like Patsy trying to raise awareness of El Paso's serious threat to their children.

"Would you like something to drink?"

"Sure, water would be great." Leo laid his head back and stared at the ceiling where the lighting from the overhead filament flickered off and on and caused his eyes to water. His head ached, and he could feel the blood pounding against the back of his neck. *Isn't this how strokes happen?* He massaged his neck and blew out a long breath of frustration.

Patsy returned with a cold bottle of water and left Leo alone. It was another fifteen minutes before Marshal Lujan joined him. Eugene Lujan was a lanky, six-foot-six native Texan with high cheekbones, straight brown hair, and naturally inquisitive eyes. He belonged to the

Texas Tall Club of Dallas, where he had lived before being transferred to the El Paso district. He was proud of his height and enjoyed hanging around with others similarly endowed. At six foot two, Leo always felt diminished in his presence.

Eugene made up for his looming stature by being a very nice guy and a very capable US marshal. And Leo would be forever grateful to him for taking a chance on Penny's remote viewing skills. Working as a freelance writer, Penny had been in dire financial circumstances before teaming up with the El Paso County Sheriff's Office to track down a Russian crime ring moving Mexican children into the United States and to other parts of the world for the lucrative sex trades. Penny's viewing skills had been instrumental in shutting it down and killing the kingpin. In fact, it was Penny who shot and killed Sergei Andulov. There had been a bounty on Andulov's head as one of America's most wanted, and Penny had been the recipient of a $100,000 reward. She had gained the respect of law enforcement agencies across the Southwest and a bidding war for her talents ensued.

Eugene shook Leo's hand and asked about recent cases. Leo wanted to dispense with the small talk because he was eager to find Penny and make sure she was not heading into a perilous situation, even with Johnny Trejo at her side. If anyone was going to protect Penny, it was going to be Leo. He felt a twinge of jealousy, mixed with unrequited guilt over letting Penny down when she was jailed last night. It only aggravated the urgency he felt to save her from herself.

Eugene sat on the leather sofa in his office, and Leo remained seated in the matching armchair that reminded Leo of Adriana's sofa. As he sank back into the deep cushion and laid his right hand on the padded arm, he tried to remain still but found his fingers tapping nervously against the soft, brown leather upholstery.

"Eugene, I've got an issue, and I hope you're going to help me solve it."

"What's up? I'll do my best."

"It's about Penny. I know she's been on a top-secret assignment for your agency, and she hasn't told me much, but I've learned she and Johnny Trejo have joined forces. I am truly curious as to why you've called in a New Mexico State trooper to help her."

"Captain Trejo has been working undercover for me for about four months, and as it fortuitously turned out, Penny's wrongful arrest for the death of the Luna County jail guard brought her in direct contact with one of the other team members who was also assigned to this mission."

"I'm hoping you'll provide me professional courtesy and share just what the heck is up."

Leo dug his nails into the leather, leaving marks on the arm of the chair.

Eugene stood and walked to his desk where he found a set of keys that opened a large file cabinet. "I've known you for a long time now, Leo, and I am certain you're not involved, but we have reason to believe that a law enforcement officer in our region is spearheading the sale of firearms to the Mexican cartels."

Leo took in a big gulp of air. A decade ago, this news would have been unthinkable for a law enforcement officer to go against his own country in exchange for a wad of cash. But with today's uncertain economy, he knew anything was possible.

Leo could not imagine Penny's life being jeopardized this way. The cartels were ruthless and had little regard for life. If you got in the way, you were eliminated. Leo's brain hit overdrive. He stood to make his point with Eugene. "I question the judgment of sending Penny into such a dangerous situation!"

"You know firsthand how good Penny is at locating fugitives," Eugene said. "I have confidence in her. And with Captain Trejo at her side, he will not let her get hurt."

The thought of Johnny Trejo getting close to Penny lit Leo's anger into a bonfire.

"For God's sake, Eugene, let me in on this so I can go help them!" Leo pounded his hand on the back of the leather chair.

"Are you sure you can handle your emotions concerning Penny? I know you are very fond of her, but the country's security is at risk. I was getting desperate to find the gunrunner—so desperate that I brought Penny in on this one. We had given up hope of solving it without an extra edge."

"But Penny has had little experience with guns, and she may have to defend herself!"

The marshal dropped the file into Leo's hands and stood silently as Leo perused it.

The evidence was sketchy, but a reliable mole reported that two sales of firearms and munitions were scheduled sometime in the next week, near Columbus. Unfortunately, the mole, Harold Moreno, a Luna County jail guard, was now dead. He had died of a gunshot in front of Penny's Mustang.

"Somebody went to a lot of trouble to implicate Penny," Leo said.

"Yes, and this is why I've got to have her on the case. She's connected now, and maybe she will have special insight into who is responsible for moving these guns south."

"But you're taking a big risk! She's new at this stuff, and you know it."

"Give your girlfriend a little more credit. She's brought in more fugitives in three months than my most senior agents. She didn't tell you?"

"No. She didn't say anything." Leo pondered the marshal's comment. Penny was good at this. Why wasn't he ready to accept that she might not need him?

"Initially, I asked Penny to locate an amateur gun trafficker named Juan Rico. He is small potatoes to us, but we figured if she could find him, we might have a lead on the jefe on the Mexican side of the border. But…"

"But what?" Leo didn't like the marshal's hesitation.

"We had an episode at the Luna County Medical Center last night. An American citizen, Dean Anderson, was wounded in Mexico, just south of Palomas, and he managed to get across the border. An ambulance in Columbus loaded him up for transport to the hospital in Deming for emergency surgery to remove a bullet from his stomach. The EMTs reported that Anderson was in and out of consciousness while in route, but he kept begging them not to take him to the hospital because the sheriff would finish him off."

"The sheriff, as in Jack Pritchard?" Leo asked incredulously. "I'm not sure what he meant, but the Mexican hit men barged across the border at the Columbus crossing and followed the ambulance to the hospital. Four Deming police officers were killed, as well as one of the gunmen and the victim, who was shot dead while in surgery.

Amazingly, the shooters left the surgeon alone and ran out of the hospital by another door. It appeared well planned."

"You sent Penny and Captain Trejo in to investigate?" Leo could hardly believe that Penny would be subject to such a stark circumstance as the aftermath of a gun battle. He could only imagine the condition of the bodies and the blood.

"We need Penny to examine the crime scene and see if she can view anything that happened. To complicate things, Sheriff Jack Pritchard has taken over the lead role in the investigation of the shootings and has refused to relinquish it. So we need Johnny to look into Pritchard's motives as well."

"That jerk!" Leo had never trusted Pritchard. There was something evil about the old guy, but voters kept reelecting him.

"We're not surprised he's not cooperating. He hates anything to do with federal agents. But we've got him dead to rights. This became a federal crime when the shooters crossed into the United States. Johnny and Penny were the closest to Deming, and I sent them to execute a search warrant and get the investigation underway. They shouldn't be alone for long. FBI agents are on their way from Tucson, even as we speak."

"You've got to let me back up Penny and Johnny. I can be there in a couple of hours."

The marshal sat back down on the sofa and leaned forward. He spoke in a low voice, and when he bent his body at the waist, Leo swore he looked even taller. "Leo, this is the most important operation of my career. I've got to get this dirty cop out of our midst. It's only a matter of time before we get blowback. If someone gets killed on the United States side with a weapon that was stolen or smuggled from the states to Mexico and then back again, we're toast."

"As much as I despise Pritchard, I've worked with him in the past," Leo said. "What if I told him I heard about the gun battle, and I wanted to see if he needed any help? You may remember we've got a mutual aid agreement between our two departments. He loaned me some of his deputies last year when we were protecting a Mexican shooting victim from across the border at the University Medical Center. We had to guard the hospital for two weeks, inconveniencing hospital staff and visitors. We needed and appreciated his deputies' presence."

"That is a capital idea, Leo, but our victim is dead, and there is no protection needed."

"Yes, but it looks like Pritchard's not willing to let go of the hospital, even with the FBI on the way. And from what you say, the Deming Police Department has been decimated."

"Okay, give the sheriff a call and offer your help. But from all we know, he may be implicated in the gun running. Watch your back!" Eugene dropped his arms to his sides, as if he were done arguing with Leo.

"Thanks!"

"And you can head to Deming only if he accepts your offer. Otherwise, you have to stay away from Penny."

CHAPTER 30

Johnny was thoroughly disgusted with Sheriff Pritchard, but his orders were to humor him until the FBI could get to the hospital, but that might be hours from now. The sheriff was doing everything possible to keep him and Penny from conducting a search of the property. They had moved down the hall, far enough away from the toxic mixture of bleach and ammonia, and were awaiting a special hospital team to clean it up. How long was that going to take?

Johnny put his hand on the sheriff's shoulder. "Sheriff, do you want Penny Larkin and me to do the search of the hospital, or do you want to wait for the FBI? They should be here within two hours."

This request stopped Jack Pritchard in midrant. He seemed to be contemplating the possibility of having these two local officers check the medical center rather than the FBI. Since Pritchard hated federal agencies, Johnny figured if he promised to take the lead on the search, it might appease the argumentative sheriff.

"You've got a point there, son. Okay, you can search the hospital, but I request that one of my deputies accompany you."

"That is fine!" Johnny was overjoyed to be able to get on with the investigation before the scene became more compromised than it already was. Hospitals by virtue of their business operated on cleanliness, and the cleaning staff was probably already scrubbing the operating room where the shooting victim had finally met his demise.

The sheriff called to a deputy who had been standing guard outside of the emergency room entrance. "Pedro, contact head-quarters and see about bringing in another officer to help protect this place."

"There is no need, Sheriff. We're down on men. Remember that Delgado and Garcia are on vacation. Other than Rocky guarding the front door, I'm all you've got."

Johnny didn't want to lose any more time. "Sheriff, we've got to get this search underway!"

"Give me ten more minutes," Pritchard said.

Johnny was not happy about cooling his heels any longer, and he hated to waste Penny's time either. He looked at Penny, who seemed just as annoyed but also curious about just how law enforcement worked a case.

The sheriff's phone rang as the trio stood in the hallway. "This is Sheriff Pritchard.

"Well, hello, Leo. How are you? What? Well, you are a sign from God. Yes, we need your help. How many deputies can you spare?"

Johnny couldn't help overhearing the sheriff. He was making a big deal out of Leo's call offering to supply him with deputies to stand guard at the hospital. Johnny watched Penny's face as she studied the sheriff. Was Leo coming here or just sending his deputies? For some reason, having Leo's help bothered Johnny. He liked working with Penny and thought when Leo arrived that he would lose his partner or, at the very least, Leo would be a major distraction.

"It looks like I can accompany you on the search and leave Officer Gomez in place. My other deputy is still at the front entrance, and there is no reason to change things now. Sheriff Tellez is coming and bringing an officer to relieve mine. That's what sheriffs do. They take care of their own."

CHAPTER 31

Juan trudged back up the grassy hill. He looked like he had been on a bender, but he was stone-cold sober. His eyes were red and swollen, and his jeans were torn at the knees where he had snagged them on the root of a tree during his roll down the hill. The fingers of his left hand were stiff, and his knuckles were puffy. He could move his right hand, but it hurt so much, he was forced to hold his pistol with the tips of his fingers. Juan had to get his gun back in his holster inside the waist of his jeans. His right hand was shaking as the pain shot through the nerves in his fingers and up through his wrists, before exploding like a ball of fire in his elbows. He finally managed to shove the gun behind his back, bringing tears to his eyes. He wiped them with his shirtsleeve and stopped long enough to check to see if he had done more damage to his fingers. They were as purple as the spiky chia flowers he used to pick as a kid and munch on the seeds. A fleeting memory of growing up in the desert blew through his brain like a hot, dry wind. He knew how to survive here, and chewing chia seeds was just the start. If he had to, he could, but he hoped it wouldn't come to that. His family couldn't live with his in-laws forever.

Juan took stock of his situation. If he lost the use of his hands, he might as well give up selling guns. If the cartel realized he couldn't defend himself, he would be shot on the spot whenever he stepped foot in Mexico. Life was cheap there, and your safety depended on being able to defend yourself. People were murdered like dogs, and there weren't enough police to even spend time hunting for the killers. And who wanted to find the killers anyway? In Juárez, you sometimes couldn't tell the good guys from the bad guys, and investigating a murder could leave a policeman dead. It happened all the time.

José Lueres, a friend of Juan's, was a guard at the Juárez city morgue. One night over a beer, José had confided that bodies were piling up waiting for autopsy. The coroner couldn't keep up and, in many cases, just gave up. The bodies were often mutilated and headless, with the hands chopped off, making them impossible to identify. When family members came to ID a victim, they had to do so behind bulletproof glass. Sometimes they ran out of the morgue sobbing because their relative's clothes didn't match the body. It was all so confusing. Juan couldn't blame the many residents of Juárez who were fleeing to the United States. Sadly, only those who could afford it crossed the border and bought or rented houses in El Paso. The poor, uneducated people of Mexico remained to bear the brunt of the violence.

José also told Juan that the shooters, or asesinos, often tried to steal the dead bodies right off the autopsy tables, hoping to keep the police from finding any clues that might lead to their arrest. "As if anyone would investigate the killing," Jose had said, giving Juan a caustic chuckle as he downed his beer. Juan knew it was no joke. It was a dangerous job but like Juan, José was uneducated, and this was the only work he could find. He was trapped in Mexico, and he would keep his head down and hope for the best. Juan didn't think the violence would ever end. There was just too much good money to be made selling drugs to Americans. He thought it was just a matter of time before the killing spilled over the border. Maybe what happened at the hospital last night was the start of something real bad. Juan shivered at the thought of it. When the killers came, there would be no stopping them. The US police were often outgunned. He was glad he had been able to save one of the officers with his Herstel. It was the least he could do.

XXX

As Juan walked through the hospital parking lot, he could feel his pistol rubbing against his back. He didn't have it in the holster right. *Damn it!* He took a deep breath and shoved his arm around his back, fighting the urge to scream. His fingers were throbbing as he adjusted the gun until it felt more comfortable. He also took the time to scrape the muddy soles of his boots on the pavement. *Should I have my hands looked at?* He was right here at the hospital. *What could be easier?* One way or another, he had to get back to his Uncle Martín anyway.

Juan chose the emergency room as his first stop. He was relieved to see that the yellow police tape had been removed from the door and the broken window was being replaced with new glass. He nodded to the deputy who asked for his identification before allowing him to step around the worker in blue overalls. Juan showed the officer his hands, and the deputy waved him on through.

Inside the urgent care waiting room, Juan stopped just short of a bucket and a mop. He knew this was where one of the police officers had been lying, bleeding out, and where he had killed the armed masked man, saving the life of the other officer. The metal desk had been moved back into its usual place, which left the bloodstain on the aging linoleum looking like an open sore. *What is that awful smell?*

Juan heard the sheriff yelling before he saw him standing down a hallway on the far side of the waiting room. He was waving his arms at a New Mexico State trooper and giving dirty looks to a beautiful blonde woman, who was standing there with her arms crossed. She looked briefly at Juan and then turned back to the sheriff, whose voice was getting louder.

Juan reconsidered whether it had been a good idea to walk right back into trouble, but he was here now, and it was too late to turn around and leave the hospital. He would just draw more attention to himself if he left in a hurry. He had to look normal. But what was normal these days? And he wondered how the sheriff would treat him when he noticed he was there. Certainly, he would be nice, having saved the sheriff's life. When had he ever seen the sheriff be kind to anyone?

Juan walked slowly to the receptionist's desk, but there was no one there to help him. How long should he wait for someone to come? This was stupid idea to come in there. *No one is even here to help.* Maybe every one took the day off. Maybe they were scared to come in after the shooting. He couldn't blame them.

Juan walked back toward the emergency room entrance, stopping again at the bucket and mop and feeling confused about what to do next. The lights of the hospital waiting room magnified his purple and yellow fingers and his swollen knuckles, which stuck out like those of a wounded prizefighter. He placed his hands behind his back before he remembered the killer pain this would cause. "Ugh!" He didn't mean to cry out, but the soreness was overwhelming him. The young woman turned to look at him again. This time her eyes stayed on Juan for what seemed like too long. He broke her gaze, bent his knees, and rested his hands on his thighs. The aching in his fingers was now unbearable. He was lightheaded, like when he played with his kids on the merry-go-round at the park. Sweat bubbled up on his forehead and spilled over his eyes and nose. He was breathing way too fast. He knew it, but he could not control it. His heart felt like a sledgehammer hitting his chest. *I have to get out of here!*

The smell of bleach burned his nose and reminded Juan of the times his children were born. He had fainted in the delivery room for both of his daughters, and now he felt like it might happen again. He planted his feet trying to keep his balance and prevent his world from breaking apart. *What is happening?*

Juan brought a crippled hand to his nose trying to block out the sickening odor of bleach and something else just as gross. The walls of the room began to spin. He looked at the floor, which wasn't moving, thank God. But when he looked up again, the sheriff, the trooper, and the nice-looking lady were twirling around him in a rainbow of twinkling lights. They had mounted the flying horses on the carousel at the county fair. He could hear the organ music pumping in time with his heartbeat as he climbed on board. Juan knew there were no brass rings and no mother looking on to catch him in case he fell from his favorite white stallion. He must ride on without her.

He squeezed his knees against the stallion's belly and reached for the horse's mane in an effort to hang on, but his fingers let him down. He had no choice but to let them slip through the horse's stringy black hair, caked with the filth of other children's hands. He released his boots from the stirrups one by one and began a downward slide to the floor. He yelled for the carousel to stop, but it kept moving in circles upon circles. He could see the feet of other riders still secure in their stirrups, and it made him angry. Why could they remain mounted when he could not? Their dancing horses mocked him as they moved up and down their chrome poles to the rhythm of the music. He thought he saw one horse show his teeth as it passed him in the turn. He looked away, starring at the filthy splintered floor, afraid even now to admit that he had failed as a son, a father, and a husband. At last, he gave into the incessant beating of his heart and looked out across the fairgrounds where the holiday fireworks were exploding in the dark sky. At first, the voices in the distance were small and faint as they tried to compete with the organ's cries, but finally, he heard his children calling his name. "Daddy! Daddy!" The last thing Juan remembered was knocking over the bucket of soapy water as he rolled off the merry-go-round onto the blood- stained floor.

CHAPTER 32

Penny reached Juan Rico ahead of the emergency room nurse. She held one hand over her mouth and turned Rico's head toward hers. She was satisfied that this was her fugitive, and now she only had to keep an eye on him. Penny heard the hospital speaker call for a code yellow. She had never heard it before and wondered what it meant.

A rotund nurse with curly black hair, a perfectly round face, and massive arms arrived wearing a respirator mask. She handed one to Penny who pulled it over her nose and mouth. Penny noticed the nurse's ID badge read "Molly Peters RN." Her identification rested on her large, heaving chest. She was out of breath.

"Miss, we need to get this young man on a cart and get him treated immediately for sodium hypochlorite and ammonia exposure."

Penny backed off and watched as an additional nurse named Juanita Rocha, also wearing a mask, helped pick Juan Rico up from the floor and hoisted him onto a cart. He reminded Penny of a rag doll. His arms dangled off the side of the bed. His mouth hung open, and his lips formed an angry oval, allowing bubbles to seep out onto his chin. As he was being rolled toward the waiting room, a doctor in green scrubs and Nikes also protected by a respirator mask and surgical gloves arrived from somewhere in the hospital and ran with them down the hall.

Johnny arrived with a handkerchief over his mouth and motioned for Penny to return with him down the hallway, where the sheriff was still waiting. Penny shook her head *no*. She wanted a gulp of fresh air and grabbed Johnny by the arm. She pointed to the door leading outside. He wasn't moving fast enough, and Penny removed her mask and shouted, "Let's get out of here!"

Johnny pushed her forward, and when they were outside, she was gasping for air. Tears ran down her eyes, and she wiped her nose with her sleeve.

"I'll get you a bottle of water." Johnny rushed back in the hospital, this time with his hand over his mouth. Penny was standing next to a weather-beaten truck whose fenders were scratched and dented. She breathed in deeply. Her throat and her nose were on fire. Johnny returned with a cold bottle of water, which Penny ran over her face and forehead before taking a drink.

"You breathing okay?" Johnny asked.

She ignored the question. "This is our fugitive. I'm certain of it." Penny took another big gulp of water and pulled the photograph out of her jeans pocket and showed it to Johnny. "I know you didn't get a good look at him, but I did. This is Juan Rico."

"Are you sure? If so, then we need to call Lujan."

"Let's hold off making any phone calls while Pritchard is nearby. I don't want him to know what we know."

"But don't you think we should stick together?"

"You go with the sheriff and execute the search warrant. You can tell him that I'm waiting for the FBI to arrive. That will get him to hustle because he apparently doesn't think much of them." Penny could see that Johnny had reservations about the plan.

He folded his arms, resting them on his chest. "I still think we need to alert the marshal."

Penny wasn't about to give up. She needed to bring in Juan Rico by herself. "I want to wait on our fugitive. We can't let him out of our sight. And when the FBI gets here, I'll send them to look for you. I promise."

Johnny was shaking his head. He didn't look convinced. "What are you thinking? You can't haul Rico out of a sick bed and have him arrested."

"While you've got the sheriff busy with the search, I'll contact Marshal Lujan, and then keep an eye on the room where they are treating Rico. We can't afford to lose him."

Penny could tell that Johnny still wasn't too keen on leaving her alone, but he dropped his arms to his sides and walked back inside. She inhaled and blew out a long breath and decided she should have some kind of plan for arresting Juan Rico. She had her cuffs, and Johnny's gun was still safely hidden in her bag. What else would she need? She ran her hand over the hood of the truck and realized that it reminded her of Leo's junk truck, as he called it. He used it for hauling things to the dump. Penny sighed. *Leo will be here soon.* She felt a little flutter of anticipation in her chest at the thought of seeing him on the right side of the law. She brushed the hair out of her eyes and finished her bottle of water. Leo had been disappointed in her. Otherwise, he certainly would have returned to the jail last night to take her home. Why else didn't he show up?

XXX

With the reassurance that both the FBI and Leo were on their way, Penny's courage grew. She decided to check out Juan Rico's hospital room. She knew she had promised Johnny she would call Marshal Lujan first, but she was too anxious about losing Rico. What if he had checked out okay, and they were releasing him already? Penny would call the marshal later. Besides, she wanted to keep her job, and that meant finishing what she had started.

Penny followed the path that Rico's nurses and the emergency room doctor had taken, which turned out to be a long, dimly lit hallway on the east side of the hospital. Johnny and the sheriff had exited the emergency room and headed to the west wing, so she knew it would be quite a while before they got around to emergency treatment rooms. This would give Penny plenty of time to scope out Rico and devise a plan for arresting him.

She crept down the hall until she saw a partially opened door. A shaft of bright light spilled into the hallway, casting her shadow against the opposite wall. This had to be the place as eerie as it felt. Penny took out her cell phone and pretended to be sending a text message as she stood next to the door. This would give her some cover as she tried to overhear the conversation about Rico's condition.

"Doctor, his eyes are swollen and red, and he is delirious. His blood pressure is 70 over 40 but stable."

"Insert an endotracheal tube and order a bronchoscopy to look for tissue burns."

"Okay. Should we admit him?"

"I'll be back in a few minutes. I've got to check on Mrs. Roland, the heart attack at the end of the hall. She's been here all night, and maybe it's safe enough to move her to a regular room." Penny heard the snap of the doctor's surgical gloves and the clank of a trashcan. The doctor barreled out the door with such force that he knocked them both to the floor. They wrestled around on the cold linoleum trying to separate their arms and legs before they both managed to stand. Penny's face was red with embarrassment. She could feel the heat rising from her neck and spreading over her face.

"I'm so sorry, miss. Are you hurt?" The doctor, in his midfifties, had green eyes and worry lines around his eyes and mouth. He ran his fingers through his thinning gray hair and took her hand. "Please forgive me. I am way too eager to get out of here, with the shootings and all."

The doctor held onto her hand as if she were a lifeline. "The fault is mine doctor…"

"I'm Doctor—I mean, I'm Bob, Bob Ranger. I substitute here on the weekends as a break from my regular job in Las Cruces at Memorial Hospital as an orthopedic surgeon."

Penny heard shouting coming from Juan Rico's room.

"No, sir, you've got to remain still!" Nurse Peters was trying to calm Juan Rico.

"He's got a gun!" Nurse Rocha screamed. "Help us!"

Dr. Ranger's body stiffened, and his eyes grew wide with fear. Without giving it another thought, Penny grabbed her revolver from her purse, flashed her badge at the doctor, and motioned for him to step aside. He mouthed some words of protest but then got out of her way. His hands were shaking, which was not a good thing for a surgeon, Penny thought. She eased her way through the door where both nurses were crouched on the floor. Nurse Peters continued trying to negotiate with Juan.

"Please, Mr. Rico, you are very sick. Put the gun down!" Luckily, Juan had his eyes on the nurses and didn't notice that Penny had entered the room. She felt the heat of the doctor's body hovering behind her. He was breathing heavily. Nurse Rocha gasped when she saw Penny with her gun drawn. Rico turned his head and lunged toward Penny.

She jammed her revolver into the side of his neck and then grabbed his arm as he nearly fell off the bed. "Juan Rico, put the gun down, or I'll shoot you." Rico's eyes looked funny to Penny. His pupils were as big as nickels, and tears ran down his cheeks. "I'm sorry," he cried as his body slumped forward and he began to shake.

"He's having a seizure!" Nurse Peters jumped to her feet, trying to contain Juan Rico. His body was jerking from side to side, but he miraculously still had his pistol in his right hand. Rico's seizure turned out to be too much for even the broad arms of the RN. The doctor rushed over to help her.

In the melee, Juan's pistol fell from his hand and bounced off the emergency room cart, banging on the floor. The hair trigger of the pistol released a bullet into the portable oxygen unit standing in the corner. The tank launched like a rocket ship through the dropped ceiling and then fell back to the floor clanging against the linoleum. Jagged pieces of acoustical tile and beads of insulation fell like hail, and the dust from a thousand other emergencies floated in the air. Penny noticed that Nurse Rocha was struggling to get her cell phone out of her uniform pocket. "I need to call for help!" she shouted.

Penny could hear the hissing sound of the oxygen tank, which was still vibrating on the floor, but nothing was going to keep her from arresting Rico. She would take her chances.

Nurse Peters had her hand in Juan's mouth, trying to keep him from swallowing his tongue while the doctor grabbed what looked like a tongue depressor from a drawer at the back of the room. Rocha abandoned her medical training and ran screaming from the room.

"Help, somebody! An oxygen tank might explode!"

The frightened nurse must have pulled the fire alarm in the hall, because the horn was deafening.

The doctor, suddenly filled with courage, yanked on Penny's arm, trying to take the gun from her. "What in the hell do you think you're doing? Bob, I'm a Federal agent. Go get help!"

Dr. Ranger dropped his hand. His face was streaked with red from his embarrassing mistake. "I'm so sorry." In an effort to make amends, he gave Penny some parting advice, which she did really appreciate. "Don't worry about the oxygen tank. It won't blow." Then Bob Ranger ran from the room.

CHAPTER 33

Leo was pulling into the emergency room parking lot at the hospital when he noticed a cluster of employees dressed in white coats and green scrubs streaming out of the building. Hospital beds on wheels were being rolled down the sidewalk and into the parking lot, leaving Leo with no place to park. Trailing behind him was Deputy Thomas Portales, who was driving a patrol car from the El Paso County Sheriff Department. Leo was scheduled for a ten-hour stint, relieving the Luna County Deputy who was standing at the entrance to the emergency room trying to help steer confused employees and visitors away from the building. Officer Portales would fill in wherever Sheriff Pritchard needed him. Leo wondered about the reason behind all this upheaval. This would be a perfect ploy by the drug cartels to take over the hospital. Hopefully, there wasn't anything more serious going on than a false alarm.

On the heels of Leo's arrival, the Deming Volunteer Fire Department truck roared into the circular drive in front of the entrance to the emergency room. The truck's presence only served to enflame the confusion and make for a greater traffic jam.

Its siren was blaring, the lights were flashing, and people were running in all different directions, some in the state of anxiety and others taking all the chaos as a joke. Volunteer firemen began pulling up in their private vehicles.

From his car, Leo perused the parking lot for Penny, but she was nowhere to be found. He motioned for his deputy to follow him in his car. They drove across the grass and over the curb to exit the lot and parked on the city street. When Leo and his deputy returned, the hospital fire alarm was still blaring, but the fire truck siren had thankfully stopped. Leo watched as the firemen charged into the facility, dragging a long hose attached to the pumper on the side of their truck.

Leo saw Johnny Trejo and Sheriff Jack Pritchard exiting the hospital, stepping over the hose and heading toward the large group of employees congregated under the hospital's one shade tree. Leo joined them, shaking hands with both men. Sheriff Pritchard was very happy to see Leo and pointed to the officer he would be relieving. "Thanks so much, Leo."

"You've done the same for me, Jack. I also brought Deputy Portales along, to give you some more help. Sheriff Pritchard pounded Leo on the back. "You're the best, Leo."

Leo introduced Officer Portales to Jack Pritchard, and it was decided that Portales would take the evening shift at the hospital's main entrance.

Leo still could not find Penny. Where could she be? He tried not to sound overly concerned. "Hey, Johnny, have you seen Penny?" If Johnny seemed worried that Penny wasn't around, he didn't act like it.

"No. The last time I saw her she was hanging around the emergency room waiting for the FBI to arrive, while the sheriff and I executed a search warrant. Leo left them to discuss the plans for the evening watch and walked over to the emergency room door. He had to find Penny! Something just didn't feel right. He flashed his badge, but the deputy refused to let him in. "Sheriff, I've got orders to keep everyone except essential personnel out of the building. I'm sorry."

"But I have to get in there."

"I'm sorry, but they won't even let me inside." The deputy responded with respect and concern for the sheriff, which Leo greatly appreciated.

Johnny joined Leo at the door.

"Is everything okay here?" Johnny asked.

"I'm checking on Penny." If Johnny didn't know where Penny was, maybe the deputy had seen her. "Did you see Penny Larkin exit the hospital?"

"No, sir. That last time I saw her she was helping a man who had collapsed on the floor of the waiting room. I swear the dumbest orderly on the planet created a toxic mix of ammonia and bleach and started mopping. Everybody had to leave the waiting room until a HAZMAT team could clean it up—which they were attempting to do when the fire alarm went off."

Johnny motioned for Leo to follow him into the parking lot. "I didn't want to say anything in front of the deputy or Jack Pritchard, but Penny recognized the fugitive she was on the lookout for and wanted to remain in the emergency room until he could be treated."

"He was the one who fainted? Where is he now?" Leo could feel the sweat gathering under his arms. His stomach churned, and he could feel a panic attack coming on. He wished he had brought his Maalox. Leo shoved his hand in his pants pockets searching for a Tums, but he came back empty handed.

"We've got to get inside. I don't like this." He was pressing Johnny and didn't care if he appeared overly alarmed. He had to find her.

Nurse Peters, whose body looked like she had taken a shower in dust, came running out of the emergency room door. Her face was red and puffy, and her uniform was torn. Ribbons of sweat ran from her face and arms. "Somebody help! A male patient has a gun!"

CHAPTER 34

Penny wasn't sure how Juan Rico managed to get her gun, which he waved in the air with his left hand, and pointed a large pistol straight at her chest with his right. She couldn't imagine how it was possible to hold both guns because his hands looked like they'd been through a meat grinder.

It had happened so quickly that Penny barely got a chance to react. Nurse Peters, who was kind enough to remain with Juan to keep him from choking, received the brunt of his anger. Without warning, Juan who appeared to be unconscious rose from the bed, shoved the nurse into the wall, and grabbed Penny's gun, knocking her to the floor. The nurse escaped and ran from the room. When Penny tried to follow, Juan yelled at her to stop. He was aiming his pistol straight at her, but he was having trouble keeping his balance.

The fire alarm made it hard to hear him. He was mumbling and was clearly out of his mind. *Is this what bleach and ammonia do to your brain?* Penny counted on being able to outsmart him. After all, she still had her faculties, but she had to act fast. She moved closer trying to test his agility. He lunged at her, his hands trembling. When he fell forward, the revolver flew out of his hand and bounced on the floor. Penny crawled toward the gun, but Rico stomped on her hand with his bare feet. "Ugh!"

The pain was intense, and now her fingers were numb. It was a good thing he didn't have on his boots. She tried reasoning with the unreasonable man. "Look, Juan, I am here to help you."

"No, you said you were here to arrest me! I'm no fool!" He grabbed her by the arm and pulled her to her feet. "Turn around and hold your hands behind your back." Juan laid her revolver down and grabbed a pair of scissors and cut a pillowcase, ripping it into strips and tying her hands.

Now Penny was really mad. She spun around and hit Rico in the groin in a double-fisted play. He fell forward. "Damn you, woman. You've done it now!" He charged her like a bull. Penny dodged him, causing him to crash headlong into the cement block wall. He collapsed on the floor.

Penny would be wise to leave now and have someone else take Rico into custody, but she was feeling territorial. She wriggled her hands free of the clumsily tied knot and rummaged through a drawer where she found some large plastic trash bag ties that she made into a makeshift pair of handcuffs.

Penny picked up her gun and his and then pulled up a straight-backed chair and sat down, resting the guns in her lap and her feet on Juan Rico's belly. Her head was pounding out a bad headache. Her whole body was lathered in perspiration, and her chest ached from Rico using her as a battering ram. Her hand looked bruised, but she could still move her fingers. Everything would heal in time.

She thought back to the last forty-eight hours. The capture of Juan Rico had not been pretty, but Penny Larkin had just experienced her first real take down of a fugitive. Life was good.

CHAPTER 35

Tom Raney, a volunteer fireman, found Penny sitting in a chair in a treatment room with her one good hand cradling her forehead and her feet resting on Juan Rico's stomach. Raney was a young man, about twenty years old who still sported braces on his teeth. When he took off his helmet, his cropped brown hair jutted out of his scalp in all directions, but his touch was kind. He examined her left hand, which was bruised and swollen. As he leaned in to apply an ice pack, he saw the weapons in her lap. "It's okay. I'm a Federal agent." Penny tried to assure him that everything was okay. She pointed to her badge, which had fallen on the floor.

Raney looked puzzled but didn't ask her any questions. "This should give you some relief until we can get you to the doctor." He looked around the room, and realizing where he was, he added, "Well, heck, that won't take much, now will it?" He laughed and wiped his face, which had broken out in beads of sweat, leaving a smear of something black across his nose.

"Can you turn off that infernal fire alarm? I'm about deaf!" Penny yelled at the fireman and dropped her hand to her lap to get a better grip on the guns, which were sliding down her legs.

"Sure! I'll be right back after I find the alarm and shut it off." The commotion caused Juan to stir, and he tried to roll on his side, but he was still out of it. Penny adjusted her feet and shoved her boot heels against his hipbones. If it hurt him, he never reacted. In fact, she thought she could hear Rico snoring.

XXX

Leo and Johnny had coaxed Sheriff Pritchard into letting them in the hospital in order to search for Penny. He agreed to it as long as he accompanied them. All three men arrived at Juan Rico's room just as the fireman was leaving to find the alarm. Johnny moved in to check Penny's hand, which she was nursing with the ice pack.

"What in the world happened?" Johnny reached down to check her face and arms for other injuries. He heard Leo clear his throat. Leo didn't sound like he approved of Johnny's examination of Penny, but Johnny felt responsible for what had happened with Juan Rico. He had left her alone to wait for the FBI to arrive and to find a way to detain Rico. He just didn't expect her to brandish her weapon and try to arrest him while he was being cared for in the emergency room. Johnny was learning more about Penny by the minute, and he now understood, nothing would get in her way of bringing in a fugitive even at the risk of her own life.

It had been a dumb move to leave Penny to her own devices. She could have been killed. Johnny hoped the marshal didn't report this to the superintendent of the New Mexico State Troopers in Santa Fe. He had just been made captain last year and was charged with running the Las Cruces office. He didn't want to lose his promotion or his respect within the agency.

Johnny saw Leo coming around his left side, apparently trying to see to Penny's injuries for himself. Johnny remained standing squarely in front of Penny's chair. He was not about to be moved when Leo had all but abandoned Penny at the jail last night. As far as he was concerned, Penny deserved better.

Penny looked into Johnny's eyes and smiled at him. "I'm fine, Johnny, I just need help getting this guy to jail." Then Penny looked at Leo. "It's okay, Leo. I am just doing my job."

The fireman must have found the alarm because the room became quiet. The silence made for an awkward moment among the three of them. Johnny could hear Juan Rico snoring. It was miserably hot in the room. Johnny looked for the air ducts and saw that the ceiling had collapsed. He also noticed what looked like some sort of green tank lying in the corner. "What happened in here?" He pointed up at the dismantled ceiling.

Before Penny could answer, Sheriff Pritchard, who had been leaning against the doorjamb, stepped between Johnny and Leo to confront Penny. "Just what are you charging this man with?"

"He's wanted on a warrant from the US Marshals office," Penny said. "I have been tracking him, and he's mine."

"Well, in case you haven't looked, you crossed into Luna County when you exited the interstate. This is my arrest. He goes to my jail."

Johnny couldn't see any harm in that, at least for the time being. But he could tell Penny was unhappy as the sheriff pulled Rico to his feet and cuffed him.

Rico began to moan. "What are you doing to me? I've done nothing wrong."

"Rico isn't going anywhere without me," Penny stood, handed Rico's gun to the sheriff as a peace offering, and tucked the .38 revolver back in her bag.

"Sheriff, I want to take him back to El Paso right now." Johnny pulled Penny back, before the sheriff got really angry.

He could see his face getting red. Pritchard tightened his hold on Rico, whose head was bobbing, and his eyes were glazing over. "Penny, how about a compromise? We let the sheriff take Rico to jail, and we pick him up on the way home."

XXX

Leo was seething. He stood in the corner and watched this whole Juan Rico thing go down. Sheriff Pritchard was pushing Johnny and Penny around, and Leo could do nothing but stand by and dig his fingernails into his palms. He would never allow Pritchard to pull that kind of crap if this were his case.

Leo also didn't like the way Johnny looked at Penny. His brown eyes seemed to light up whenever she smiled at him. Leo hoped this was lost on Penny, who looked haggard and tired.

Leo was desperate to inject himself into the investigation so he could keep an eye on her, but he was stuck taking the night shift at the emergency room door. What had he been thinking? Now he was trapped while Johnny and Penny took custody of Juan Rico and headed back to El Paso. Maybe he could call his office and order another deputy to come and relieve him. As Leo pulled out his cell phone, it vibrated. It was Adriana. He would have to let it go to voice mail. Leo didn't have time for more aggravation right now.

CHAPTER 36

Johnny was having a difficult time convincing Penny that it was okay to have Juan Rico transported to the Luna County jail for safekeeping. She knew that a sale of semiautomatics was imminent and that she should get him back to El Paso as soon as possible. Any further delays might mean more innocent or even culpable shooting victims in Mexico.

"Juan Rico is not going anywhere without me," Penny said defiantly.

"Penny, the FBI will be here any time, and then we can hand over the hospital investigation to them. I don't think the marshal would like us to leave the sheriff to his own resorts." Johnny was pressing his case and did not appear to Penny to be letting up.

Penny looked at Leo, who was not taking sides, but then he couldn't. He had no authority here. Penny thought it was wise of him to keep his mouth shut.

Johnny's cell phone rang, and he walked into the hall to answer it. The call only lasted a few minutes, but when he returned, he drew Penny aside. "Penny, can I speak with you alone?"

Penny walked with Johnny into the hall, leaving the Sheriff and Leo with Juan Rico, who was cuffed and ready to transport. "That was Marshal Lujan on the phone. According to a report from the FBI's chief firearms examiner, the serial number on the gun and the casings from the AR-15 found on the dead shooter was one of several stolen from a National Guard Armory in Phoenix last year. Also the ATF reports that this aligns with a report they sent to the Mexican Federal Police. This same automatic weapon was one used to kill a bunch of people at a drug rehab center six months ago in Juárez."

"Ouch!" Learning this only made Penny more determined to stick close to Rico.

"Marshal Lujan is flying in an agent along with the ATF officers to question Rico in the Luna County jail since we're on a short fuse to stop this second sale. Moreno had warned that the sale was going down tonight, but since he's dead, it's just a guess. Oh, and by the way, Lujan said to tell you congratulations and good work!"

"I'm going to see this through and ride with the sheriff to the jail." Penny had moved squarely in front of Johnny and leaned in to him. "Can I keep your revolver?"

Johnny threw up his hands as if he was surrendering. "Sure, Penny. Why not!" Penny could hear the sarcasm in his voice and thought she saw his eyes moisten. She couldn't figure why he was so reluctant to let her go.

"Am I doing something wrong?"

"No, you're right to want to see it through. I probably would do the same thing. I'll stay and finish up the warrant with the FBI's help, although much of the hospital has been contaminated, as far as any measurable evidence is concerned. And honestly, I'll be glad to have Jack Pritchard out of my hair."

Johnny laughed and placed his hand on her shoulder. "You be careful, okay?" Johnny gave her a hug and then refused to let her go.

Penny pulled out of his arms and made light of the moment. "What kind of trouble can I get into? I'm heading to jail!" Penny laughed, but it was no joke. It would be the second time in two days that she had seen the inside of a jail.

CHAPTER 37

Penny and Leo walked out of the hospital and followed Sheriff Pritchard to his patrol car.

Leo had not had time to speak with Penny alone, and this was the best it was going get until they both got back to El Paso and back to normal. And normal meant confronting Adriana too.

Just the thought of Adriana caused a chill to race down his arms. It excited him to think of her, but it felt wrong to do so. Being unfaithful to Penny was just too much to contemplate right now. He began massaging his fingers, which felt numb. He shuddered and hoped Penny hadn't noticed.

Leo let Sheriff Pritchard and his prisoner get a little further ahead and spoke softly to Penny, "I want to apologize for not being there when you were released from jail."

"What happened?" Penny seemed genuinely concerned and not angry that he hadn't shown up.

Leo hated to lie to her, but otherwise, his relationship with Penny would be irretrievably damaged. "On my way home to El Paso, I got a call about a hostage situation in Monte Vista. I took Adriana home and headed to the far east side to back up my SWAT team."

"Didn't you check your cell phone? Mine was dead, but Johnny said he tried to contact you."

"I had no cell phone service in Monte Vista. You know it's halfway to Carlsbad! And by the time I got within cell range, my phone had run out of juice from roaming for service. I drove straight to my office, and that's when I heard Johnny's message." Penny placed her bruised hand on his arm. "I understand, Leo.

I do. It's just that while in the jail, I had a dream. I thought I saw Adriana's long black hair brushing over your arm. It worried me." Leo looked down at her bruised and swollen hand. "My God, Penny! Why didn't you have the doc look at your fingers? Can you move them?" He had been right. Penny could see what he was up to, and that sucked.

Sheriff Pritchard put Juan in the backseat of his patrol car and slammed the door and then climbed in the driver's side. Leo walked Penny around to the passenger's side and helped her in. He leaned down and whispered in her ear, "I love you, Penny. Call me when the marshals guys get to the jail, and I'll swing by and take you home."

"Johnny was planning on picking me up."

"Don't worry about Johnny. I'll make sure he knows I've got this." Leo shut the car door and watched the sheriff pull out of the hospital parking lot. Leo would do whatever he could to make this up to Penny.

CHAPTER 38

The Luna County Detention Center was on Fourth Street, several miles east of town, where the closest neighbors were stray cows who managed to munch their way to the fence that separated the captives from the free rangers. Just two days ago, Penny and the team of trackers assembled by the marshal's office had met in front of the jail at 6:00 a.m. before they scattered to follow the leads to which each of them had been assigned.

Since Penny was already familiar with the jail, she was not concerned about going there with the sheriff alone because the place she had seen in her dream while at the state trooper's headquarters was nothing like where she was headed.

In her research, she had learned that the center held more than four hundred inmates, and like the Doña Ana County jail, it had mostly glass partitions for better supervision. The place she had viewed was old and rundown. And the prisoners were held behind bars that had been repainted many times to cover over the initials and filthy language etched into them. And there were bunks in each cell, like something you'd see in the *Shawshank Redemption*, not the single beds in the modern pods that each prisoner occupied.

The sheriff didn't make any small talk with Penny, for which she was grateful. He spent most of his time on the radio following up on some old messages and ordering a deputy to meet him at the side entrance to transport a prisoner into a holding cell for pick up by the US Marshals Service.

The sheriff pulled into the circular driveway and then made a right and headed toward the back of the center. He stopped at a side door where the deputy stood, dutifully prepared to take in the prisoner. The sheriff remained in the car as the deputy pulled Juan Rico out of the backseat and walked him inside the jail. Then the sheriff continued driving toward the back of the center where there was a large parking lot that held a dozen private vehicles, which Penny presumed belonged to employees.

"We'll head in the private entrance," the sheriff told Penny.

Sheriff Pritchard helped Penny out of the car, and they walked side by side to the back door. He knocked, and within a minute, the door opened, and a woman guard opened the door and let them in. She was stone-cold serious and didn't even look Penny in the eye.

The hall was dark and had a musty smell, which Penny thought was odd. For a new place, it had an odor of old, wet towels. It was also extremely warm, like the air conditioning had been shut off. Penny's feet were sweating. She could feel the dampness between her toes. She walked behind the sheriff who seemed to be intent on getting somewhere fast. The itching in her boots was driving her crazy. "Can you wait a minute, Sheriff?" She bent forward and tried without success to reach the irritation with her fingers. Disgusted, she gave up, and continued down the hall, making a right turn around a corner, where she'd watched the sheriff go.

She took the corner, fully expecting to see the sheriff, but he was gone. Penny headed to the large metal door, which she presumed led to the main part of the detention center. She knocked and waited, but no one came. She knocked again. The lights in the hallway went off, leaving her in darkness.

Did the sheriff not realize I had stopped? Certainly he wasn't so distracted that he forgot me? Penny felt for the door and pounded as hard as she could. The noise echoed against the empty hall. But no one apparently could hear her.

Finally, she yelled, "Sheriff, it's Penny! You left me behind!" Still nothing. The jail was strangely silent for being in a facility with hundreds of prisoners. Finally, she gave up and turned around, retracing her steps until she found the door that led outside to the parking lot.

She shoved on the door, but it was locked. She was trapped!

She could feel her heart racing. She tried not to panic, but she was completely alone. Certainly, there was an explanation for this. Penny tried hard to think what that explanation might be. She heard the sound of metal rubbing against metal and then a clanking noise. The sheriff had returned! She let out a sigh of relief and moved toward the sound, as carefully as she could in the darkness. A door in the middle of the hall opened, letting in a splinter of light. *A door? Where did that come from?* Penny could see that it was cleverly hidden within the wall, surrounded by carved panels.

A shadowy figure stepped into the hall and turned to face her. With the small amount of light at his back, Penny could see that he was at least six foot five and weighed close to three hundred pounds. He lumbered closer, and she could hear his chest rattling, as he heaved himself toward her. She smelled the lingering odor of cigarettes. His black knit cap covered a huge head that held his lips, nose, and dark eyes in check. He flicked on a flashlight, which revealed his black shirt and pants and black boots. He carried a rifle in his right hand. Was he on a SWAT team?

Penny was paralyzed with fear. There was nowhere to run. She had to face whatever was about to befall her, and it was her own darn fault. Leo's face flashed before her, and that brought her some comfort in the wake of what was surely going to be the end of her life.

"Who are you?" Penny called out to him, but he said nothing although she thought she heard a groan as he dropped his flashlight and let it roll across the floor. When the light stopped, the beam grazed the floor and ricocheted off the paneled wall, exposing Penny with a burst of light. He could see her clearly now, but she could not see him well at all. He hung in the shadows like a coward.

Penny gasped for air, but the heat in the hall and the lack of circulation was suffocating. Sweat oozed from her every pore. She fought the urge to scream, not wanting him to see that she was afraid. She fumbled around trying to unzip her purse, but it was stuck. She couldn't get to her gun.

When he reached for her, she took several steps back, hoping to bring his face into the light. His fingers were fat and thick, and his nails were long but not quite long enough to touch her. The itching in her boots returned, and she scuffed her shoes back and forth on the floor, laughing at herself for worrying about a tiny itch when she was about to die. She had to fight back!

She lunged toward the bulky, black figure, hoping that the surprise move would knock the rifle out of his hand, but he grabbed her with his left arm and closed it around her chest. He was slowly compressing the air out of her lungs. She felt him taking her life an inch at a time. She was grateful for a thread of air still running from her nose to her lungs, but she wasn't sure how long it would last.

Penny looked up to see her killer's face, now in the center of the shaft of the flashlight. She could see into the nostrils of his broad nose. He was breathing hard, and the moisture blew onto her face and neck. His breath smelled of rancid salsa and raw onions.

Penny braced herself for what might come next. He smiled, revealing his nicotine-stained teeth. The man groaned louder as he lifted her face level with his. His dark eyes were full of rage, as if he sought to rob her of her soul.

CHAPTER 39

Officer Portales had Leo on the phone, explaining he had to leave his post. "My wife was in an auto accident. She's at the hospital. I've got to get there. She needs blood, and I've got to sign for permission to have it done!"

"Of course, Thomas, please get on the road now. I'll relieve you of your watch."

Leo had to let Deputy Portales get to El Paso, but now he was stuck for the next ten hours at the hospital even though he had found a replacement, Deputy Frank Reynoso, for his own watch. How could he pick up Penny when she called? It aggravated him to think that he would have to ask Johnny to take her home once again. He called Johnny on his cell.

"Hey, Johnny. I'm going to have to stay at the hospital to relieve my deputy who has had an emergency."

"Don't worry, I can run by and pick up Penny when I'm done here. We're just reviewing everything we found with the FBI. I'll copy you on the e-mail with my report. It was definitely an inside job."

"Great. Thanks, Johnny. I'll call Penny and tell her there has been a change of plans."

Leo had to come to grips with the fact that he was jealous of Johnny. He was thirty-five, nearer to Penny's age, and extremely handsome, even for a guy's standards. Johnny looked like he actually took the time to go to the gym, which Leo always found a good excuse to avoid. Leo, who had just turned forty-two, had a difficult time disliking him. Johnny was well respected in law enforcement circles and had a great career ahead of him. He just didn't want Johnny sharing that career with Penny, as his wife. He regretted not expressing his desire to Penny earlier that he wanted to get married. She had been very understanding when he had told her he needed time to heal from the loss of Alejandra and Marta, but now he realized he had made a mistake. He hoped he hadn't waited too long.

Leo pushed speed dial on his phone. Penny's voice mail came on. "This is Penny Larkin. Please leave a message and the time you called. Thanks."

"Penny, please call Johnny when the agents get there to question Juan Rico. I've got to pick up Officer Portales's shift because his wife was in an accident, and he has to rush home. Johnny has agreed to take you back to El Paso. Regardless, can you call me back when you get this message? I want to make sure everything is okay."

Leo had never trusted Jack Pritchard. He had been in office for twenty years and had a stranglehold on the county. Nothing got done without his approval. He was not sure how he got reelected, but Leo had his suspicions that it involved money in the right palms.

XXX

Leo was starving. He stopped in the hospital cafeteria to grab a cup of coffee and a bagel, before heading back to the emergency room to relieve Deputy Portales, who had moved from the front of the hospital to the emergency room door after Deputy Reynoso had arrived. It had taken an hour to get everyone back at work and tucked back in bed after the fire alarm emptied the hospital, so the coffee had gone cold, but Leo took a cup anyway. He shoved the bagel in his mouth and washed it down with the brew, which tasted bitter against his tongue. It matched his mood, cold and acrimonious.

Leo managed to put on a positive face when he reached his deputy.

"Get going. I'll call the emergency room at Las Palmas and tell them you're on your way." He shook the officer's hand and then hugged him and pushed him toward the parking lot.

"Thank you so much, Sheriff. I'm really worried about her." Thomas ran down the ramp leading to the parking lot and onto the street where he had parked the patrol car.

Leo looked around the back end of the hospital and wondered how long it would have to have protection. Generally, when a gunshot victim from Mexico was discharged, the sheriff's office remained stationed at the hospital for another thirty-six to forty-eight hours just in case the cartel returned. In this case, the shooters had been successful in eliminating their target. It could be that the need for protection might end once the FBI finished their investigation, which could be at any time. Leo could hope. He wanted to get back to El Paso and set things straight with Penny.

CHAPTER 40

Johnny shook hands with FBI Special Agent Don *Little* Richards and escorted him around the hospital, showing him the places where he and Sheriff Pritchard had already executed the search warrant and what had been interrupted when the fire alarm went off. Then Johnny called Marshal Lujan to tell him that he'd also learned that a hospital orderly named Roberto Renteria had not reported to work this morning.

"Marshal, when a Deming City Police officer went to check out Renteria's apartment, he was in the midst of moving out, and he had $5,000 in cash lying on the bed. He started singing like a canary about not having anything to do with the hospital shooting. The officer took him into custody on suspicion of conspiracy to commit murder. Do you want to have your agents question him at the jail while they are also meeting with Juan Rico?"

"Of course. I'll give the order when we hang up. This confirms a tip we had last month from Officer Moreno."

"What was that?" Johnny asked.

"Anderson Dean, a.k.a. Rio, a notorious American gunrunner for the Chihuahua cartel was setting up the next two buys for shipment to Mexico. We had a warrant out for his arrest, but he was always running under our radar. While in Mexico, he had the misfortune of finding himself in the cross hairs of the Betas cartel. Then their hit men followed his ambulance to the Luna County hospital where they finished him off."

"Do you want me to see about getting Dean transported to El Paso for an autopsy before Sheriff Pritchard gets wind of it?" "Yes, you read my mind," the marshal replied. "But, Captain, I've got to warn you to be cautious. Officer Moreno had strong suspicions that

Sheriff Pritchard was Dean's gun supplier. Moreno was killed before he could confirm it for us."

The news from the marshal rattled Johnny's eardrums. "Oh, no! Penny left with Sheriff Pritchard to accompany Juan Rico to jail. She refused to let Rico out of her sight."

"Don't panic. We've got every federal agent in the region headed to the jail. There's not much the sheriff could do to Penny from that venue."

Johnny disagreed. There was plenty the sheriff could do. His brain was in chaos as he disconnected his call with the marshal. Why had he let Penny head to the jail with Pritchard and Rico? Johnny punched her number into his cell phone, listening to the phone ring and waiting forever for her to pick up. The man who answered was not happy. He had been in the shower. "No, I'm not Penny! Get some new glasses, buddy, before you dial me again!"

Johnny felt like all thumbs when he pressed in her phone number again. This time he heard Penny's voice mail. She was not answering her phone! Something isn't right!"

Johnny went looking for Agent Richards to tell him he was heading to the Luna County jail to connect with Penny Larkin.

"Oh, you know Penny?" the agent asked.

"Yes. We were both ordered by the US marshal to keep an eye on the hospital until you, uh, the FBI arrived."

"Where is she now?" Richards asked.

"Penny just headed to the jail with her fugitive, Juan Rico, whom she apprehended in the emergency room. Penny is pretty much of a bulldog when it comes to hunting down fugitives. She is refusing to let Rico out of her sight."

"Oh, yeah. The marshal had tremendous luck hiring her. We wanted to hire her too. She's brought in four hard-to-find fugitives for him. Without her viewing abilities, they'd still be searching for them."

"So you believe in that stuff?" Johnny had yet to reconcile Penny's expertise as a remote viewer with serious police work.

"Didn't you hear about her work tracking down the kidnapped kid and breaking up the Russian child trafficking ring?"

"She was involved in that?" Johnny was amazed and surprised Penny hadn't mentioned it. Everyone had been talking about that case for months, especially since New Mexico's Doña Ana County Sheriff Ted Rodriguez had almost died of a gunshot wound. "I read that the FBI was responsible for ending it."

"Yeah, that's what we said, but it was all thanks to Leo Tellez and Penny Larkin, with the help of Sheriff Rodriguez of course." Johnny was blown away by this information. He had underestimated Penny and regretted not knowing this from the start. Now he understood how Penny and Leo had become so close. They had faced danger together and brought down a big case that made national news—only they didn't get the credit for it. The FBI was like that, sometimes, taking the credit for solving cases on which his own troopers had broken their knuckles bringing fugitives to justice.

Johnny looked at Agent Richards with suspicion. Were all FBI agents so greedy for credit? He didn't have time to worry about who got credit and who did not. He had to make sure Penny was okay.

"I've got to go!"

Johnny ran out of the hospital with his cell phone on his ear. He had a local mortuary on the line to arrange the transport of Anderson Dean's body to the morgue in El Paso. Then he dialed Penny's number again. The call went immediately to voice mail. Johnny thought it strange since she had charged her phone in his car on the drive to Deming. It shouldn't be dead yet.

CHAPTER 41

The Luna County correctional officer led Juan Rico into the detention center and then into a room where he was asked to empty his pockets. The guard took Juan's truck keys and dropped them in a brown paper bag. Then he picked up his cell phone, punched a few buttons, and looked at the screen. "I see somebody named Alicia called."

Juan looked at him in surprise. He had not heard his cell phone ring, but then he had been a bit busy going crazy. Maybe his wife had news about Nancy. He hoped and prayed his daughter was okay. He could handle jail time, but he could not stand learning his family was hurting.

The officer rubbed his hands up and down Juan's legs, and when he reached his waist, he found his empty holster hidden in the back of his pants. "No gun today—eh?"

"No, the sheriff has it." The gun had been his lifeline. He had used it to save the sheriff's life, as well as Officer Jackman's. He hoped the sheriff would remember all that and go easy on him.

Juan waited for the officer to take him to a room to change his clothes and put on a jail jumpsuit. This was the most humiliating part of being behind bars. He hated the orange or yellow suits inmates had to wear. Instead, the officer walked him into an office where there was a large wooden desk and a swivel chair with arms.

"Sit here and wait. The sheriff wants to talk to you." The guard left Juan alone in the room and shut the door.

Juan sat and waited. The sheriff had mercifully cuffed his hands in front and not behind his back. He couldn't have stood the grief of that. He examined his hands, which had never been treated. His injured hands were the reason he had gotten into all this trouble. If only he had not gone into the hospital.

His left hand was badly bruised, but it didn't appear to be broken like he first thought. His fingers were bending now, which to Juan was a relief. On his right hand—his shooting hand— the purple bruises were turning yellow. He thought he would be okay, although the cuffs were not helping him heal. When he tried to move the steel bracelets further up his wrists, a throbbing ache began in his left hand again, bringing tears to his eyes. He wiped his face with his sleeve and sat back in the chair, trying to imagine what his wife had to tell him about Nancy.

XXX

Juan only waited about ten minutes for Sheriff Pritchard. The sheriff unlocked Juan's cuffs and handed him a cold soda. Juan was very grateful. His throat was dry, and it hurt to swallow. He tried not to drink it too fast, but he was so thirsty, he chugged it, dribbling some on his chin. He belched and thought he might vomit but swallowed hard.

"You know, boy, you had quite a seizure. I never saw one before. You were foaming at the mouth, just like a rabid dog. Good thing we didn't have to shoot you!" The sheriff roared with laughter and slapped his thigh.

Juan didn't think it was funny, but he forced his lips to curve upward and nodded his head, like it was okay to make fun of him for getting sick over the fumes in the waiting room.

"Well, Rico, I've got some very good news."

"We're going to leave by the side door where my deputy is waiting to take you to your car on your uncle's ranch. Martín isn't home yet, but he's making good progress, so you don't have to go back to the hospital."

"You letting me go?"

Juan thought there was some catch. The sheriff never did anything without strings attached.

"I pay my debts, and I owe you. Now we need to get a move on, before the Feds get here to question you." The sheriff helped Juan to his feet and guided him down a long hall. "You can open this door and find a young man waiting for you. He'll take you where you need to go."

What choice did Juan have? If the sheriff chose to shoot him in the back, claiming he was trying to escape, he could.

Juan opened the door slowly. The sunlight lit up the hall and blinded him. He placed his hand across his eyes, trying to focus. He was afraid to step outside. His ears were ringing, and his head was pounding. Though the fumes were gone, he could not breathe. He turned back around and stared at the sheriff, hoping for some assurance that his life would go on.

"Oh, wait just a minute," the sheriff said. "Here's your pistol, your wallet, and your cell phone. You never know when you might need your gun."

As Juan climbed in the patrol car, he could still hear the sheriff laughing. The deputy burned rubber, throwing Juan's head back against the leather seat. "Buckle up, buddy! We're in a hurry!"

CHAPTER 42

Penny opened her eyes and was surprised to find that she was still alive. But that was about all that was good. She could only inhale in short little breaths because the pain in her chest was excruciating. The last thing she remembered was a big man, dressed in black, squeezing the life out of her.

She was stretched out on an old mattress, and with each attempt to pull herself into a sitting position, little puffs of dust erupted out of the ticking like smoke signals. Her eyesight wasn't all that great either. Her eyeballs felt like they'd been rolled in sand. And her left hand, still black and blue, ached from the altercation with Juan Rico. And where was Rico now?

When Penny was finally able to focus her grainy eyes, she noticed a light streaming from an unknown source. Tiny particles of dust floated in the trail of light, which exposed filthy walls and created a ripple of shadows. Penny rolled on her side and, with some effort, brought her body to a sitting position and then managed to stand, with her knees resting against the bed. She took short steps in the direction of the light, her arms straight out, testing her path for obstacles. It was strangely hot, and yet she felt the chill of a draft somewhere.

Without warning, her right hand crashed into a something hard. "Oh, dear, God!" She couldn't help but cry out. Penny pulled her injured hand to her chest and then brought it to her lips, sucking on the open wound and trying to make the pain go away. It hurt so much the tears ran down her cheeks. She shook her head in disgust. She had to go on. She could see the source of the light just ahead, but what was blocking her way?

Penny stretched her arms out once more, but this time, she curled her fingers into fists to protect them, and took a step forward.

Her fists and feet found nothing but air, causing her to stumble. Penny managed to grab what appeared to be metal bars, but she could not keep from sliding down onto the cold cement floor. The sensation of the hot room and the cold floor reminded her of how the desert gives up its heat at the end of the day. No matter how hot it got in the afternoon, you knew you would get a break at sundown. That is why she loved the harmony and the restoration of the desert so much.

It took a few moments for it to register. This place of hot and cold was not about harmony but rather years wasted from poor choices. She was in a jail cell—an old jail—not the modern one belonging to the Luna Detention Center. She placed her forehead against the ribbons of iron in full recognition of where she was. Penny had seen this jail in a vision while waiting for Leo to arrive at the New Mexico State Trooper's headquarters. She also remembered that the dead corrections officer had been in this very jail. *Had someone been holding him here against his will?*

Penny ran her hand over the bars, which were pitted with age and caked with grime. A halo of light allowed her to see the initials of inmates from years past. She traced her fingers over a "1979" etched through the countless coats of paint. When was the new detention center built? Where was the old jail? It would help her to keep her sanity if she at least knew where she was right now.

Penny retreated to the mattress and sat down, trying to figure out what her options might be. Of course, they were few, but she had to believe she could still get out of there. She tried to form a plan, but her brain felt like a wad of rubber bands. She couldn't follow a single logical thread of thought. That changed when she heard heavy footsteps in the hall. Suddenly, her mind became as clear as the southwestern sky. She would and could fight back. This time, she would be prepared.

The dark, hulking silhouette stood in front of her cell. She heard the clanking of the keys against the bars and then the heavy door rubbing against the floor as it slid open. It did not open easily due to its years of disrepair.

Penny was panting now, and the pressure from the air pumping up her lungs pummeled her bruised ribs with pain. "What in the hell do you want from me?" She thought she had yelled at him, but on second thought, perhaps she had only managed a whisper. Penny recalled the strength of the man's arm as he had squeezed the air out of her chest. What did he want now? If he didn't kill her the first time, maybe she still had a chance of staying alive.

CHAPTER 43

A short, skinny man exited the hospital via the emergency room door. He stood out in his dark suit, white shirt, red tie, and shiny black-laced shoes. Leo, who was standing guard at the door, recognized the FBI *look*. He would never forget it. His good friend Special Agent in Charge Peter Brooks had betrayed him six months ago during the kidnapping of Rosa Garcia. Brooks was dead now—gunned down on the streets of Juárez for being a dirty cop. Since then, Leo's opinion of the FBI had soured, and he had no desire to make conversation with this guy.

"I remember you," Agent Richards said, looking squarely at Leo. "I was on the helicopter that took you and Penny Larkin to University Hospital. I'm Don 'Little' Richards."

Richards extended his hand, and Leo reluctantly shook it. Leo didn't remember Richards, probably because he had been so upset about Penny's injuries at the Santa Rosa Airport in New Mexico when she was thrown out of a small plane as it crashed. He had run through flames searching for her. He found Penny lying on the tarmac and scooped her up just before the aircraft exploded in a ball of fire. Both arms of Leo's jacket were smoldering as he carried Penny to safety, and an FBI agent had convinced him to give Penny to one of the EMTs so he could douse Leo with fire repellent powder. Leo joined Penny in the helicopter as they flew to the hospital, all the while praying she would live. The road to recovery was difficult for Penny because she had to spend a couple of months in rehab for a broken leg and a cracked hip, while Leo got off with minor burns.

"I never thanked you for getting to the airport when you did," Leo said, coming out of his reverie. "I'm thanking you now!" He smiled and shook Richards's hand again. "And I'm sorry about Agent Brooks."

Agent Richards looked down at his shoes and then nodded his head before looking back up at Leo.

"It's a shame when an agent goes bad," Leo said. He knew Peter Brooks had disgraced the agency for his double-dealing with the Chihuahua drug cartel, and he had paid the price. Brooks's body was found riddled with bullets in a Juárez park the same day he was supposed to be sending Leo back up to the airport in New Mexico.

Leo watched Agent Richards walk into the parking lot where he met another agent, also dressed in a dark suit. *They must boil in black*, Leo thought. He was never so happy to be a sheriff and get to wear sensible clothes.

As the agents drove away, Leo pulled out his cell phone and pressed Penny's number on speed dial. It went to her voice mail again. *Darn it!* Maybe she was sitting in on the interview of Rico. The agents must have arrived by now, and Leo would hear from her soon.

CHAPTER 44

The sun was shining directly into Leo's eyes as the afternoon dragged on. He wiped the beads of sweat from his upper lip and reached for his coffee cup. He took a sip of the cold coffee and let it roll around in his mouth. It did little to quench his thirst. Why hadn't he had the sense to bring a bottle of water with him?

There had been no word from Penny, and the heat and tension in his body dropped over him like a hot towel in a steam room. He had been standing for three hours at the emergency room door. His knees were aching, and his toes were tingling. He hadn't spent this much time on his feet in years, and the cement was taking its toll. Leo leaned against the building for a few minutes, trying to relieve the throbbing in his knees. His toes were numb. Maybe it was his old boots. He had promised himself that he would invest in a new pair but never found the time.

A black Cadillac Escalade pulled into the emergency room parking lot, circled around the parked cars, and then drove back on to the street. In this middle class community, an Escalade was unusual, especially with darkly tinted windows. It brought Leo to attention and made him forget his discomfort. He called Deputy Reynoso who was still on watch at the front entrance. "This may be nothing, but a black Cadillac Escalade drove through the parking lot. I think maybe the driver saw that I was standing watch and drove away. Be prepared for anything!"

While Leo was speaking with the officer, he heard gunfire over the phone, and the officer shouted, "I've been hit!"

Leo had no choice but to leave his post. He sprinted around the outside of the hospital toward the front door. He climbed over a cement barrier, tearing a hole in his pants, and knocked over a metal trashcan as his feet hit the ground near the side entrance. The racket of the metal crashing against the pavement would announce his arrival if anyone was waiting for him to come to the officer's aide. Leo recovered and picked up speed, ignoring the blisters forming on his heels. The worn soles of his boots caused him to slip on the pile of cigarette butts on the walkway. He fell to his knees but was quickly on his feet again.

Leo jerked to a stop just before he reached the front of the building and peered around the corner. Through the tall shrubbery, he could see his deputy lying on the porch in a pool of blood. Visitors were running out of the hospital in the direction of the parking area to the south. He moved cautiously toward the entrance under the protection of the bushes. Now he wished he had more than his 9 mm Glock and a couple of cartridges on his belt. He had his AR-15 semiautomatic rifle in his Tahoe, which was not much help now.

Leo moved steadily closer to the front entrance and was just about to climb the steps to the porch when he saw two men pushing a hospital cart into the lobby. Automatic weapons lay on the gurney as they rushed the patient toward the door. The man on the cart was about sixty years old and appeared to be hooked to an IV. Leo took cover again behind what he now recognized as juniper trees. He was very allergic to juniper trees, and he felt a sneeze coming on. His eyes were stinging, and tears ran down his face. He could barely see the gunmen as they rolled Officer Reynoso out of the way and shoved the cart down the ramp. The wheels of the cart ran through the deputy's blood, staining the sidewalk as they charged toward the black SUV.

The men opened the tailgate and transferred the patient onto a stretcher that they had stored in the Escalade. Now was Leo's chance to stop this kidnapping! The guns were still on the cart, which stood alone at the back of the Cadillac. Leo inhaled deeply and aimed his pistol at one of the men. The hallow point bullet pierced the gunman's Kevlar vest, and he fell to the pavement, hitting his head on the tailgate door. The other perpetrator reached for his rifle and fired at Leo. Leo ducked behind the grove of trees but not in time. The bullet shattered his left shoulder, dropping him to the ground. Leo rolled onto his side in time to watch the surviving kidnapper push the stretcher further inside the vehicle and close the tailgate. He checked on his partner, who didn't respond, and ran to the driver's side, which was out of Leo's view. The SUV's engine was running, so the kidnapper threw the car into gear and drove out of the parking lot, screeching his tires and leaving a cloud of smoke where the tires had rubbed hard against the pavement. All that remained was his dead or dying partner lying on the sidewalk and a gaggle of bystanders who had been hiding behind other cars.

Leo was freezing from the sweat pouring from his arms and legs. He was shaking so hard, he wasn't sure he could call for help on his cell. He lay hidden from view and was still afraid to call attention to himself for fear another gunman remained on the property. He finally managed to dig into his shirt pocket with his right hand. His cell phone was gone! He searched the ground around him, which was covered in several inches of tiny, fanlike pine needles and piles of juniper berries, which made his whole body itch. He felt his chest constricting. An asthma attack was almost certain. He had left his inhaler at home.

He saw his cell phone about ten feet away. It must have flown out of his pocket when he was shot. He tried to crawl toward it, but the blood was oozing out of his shoulder and forming an ugly pattern across his shirt. He knew he needed help immediately, or he would bleed to death. Leo was surprised that he felt no pain as he moved in and out of consciousness.

XXX

Did Leo yell for help? He couldn't be sure. He was so very weak, and his mind was a jumble of disconnected voices. He thought he was in University Medical Center waiting outside the delivery room for Alejandra. There had been complications, and he couldn't go in for the birth of their first child. He paced outside the operating room, watching through the windows as the doctor and the nurse worked frantically to save her. He saw little Marta being scooped up and carried out. He shoved his way in the room just as the doctor tore off his surgical gloves and threw them on the floor. "We've lost her!" he yelled into the ether. "Alejandra is gone, but the baby is still alive."

Leo came to, and he remembered he was not in a hospital at all but lying outside one—so close and yet so far from the kind of help he needed right now.

CHAPTER 45

The Luna County sheriff's deputy driving Juan to his truck was not your typical cop, Juan thought. He was not more than five feet tall and reminded Juan of a mouse he had seen hiding behind the bed in his Uncle Martín's cabin. His hair was brownish gray, slicked back with hair gel. His face was narrow, and his black eyes, which darted between Juan and the road, looked like they'd been squeezed together with a vise. His nose was so long and pointy, Juan checked for whiskers growing beneath it.

"Where are you taking me?" Juan asked

"I'm under orders to get you back to your truck."

Juan relaxed at bit and released his grip off the armrest on the passenger door. He looked more closely at the officer's uniform, trying to find his badge number, but there was none. The young man must have noticed Juan staring at him.

"What's your name?"

"I'm Granger. Granger Pritchard."

Juan was stunned. *Is the sheriff setting me up again?* "Are you related to Sheriff Pritchard?" Juan tried to remain calm.

"The sheriff's my uncle. He hired me as an intern so I can learn the ropes. I graduate from high school next spring and want to become a deputy."

This wasn't lost on Juan who wondered where he had gone wrong. He had a high school education and so did this guy. Why hadn't he thought to follow the same route? Instead, Juan chose to operate on the opposite side of the law. Juan sighed and then looked straight ahead, hoping this country road was taking him closer to his truck.

It took them thirty-five minutes to arrive at the City of Rocks State Park. "You'll have to tell me where to let you off," Granger said as he pulled into the road that curved in and out of park's boulders of various shapes and sizes. When Granger smiled, he revealed a set of crooked teeth, one of which looked dark, making it appear that the tooth was missing.

"Around the next curve, you'll see a gravel lane to the left. That's the way to my uncle's cabin."

Granger pulled slowly up to the gravel road and rolled to a stop. "I don't want to dent up the patrol car. I gotta make sure I bring it back in one piece!"

"That's fine," Juan said. "I can make it from here. Thanks." He opened the passenger door and stepped out into the desert.

"I'm to call the sheriff as soon as I drop you off," Granger said. He gave Juan another one of those smiles that only reinforced Juan's feelings that the standards for hiring Luna County sheriff's deputies might be lower than he had thought.

Granger turned the car around at a pullout and slowly moved toward the paved roadway. He turned his head and watched Juan for a few seconds before driving away.

Juan blew out a breath of relief and began the trek to the truck, which was tucked behind a large boulder in between the cabin and the mine, where he had hidden his guns. He checked his cell phone, which was dead. And his truck keys had gone missing in all the confusion.

Juan got to the truck and looked under his front bumper for the spare key his wife had insisted he keep there in a magnetic case. He was relieved to find it and opened the driver's side door.

The smell of fast food and stale beer hit his nose as he climbed inside and shoved his body under the steering wheel. He pulled out his cell phone charger from the glove compartment and plugged in his phone. The battery was so gone it was going to take awhile to get it up and running. He fired up the engine and let the truck idle for a few minutes, hoping this would kick-start his cell phone battery. When he got the phone charged, he would make two calls—one to his wife and one to his cartel contact, which he only knew as *Rio*. Certainly, both Alicia and Rio were wondering where in the hell he was.

The thought of the gunrunner being angry made him nervous. He had met with Rio one other time, and he didn't look all that scary. He was a US citizen, an Anglo, and his eyes always seemed kind. Maybe that's why Juan had the courage to stay in the business because Rio had treated him fairly.

But none of that mattered anymore. Juan had one more chance to make the exchange of guns for money, and he didn't want to mess things up. He wondered if Rio knew about the shooting of Uncle Martín. Was he outside the cabin all along watching everything go wrong? Had he seen the ambulance arrive and haul his uncle to the hospital?

A horrible thought ran through Juan's mind. After the ambulance and the sheriff had left the ranch, had Rio checked the cabin and the surrounding property for Juan's stash of firearms? If Rio had found the mine, would he have been so crazy as to climb inside? Had Juan been fooled into riding to the hospital with his uncle so the cartel could rob him of his guns? Nothing that crazy could have happened!

What would Juan do if his guns were gone? He needed the cash to leverage another purchase of automatic weapons from Federico Castañón. It was all part of his plan to build his house on his ranch and bring his family back together. He had to find out for sure. He would get out of the truck and check things out before going nuts with worry.

Juan turned off the truck, climbed out, locked the door, and stepped out into the late afternoon sun. He had no sunglasses, and the brightness made his eyes sting. He blinked and waited for his eyes to adjust. Juan looked around for any signs of intruders to his uncle's property, but even a simple desert windstorm would have blown away any footprints. He started walking toward the cabin but only took a few steps and stopped abruptly. *Maybe someone is watching me right now!*

Juan's hands were shaking. He felt tiny tears of sweat running from his forehead down to his chin. His jean jacket was hot. He certainly didn't need it now. But the sheriff had given him back his gun. He pulled it out of his holster. It wasn't loaded. The sheriff wasn't dumb enough to hand him back a loaded gun. He slipped off his jacket and left it and his gun on a boulder near the trail to the cabin. He would put it on again once he had retrieved some ammunition from the mineshaft, but for now, he had to check out the cabin.

As he climbed onto the front porch, he heard someone laughing. He dropped to his knees. Juan crept to the only window of the cabin and peered inside. There was Federico Castañón talking on his cell phone! He was smiling like he didn't have a care in the world. Juan noticed he had a Glock resting on the thigh of his jeans. *Is he here to kill me?*

Juan stood and walked to the door and knocked. Federico opened the door slowly. "Whoever it is, I'll blow your head off if you're armed. Throw your gun on the porch."

"It's Juan Rico." Juan was sucking in air in small, quick breaths and praying the mayor meant him no harm. "I'm not armed."

Federico opened the door wide and pulled Juan inside. "Good grief. You surprised me. I tried calling you, but you didn't get back with me. So I came out here on a hunch you might come back here."

"My cell phone was dead. I'm charging it in the truck." Juan wondered just how the mayor knew where he had been hiding.

Maybe the sheriff had told him.

"Well, I've got great news. I can fill your order for not just semiautomatic weapons but automatic weapons. One of my contacts bought a load of firearms stolen from a state police warehouse south of Albuquerque. But it will cost you more."

"I've got some business to do before I'll have the money," Juan said.

"When do you think you can pay me, because I forked over a bunch of hard cash—I borrowed it from the city coffers. I need to get it back in the bank before the auditor notices it's gone."

"Give me twenty-four hours," Juan said. "I can get you the money by then."

"How about my bonus?"

"I'm sure my cartel contact will be very happy to pay more. I'll give him a heads-up so he can bring more money."

"Good! That's just what I wanted to hear." Federico pounded Juan on the back and moved toward the cabin door. "I went out on a limb for you, and I expect you to follow through."

"Don't worry, Mayor. I'll come through." Juan was mouthing the words, but in the back of his mind, he had the nagging worry about the guns in the mine. *I hope to God they are still there.* Maybe his Uncle Martín had been right. This was too big for him.

Juan watched as Federico gathered a newspaper and his cell phone and walked to the door. He would wait awhile after Federico left the cabin, before making a move toward the mine. Then he would slip down to the mine and check things out. If everything were cool, he would call Rio and arrange for a place to make the exchange.

Juan took an old dirty towel and wiped his face and blew his nose. He was whipped and just wanted to lie down, seeing the quilts still a tangled mass on the bed. But timing was everything in the world of gun trafficking. He would have to act fast to turn over his current load of guns and then purchase Federico's. At least he would be able to tell Rio he had some good news. The weapons were coming from the New Mexico State Police, and they would all be military and police issue. The thought of putting all this together in a short amount of time made Juan shudder. He considered pulling a quilt around his arms and rolling up in a ball.

Instead, Juan threw the towel on the floor and opened the door to the cabin. Everything seemed calm. Even the wind had slowed. The dry grass was barely moving. As he walked to the mine, he took a good look at his hands. He would be handicapped with the badly bruised fingers on his left hand, but he would manage somehow, even if he had to pull the firearms and boxes of ammunition out a few at a time.

At the old copper mine, everything looked okay. But the large prickly pear cactus had one arm lying on the ground. *Has someone been snooping around?*

He inched his way around the arms of the cactus and slid downward to the face of the mine. He felt the gravel scraping his back through his shirt. *Why did I leave my jacket above?* It was only about a four-foot drop, and even with mangled hands, he could manage that. The trick would be crawling into the long shaft that led about a hundred feet inside the earth. That's where he had stashed his guns and ammo.

It would be dark in an hour, and Juan needed to hurry. When his boots hit the face that served as the launching area for the mine, he waited for any rocks to settle before making his next move. He was growing increasingly nervous. He reached straight ahead and felt for his flashlight, which he had left tucked in a crevice between two pieces of granite. It was hard to turn it on with his crippled fingers, but he finally managed it and swept the torch back and forth across the face of the mine. Everything appeared as he had left it, so he knelt and began crawling into the mine, which sloped down on an angle. He pressed his injured left hand against the side of the shaft. The pain shot up his arm, and he winced.

Juan had to keep going. He dropped deeper into the mine. The cool air brushed over his face and arms, and at any other time, he would have welcomed the relief from the one-hundred-degree day. But now, he had to find his guns and ammo and get going. That meant fighting the obstacles in the tunnel, including jagged rocks hanging above him, and gravel on the floor, which caused him to occasionally slide out of control. He could only stop his free fall by jamming his right hand against the wall of the shaft and dragging one of his feet against the left sidewall. The rough sides scraped the skin off his palms.

Juan descended much deeper into the mine than he ever recalled going, and yet he did not find the weapons. He had no choice but to inch his way deeper and deeper into the bowels of the earth. He heard a trickle of water falling off the sides of stone walls, seeping in from an underground stream. Juan ran his hand across the cool, moist ceiling and wiped his fingers across his face. It made him more alert. He only wished there was a way to drink from the stream, which he knew was just a few feet away, flowing directly above him yet encased in the bulwark of granite. He was so very thirsty and ran his tongue over his front teeth. When he raised his hand above his head to search for the source of water, the flashlight slipped out of his fingers. It rolled into a spot beyond his reach. The light was pointing up from inside a deep gap in the granite. Juan cried when he forced his hand in the tiny crevice without success. "Damn it! I have the worse luck!"

The light was shooting back in his face like an evil eye and he had to look away. Juan could still see, but barely, as his eyes adjusted. He had to keep going. He placed the weight of both hands against the walls, using them as makeshift crutches, and he started downward again. It wasn't long before Juan realized that he had probably gone too far even though everything looked the same each step he took. Finally, he had to come to grips with reality. His guns were gone! He knew he had not hidden them further than thirty or forty yards inside the shaft, and he'd already gone much deeper.

The air chilled him as he leaned against the wall, the dripping water damp on his back. He didn't even have a backup pistol or ammo as he had hoped. What would he tell Federico who had taken a chance and bought those machine guns?

And worse, what would he tell his wife? His dreams of building her a home had vanished as surely as the guns. Juan was very angry, but he had only himself to blame. He shouted as many cuss words as he could remember into the depth of the mineshaft. He listened as his words echoed back at him, mocking him and reminding him that he was nothing but a worthless SOB.

CHAPTER 46

Johnny pulled up in front of the Luna County Detention Center and put on his car's flashers and got out. He noticed two guards smoking cigarettes on the center steps and walked up to them. "I'm Trooper Johnny Trejo. I'm here to pick up Penny Larkin. She accompanied Sheriff Pritchard on the delivery of a federal suspect named Juan Rico. Do you know where I might find her?" The guards looked at one another as if they were puzzled. The taller one, whose nametag read "D. Acosta", rubbed the sleeve of his uniform with his other hand, and then rested his fingers on his holster, which held a 1911 semiautomatic. Perhaps it was his imagination, Johnny thought, but the officer appeared ready to defend himself. *What have I done to insult him?*

"You'd have to ask intake," Officer Acosta replied. "I haven't seen anyone by that name, but maybe someone has."

Johnny thanked the guards and climbed the rest of the steps. He could feel the officers' eyes on his back, and he resisted the temptation to pull his own firearm out of its holster. Instead, he just returned the favor and let his right hand rest on his holstered pistol.

The intake officer was busy on the phone. "Yes, mijo." He chose to ignore Johnny, perhaps not realizing he was a member of law enforcement. Or on the other hand, maybe the intake officer just didn't care one way or another, and personal calls took precedence over county business.

Johnny pulled out his state trooper badge and laid it on the counter. The intake officer immediately hung up and addressed him with a smile. "Sorry about that. My eight-year-old was explaining how he was able to catch a desert tortoise and bring it inside the house."

That brought a smile to Johnny, who eased up a bit. "I'm looking for Penny Larkin. She came in with Sheriff Pritchard about an hour ago with the transport of a federal fugitive, Juan Rico."

"The Feds already left. Said they were heading back to El Paso because Juan Rico escaped our custody. We weren't supposed to book him, so the sheriff just put him in a holding room. He asked a guard to let him go to the bathroom, and he escaped by the side door."

"Is there an APB on the fugitive?"

"You'd have to check with the US marshal, Captain. They would be the ones taking care of that since Rico was their suspect." "What about Penny Larkin?" Johnny was finding it hard to believe that the detention center was so lax that a fugitive could simply walk away.

"I saw a good looking blonde lady get in a brown sedan.

Somebody came along and picked her up after Rico escaped." "Is the sheriff here? I'd like to speak with him."

"Sorry, but he left awhile ago. He said he was going to the home of an officer who was killed, to pay his respects."

"Thank you. Have a good day." Johnny turned around and headed out the door. The two guards were just stomping out their smokes and preparing to return to the center.

"Well, smoke break is over," Sergeant Acosta joked. "Looks like you struck out. Sorry we couldn't have been more help, Captain."

Johnny waved them off and trotted over to his patrol car and jumped in. What in the heck was going on? This county was either really corrupt or incredibly incompetent. Right now as far as Johnny was concerned, it was a toss-up. He called Leo's cell phone to report on Penny's disappearance. Maybe he had ordered a car for her without telling him.

Leo's phone went right to voice mail. Why wouldn't you answer your cell phone? Why else have one? Not reaching Leo aggravated Johnny even more. He had no choice but to head back to the hospital.

CHAPTER 47

The man in the black mask trudged toward Penny with his arms stretched out. "Venga conmigo." It will be better for you if you don't resist me. Penny moved back into the bowels of the cell. "Hazte tranquila, chica, y nada te pasa. ¡No pelear conmigo!" Be still and nothing will happen to you!

Before she could make another move, he lunged for her and grabbed her by the hair and then twisted her body until her back was jammed into his sternum. She could feel his chest moving in and out and could count his heartbeats, which were surprisingly slow. Her heart was racing like a little bird caught in a trap. Her heartbeat and his were mixing in a kind of dour musical duet that made her dizzy. Had he not swept her into his arms, Penny would have fallen to the floor. She was lightheaded, and the dim bulb that hung in the hall was a reminder of her shadowy future. She shut her eyes, which was the only physical movement she had left under her control, and fainted.

XXX

When Penny awoke, she was lying on her back, wedged between heavy wooden boxes, and riding in some sort of vehicle with no top. She could see the sun rising in the eastern sky, which meant they were traveling south. She was grateful that it was morning and not in the middle of the day, where the sun's rays would do serious damage to her body and her brain. Her long-sleeved blouse was gone and replaced with a grungy T-shirt smelling of men's sweat. It hung loosely over her filthy jeans.

Two guys sat in the bucket seats in front of her, chatting in Spanish and making what sounded like an occasional joke.

She raised her head to get a better look at them and banged it against the round metal bars welded to the vehicle. "Oh!" Penny cried out and then regretted it.

The man, riding shotgun, turned to check on her. "She's awake!" Penny tried to remember his face. She'd had an experience with the El Paso County sketch artist and knew what the computerized programs looked for in a suspect. She picked a perfectly round face from her choices on her imaginary computer screen. He was surprisingly young, maybe not over seventeen or eighteen—barely old enough to shave. She imagined herself pulling a mass of black, curly hair to the top of his head. Then she placed little stubs of hair above his upper lip and a few scraggly ones on his chin. Before she could record any more of his identity in her virtual computer, the kid turned back around and switched on the radio, which blared out Mariachi music.

The ride was rough, and every time they hit a bump, her body bounced up against one of the boxes and shoved splinters into her bare arms. An occasional puff of exhaust blew out of the tail pipe as they moved up and down and over hills. She tried to hold her breath, anticipating the fumes, when they roared up a hill, but she just couldn't help breathing in the rancid odor. With the loud music and the drone of the engine and the exhaust fumes, Penny became nauseous and dizzy. She wanted to scream for them to stop the car and let her out. Instead, she propped herself up on her right elbow and vomited all over her jeans.

"Help me! ¡Estoy enferma! I'm sick!" she screamed over the horns of the Mariachis and the roar of the engine.

Both men turned around this time and stared at her. When they saw she had vomited on the floor, the driver pulled to a stop and got out of the car. "Sácala del carro." The driver, no doubt disgusted with the mess, yelled at his buddy and motioned for him to pull Penny out of the vehicle.

The man frowned and dragged Penny out by her arms and threw her on the desert floor. She rolled into a cactus, impaling her arm in its midst. She yanked her arm out of the thorns and was left with several of them hanging from her wrist. Penny sat up and tried to remove them, wincing as she shook them free from her fingers. The driver got a canvas bag of water that had been hanging on the front of the vehicle and lugged it over to Penny. He was asking her to stand. "Up!

Up!¡Levántese! De pie! De pie!" She was so weak she couldn't rise without help. The younger man jerked on her arm until she was vertical, but she continued leaning into him. He tried pulling away from her, trying to get away from her vomit-stained clothes, but when he did, she stumbled forward and threw up again.

The driver said something that Penny could not understand but soon realized he was asking his buddy to remove Penny's clothes. At this point, she couldn't stand herself, so she stood quietly as the young man pulled the T-shirt over her arms and unsnapped her jeans, yanking them to the ground. When Penny looked at her jeans lying crumpled around her feet, she realized that her boots were gone. She was standing in her stocking feet, and she could feel the rocks bruising her heels.

He helped her step out of the jeans, but Penny continued to lean into him because she was so dizzy. She ended up in his arms. The driver heaved the heavy bag of water onto his shoulder and dumped its contents over Penny's arms and chest. It also splashed on the young man holding her up. He jumped away, and Penny dropped to the ground into a puddle of water.

"Ha ha! Felix!" The driver was calling his friend Felix. So now Penny at least knew one of the names of her kidnappers. The driver threw water over the vomit inside the car and mopped it up with the T-shirt Penny had been wearing. Then he threw the shirt into the desert. Dripping with water, Penny grew chilled and began shaking.

The driver rummaged through a duffle bag he had pulled out of the back of the dune buggy until he found a black sweatshirt and matching sweatpants. He threw them at Penny. "¡Ponga se los!"

Penny knew he was telling her to get dressed. She was happy to do so but also realized that in a few hours she would be dying in the heat. She hoped the trip wasn't going to last too much longer. Felix walked her over to the passenger seat and helped her in. "¡Ya no te enfermas, chica!" He smiled, as if he really cared that she had been ill. Of course, Penny doubted that her kidnappers gave a hoot about her, but just that one look of kindness encouraged her not to give up.

Felix climbed in behind her and knelt down, forcing his body between the two seats. When he bent his knees, Penny noticed he had a gun holstered under his jacket. Of course, she wasn't surprised, but now she knew kindness was not his intent. He had been hired to transport Penny somewhere, and he was just doing his job.

The driver fired up the dune buggy and accidentally threw the gears into reverse, bolting them backward and crashing the dune buggy into a barrel cactus. Finally, he revved the motor and threw the transmission into the right gear. Penny felt much better with the desert wind blowing across her face and through her hair. She was growing much more alert, and the nausea was gone. She examined her surroundings, and at her feet, she was stunned to see her purse! With any luck, the battery on her cell phone might still be alive. Anyone tracking her could follow the GPS device, but Penny wasn't holding out hope. Wasn't that just something she saw on crime shows?

The driver turned on the radio again, only this time it sounded like a man announcing the news. She was grateful that the Mariachis had called it a day.

Penny was feeling the full effect of the sun. She was sweating under her arms and between her legs. She wiped her forehead with the sleeve of her sweatshirt. After about an hour on the road, the dune buggy pulled up to a gated driveway, and the driver jumped out and punched a few buttons, and the gate opened. Penny was puzzled. How was there electricity out in the middle of nowhere? Then she heard what she thought was a generator running behind a small storage building near the front of the property.

The dune buggy kicked up a lot of dust as it traveled the long lane that was beaten down from constant use. On either side of the road were crude fences. On Penny's side, a single horse, whose back was swayed and his muzzle gray with age, nibbled on a sparse patch of grass. Penny put her hand over her mouth, trying to avoid the cloud of dust the dune buggy generated as they drove further into the property.

She saw a whitewashed wooden sign reading 'Romero Rancho de Mexico' arching over the roadway. It was anchored by two posts and secured with a more elaborate gate. This time, a man dressed in camouflage and armed with a machine gun nodded at the driver of the dune buggy, then held a plastic card up to a sensor, and the gate opened, allowing them entrance. Penny's eyes widened. She looked up at the sign again as they drove through the second gate. *I'm in Mexico?* Her whole body trembled. She could feel the sweat that had been boiling up under her arms and between her thighs, now rolling down her body and onto her feet. There would be no one tracking her across the border! And who would know she was here?

Thousands of women had been kidnapped in Mexico over the last five or six years. They were never seen again, or they were dug up in the desert, their bodies raped and mutilated. Penny tried to keep from shaking. She was breathing hard, and a couple of hours without water made it tough to swallow.

The driver pulled into a circular driveway and stopped in front of a stucco hacienda. Felix jumped out and opened Penny's door. She hesitated, fearful of what might come next, but Felix jerked on her arm and motioned for her to get out. "¡Ándale!" He yelled in her ear to hurry, his eyes shifting back and forth, as if he were afraid of doing something wrong.

An armed guard, also dressed in army fatigues, greeted the driver. "¡Buenas, Paco!" He offered him a mocking salute and laughed. Penny noticed that the faded patch on his shoulder, indicating he was or had been an officer with the Mexican Federal Police.

Paco was laughing as he got out of the dune buggy and stepped onto the porch to embrace the guard. Felix pushed Penny forward, and Paco reached out and pulled her up the steps. Penny's legs were shaking, either from riding for so long or from pure fright. She really couldn't tell for sure.

Felix ran ahead of them both and opened the large, oak door, whose hinges groaned from the weight.

"Bienvenido, Ms. Larkin!" Paco chuckled and stepped out of Penny's way so she could enter the home. The room was dark, even in the daylight. A couple of table lamps served as the only illumination in the room, which was as large as a dance hall. The floors were highly polished oak and matched the front door. A chandelier hung over a massive dining table, which was at least fifteen feet long. Its upholstered chairs sported tall, wooden backs with intricate carvings. It was a setting fit for a king.

Penny's eyes covered the rest of the room and finally rested on a man sitting in an overstuffed, cowhide wing chair. He was clearly relaxed. His legs were crossed, and he had a clear, iceless drink in his right hand, which Penny figured was tequila. His left arm was bandaged, and Penny noticed, it lay motionless in his lap. "Come closer so I can see you, por favor," the man asked.

He was not a large man, maybe only five foot six, if that. His English was almost perfect, if he were indeed Mexican. His curly, black hair looked like someone had sprinkled a saltshaker over it. His sideburns and mustache were totally gray, giving him a distinguished but haunting appearance. Penny approached the man cautiously. She couldn't think of a single reason for someone bringing her here—but for much of Mexico reasons weren't necessary—there were no rules, and she wasn't calling the shots.

CHAPTER 48

Johnny made pretty good time running the back roads from the detention center to the hospital. On the old Wagon Trail Road, he passed the abandoned Luna County Jail, flooding him with memories of his father. Johnny backed up and pulled into the driveway, which was now overgrown with weeds. He had accompanied his dad to the jail many times. In the early days of his career, his father was a patrolman with the New Mexico State Troopers, and his father would let him tag along on routine calls to check on the court dates for the suspects he had arrested. His mother hated this practice, but some of Johnny's best times with his dad were at this jail. His dad was totally dedicated to his career in law enforcement and never took the time to fish or hunt or even attend the state fair with him. So if Johnny wanted to spend time with his dad, it had to be in places like this.

The sheriff at the time, Roger Bennett, had been one of his dad's closest friends, and he would take Johnny around to all of the offices. "If I had a son, he would be just like young Johnny!" Everyone would laugh and offer Johnny candy from the office candy jar.

Johnny's father had worked long hours to achieve the title of deputy chief, and his mother had paid the price for it. There wasn't much room in a trooper's life for family, and now that his dad was dead, his mother would have to live alone on his dad's meager retirement. Not much of a legacy, Johnny thought. *Was it worth it, Dad?*

Johnny knew he was headed down the same professional path as his father. He had been promoted way too fast, some in the agency believed. But he proved them wrong by overworking his assignments and tracking down criminals like a Komodo dragon. Johnny had read once that there were only two animals that would stalk their prey for up to thirty days. One was the Komodo and the other a polar bear. He refused to give up until he cracked a case.

And like his dad, he had let a perfectly good relationship flounder. Joanna, his college sweetheart at the University of New Mexico, had moved onto Colorado to follow her own dreams. And he had been spending most of his nights since then justifying the loneliness as the price one pays for being a state trooper in New Mexico.

Johnny was tempted to get out of the car and walk around the property, but he knew he shouldn't. And besides, the place looked like a hazard. An old storage building had collapsed, and its wooden beams were strewn across the property. With the cuts in state and county budgets, the jail was destined to languish in the sweltering heat of the desert, someday crumbling into a pile of dust. He drove further up the driveway, trying to get a glimpse of the front entrance, where he hung out while his father was busy. He was feeling a bit foolish and decided it was time to pull up and around the circular driveway and head to the hospital. But the temptation to get out of the vehicle was just too great.

Johnny jumped out, stretched his legs, and wiped the sweat from his forehead with his fingertips. He adjusted his eyes to the bright sunlight and walked up to the front door. He rubbed his hands across the dirty window and tried to see in, but the darkness inside the front offices prevented it. He stepped back and started to return to his car when he noticed a red scarf lying at the entrance. It looked brand-new. He picked it up and brought the scarf close to his nose. The sweetness of lavender permeated the scarf. *This is Penny's!* He had bought it for her at the western store. He was surprised at the feeling of rage that welled up in his throat. That bastard sheriff was dirty, and now he was sure he had done something with Penny. That meant those guards at the correctional center were covering for him.

Johnny jerked his pistol out of his holster and walked cautiously toward the rear of the building, leaning close to the wall out of the range of any surprise ambush. He turned the corner, gun drawn, and found a desolate parking lot that hadn't seen used in years. Even the white lines had all but vanished. He walked across the lot checking for what he wasn't certain, but when he saw the puddle of oil, he pulled out his handkerchief and dropped a corner into the sticky substance and brought it to his nose. It smelled fresh. Old oil would have spread out and soaked into the asphalt over time. Someone had been there recently, and he instinctively knew Penny was involved. Johnny pulled two plastic bags from a small case he kept attached to his belt and dropped the handkerchief in one and placed Penny's scarf in the other.

Johnny pushed Leo's number in on his cell phone, but once again, it went to voice mail. No self-respecting officer of the law would let his phone go unattended for long. Something was terribly wrong. Johnny ran back to the Charger, jumped in, and roared down the driveway. He knew he shouldn't drive when he was wild with anger, but he had to get to the hospital immediately. Penny was missing, and it was Johnny's fault.

When Johnny arrived at the entrance to the emergency room, he found the Deming Volunteer Fire Department truck in the driveway. Why had they returned? Several firemen were walking around the emergency room parking lot, and a couple of guys were congregated at the door. *Where is Leo?* Johnny did not see him at his post. Perhaps Leo had finally been relieved him of his assignment and headed back to El Paso.

Before pulling back out on the street to park, he drove alongside one of the firemen to get an update on why they had returned to the hospital. "Is everything okay?" Johnny asked the young man, whom he had recognized as the one who had located Penny during her altercation with Juan Rico.

"Hi, Captain. Well, would you believe we had another shootout? Cartel hit men returned and kidnapped Martín Romero, a local rancher, who was recuperating from surgery after a gunshot to the shoulder."

"Was anyone injured?"

"El Paso County Sheriff's Deputy Frank Reynoso was killed, as was one of the gunmen. We're here to assist the police and hose down the blood in the parking lot out front."

Johnny parked and ran back toward the emergency room door. No one was on duty to check his credentials, so he barged on through the waiting room where hospital employees were trying to get the emergency room back to normal. He stopped at the intake desk and asked about where the shooting took place.

A middle-aged woman, with frizzy blonde hair and a scowling brow, looked up at Johnny and shook her head. "If this keeps up, we won't be able to hire a soul to work here. I've got to cover the desk, even though the docs need my help. I'm an RN, but a lot of good that does."

The nurse directed Johnny down the hall. "All the excitement took place in the hospital wing and at the front entrance."

Johnny jogged toward the front of the hospital, sidestepping a patient being rolled into a room for care. The foyer was jammed with people, and with all the chatter, Johnny didn't know whom to ask about what had happened. Finally, he saw a short, youngish Deming police officer in the middle of a crowd of people, trying to get statements from as many as he could, but he wasn't having much luck. Johnny could see that some of the folks were in a kind of post traumatic stress that often occurs when witnesses experience a harrowing event.

Johnny parted the circle of human curiosity and approached the policeman. "Officer, I'm Captain Trejo, with the state troopers. Can I have a moment?"

The young officer looked at Johnny with great respect. "Of course! What can I tell you, Captain?"

"What time did this kidnapping occur?"

"At 0-200 hours, sir. Two armed men took a patient from Room 220 and rolled him out on a cart to the parking lot and managed to load him in the back of a black Escalade." Johnny was pretty sure the officer was just getting his law enforcement legs because he tried to sound more official than he really was. He recalled how he must have sounded his first couple of years on the job—totally like a greenhorn.

"I understand one of the gunmen was killed? Who was responsible for the take down?"

"Well, Captain, that is the puzzle. Our detective is on his way, but so far, I haven't found anyone who tried to stop the kidnapping, and yet somebody sure did try. The dead bodies of the deputy and the gunman are just being loaded into Donovan's Funeral Home hearse right now."

"Thanks, officer. I appreciate your help." Johnny did an informal salute and made his way to the front door. He stepped outside onto the porch of the hospital. It was about twenty feet wide, surrounded by wood railings and decorated with wicker rocking chairs and a porch swing. It reminded him of a country style home you'd find out east, not in the middle of the Chihuahuan desert. The fire department had brought the pumper truck around to the front and cleared a path to hose down the asphalt. A black panel van with the name "Donovan's Funeral Home" was pulling out of a handicapped parking space.

Johnny walked up and down the width of the hospital but saw nothing out of order. The landscaping was neatly manicured. Even the tall juniper trees were expertly trimmed into spherical towers. As he made his way back to the front porch, he heard a cell phone ringing. He found it lying in the pine needles between two juniper trees. He pulled out a plastic glove and picked it up, trying to keep his fingerprints from contaminating the phone. "Hello."

Johnny saw the name of the caller. It was Adriana. The line went dead. He scanned the entire backside of the juniper trees and found Leo lying behind a brick buttress jutting out of the foundation.

Johnny called to the fireman hosing down the lot. "Get a doctor. We've got an officer down!"

Johnny knelt beside Leo and felt for a pulse. He could feel a faint heartbeat, but Leo was pale and bleeding badly from the shoulder. Within minutes, a doctor appeared in bloodstained scrubs, along with a stretcher. "I was just finished with a surgery," he said, "when I got the call." An orderly and the doctor lifted Leo onto the stretcher and then transferred him to a cart, which they rolled up the handicapped ramp and into the hospital.

"What in the hell is happening?" Johnny said to no one in particular as he watched Leo disappear through the front door. He caught up with the medical team in the emergency room where Leo had been rolled.

"He's badly wounded and has lost a lot of blood." The surgeon told Johnny.

"Doctor, please keep me posted. I'll be right here."

"Will do, Captain. Your good police work may have given the sheriff a fighting chance. We got a heartbeat."

Johnny collapsed into a chair in the waiting room and rested his head on his knees. The adrenalin rush drained from his body, leaving him completely wasted. He needed to call Marshal Lujan and give him the bad news, but he wasn't sure he could. He felt so weak. His body shook, and he recognized the signs of stress overcoming him. He had seen it countless times in victims of crime. He stood and hobbled over to a vending machine, where he tried to drop a fistful of quarters in the slot. The coins fell on the floor and scattered across the small alcove that housed the machines. Johnny crawled on his hands and knees, the sweat from his face dripping onto the floor. Finally, he had gathered enough money to buy a drink, leaving the rest of the money behind. He grabbed the handle on the vending machine and pulled himself upright. The motor on the soda dispenser was running incessantly and sounded as if the generator was about to blow. He heard a can of Coke fall into the reservoir at the bottom of the machine. Johnny pushed the swinging metal door open and grabbed the can with his fingers. It was cold and wet. He pulled the Coke out and placed it against his face, then took a big breath of air. When he popped the top, he felt the carbonated shower hit his neck. Johnny gulped the drink. He couldn't help it. He felt the tingle of the bubbles on his tongue and the sugar rush coursing into his bloodstream. He returned to the waiting room and sat down again. He needed to have it together before calling the marshal. He wasn't sure what he was going to say about how everything had gone to hell, but he was hoping Marshal Lujan had better ideas for finding Penny than he did.

CHAPTER 49

Penny slid her bare feet across the hardwood floor of the hacienda's massive living room, inching closer to the man relaxing in the leather chair. The shadows of the cavernous space, mingled with the subdued lighting, gave his face a yellow cast and accentuated his gaunt cheeks. Even from ten feet away, Penny could tell he had not been well. She was so focused on the condition of his health that another man creeping up behind her caught her off guard. Paco was carrying her pocketbook! "What are you doing with my bag?" She gasped and grabbed for it.

You are never going to get it back. "¡Si lo pierdes! You lose it!" He sent a sharp elbow into her side, causing her to stumble and fall to the floor. She landed on her knees, and a knifelike pain shot up her right knee into her thigh. "Ah!" she cried out, and the man in the chair laughed.

Paco placed Penny's purse in the man's lap.

"Gracias, Paco. Eres un buen hombre…a good man."

Penny managed to stand, determined to hold herself together, but her fingers were trembling and her eyes welling up with tears. Up until now, Penny thought she could talk her way out of this situation, but Paco, in his fatigues, black boots, and black beard, was a sinister presence in the dimly lit room.

The man waved Paco away, shoved the bag between his legs, and rummaged through it, until he found Penny's wallet and pulled out her driver's license. "You won't be doing any more driving! I'm going to keep this as a little token of our meeting." He waved her license in the air, laughed again, and then shoved his hand deeper inside the bag. "There's always something more in a woman's handbag. I've learned that the hard way." His chuckle came from the depth of his throat, causing him to choke on phlegm. He coughed several times and wiped his mouth with a napkin lying on the side table, which also held the lamp. He pulled out Penny's cell phone, which she noticed, with relief, was still flashing green. That was good news. Perhaps someone could track her after all! He saw the green light too and dropped the phone to the floor and smashed it with his foot. Penny couldn't help but express her anger. "You son of a bitch!" Her cell phone was her best chance of getting help because even if she could convince the man to let her go, how would she get back to the United States without a Google map or without someone knowing her exact location?

For the first time, hope slithered away, like a snake seeking sunlight on a cold afternoon. She felt an aching behind her eyes and a pressure inside her nose, like her head was going to explode. Penny wanted to reach over and knock this little pittance of a man back on his heels. She tightened her fists, holding herself in check, only to remember that her right hand was bruised. She refused to let him see her cry. She blinked back the tears and held her ground.

"Ms. Penny Larkin. I know you are wondering why I brought you to my ranch. And I will be up front with you, I can't let you go back home. Federico Castañón tells me you are too smart for your own good."

Penny was stunned! She had been foolish to tell the mayor she was working as an investigator.

The man rifled through her bag again until he found her US marshal's badge. "What do we have here? Federico thought you were a private detective. He had no clue you are working for the Feds! This makes life so much more entertaining."

Penny could see his teeth, all white and perfect, as he smiled at her. She had to keep her wits about her. She recognized that things would only get worse if she reacted in fear. Guys like this got off on hurting women. He may have a bad arm, but he was surrounded with bullies who could do the damage for him. All he had to do was sit back and watch her take a beating. She wiped a solitary tear from her cheek and crossed her arms. She widened her stance and waited for him to find her gun.

The man smiled as he watched Penny's aggressive body language. "Federico waited for you outside of the convenience store and followed you. He and his friends tried to stop you on the highway during the dust storm. He just wanted to scare you, but he hadn't counted on you being armed. Instead, he found a perfect way to frame you for the murder of an informant they had with them—a traitor he and his men were planning to kill anyway. *Ah*, here it is!"

He pulled her gun from the depth of her bag. "I guess the ballistics from your gun didn't match up because you're here and not in jail. It would have been safer for you to still be locked up." Penny's face flushed, and she could feel the blood pounding through the veins on the back of her neck. She felt violated! This ugly man knew everything about her, and she still didn't know his name.

"Who are you?" she asked. Her voice was hoarse, and her throat cracked. She may wind up buried in the desert, but she would not die without finding out the truth.

"My name is Martín Romero. You have heard of me?"

"No." She waved her hand in dismissal, brushing him off like the maggot he was.

"People call me El Acero. You can call me Steel. You may know my nephew, Juan Rico."

Penny was way past being stunned by this news. Nothing surprised her now."So you're Rico's contact for running guns." She had nothing to lose. She might as well as solve the case right now, even though she would probably never live to see it prosecuted.

Steel dropped her pocketbook to the floor. Her marshal's badge lay on the table, along with her driver's license and Johnny's .38 revolver. "Ms. Larkin. My great-grandfather, Rodrigo Romero, was a trafficker of weapons during the Mexican revolution. He helped Pancho Villa arm his rebels, who, in turn, fought valiantly to save the Mexican people from dictatorship and from greedy landholders. This was my great-grandfather's ranch, a gift from Pancho Villa. I am simply carrying on the tradition of being a freedom fighter for my country.

"I'm going to have my housekeeper, Margarita, walk you to your room. Please enjoy your stay until the time when you must leave us. How long that is depends on how well you behave. And by the way, we're serving dinner at eight." He pointed to the dining area across the room, where a man, dressed in a white chef's coat, was setting the table. "I've left some of my wife's clothes in your room. You're about her size. She doesn't need them anymore."

Penny didn't know if that meant his wife had left him or she was dead or ran around naked. It was just was well. She was so angry that all she could think about was getting away from this perverted animal.

She heard the tapping of high heels against the wood floor and saw a tiny woman with a long, black braid and dark, olive skin moving toward her. "You come, por favor." Margarita waved her long, bony fingers, motioning for Penny to come with her.

Penny did as she was told and followed Margarita down a long hallway, lighted with brass sconces and decorated with an expensive-looking oriental runner. The intricate pattern in the rug made Penny dizzy, so she stared straight ahead at the little woman who was walking at a fast clip. Margarita stopped suddenly, and Penny ran into her from behind, causing the servant to drop her keys. She swept them up off the floor with one hand and then placed another gaunt hand on Penny's arm.

"There's nothing between here and Ciudad Juárez except rattle snakes and wolves," Margarita cautioned. "So don't get it in your head to do anything foolish."

CHAPTER 50

Johnny let out a sigh of relief when he heard Marshal Lujan's voice on the phone.

"This is Lujan."

Johnny ran his fingers through his hair, took a couple of breaths, and then cleared his throat. He hated giving the marshal bad news. "We've got a terrible situation. Leo Tellez has been gravely wounded in a gun battle with cartel members and is fighting for his life. He was shot when he tried to keep the cartel from stealing a patient from the Luna County hospital. And worse still, Penny has disappeared. She was last seen riding with Sheriff Pritchard as he took Juan Rico to the correctional center. He insisted on holding onto Rico until your guys could get to the jail. And now Rico has escaped."

"What excuse do they have for Penny's disappearance?"

"A couple of guards on a smoke break told me they saw Penny get in a brown sedan and drive away with a dark-haired man. That is ludicrous of course. She never found her way to the hospital where she was to return and help me finish up with the FBI. On my way back to the hospital, I found Penny's scarf in front of the old Luna County Jail. That probably means she was taken against her will. Maybe she left us a clue."

"I already got the news about Rico getting away from the sheriff's custody. It looks like Pritchard is dirty, but we need more proof. I've got an investigator working on that and still another agent questioning the hospital orderly. You've got your hands full." "Is there any chance you can get a GPS tracking on Penny's cell phone?" Johnny was hopeful that they might get a break. "Let me get back to you with anything we find."

"I can't just wait at the hospital!" Johnny was angry and felt helpless. The longer it took to figure out where Penny was, the worse the outcome. He had worked countless abductions— mostly domestic issues—but the longer the person went missing, the less likely they were to be found alive.

"Okay. I'll send an agent to track Rico, and you go back to the jail and demand answers from the sheriff. Maybe we will get lucky and turn up the information we need to find Penny." Johnny didn't think the marshal sounded all that hopeful.

"And the cell phone?" Johnny asked again.

"I'll do you one better. The DEA has Predator B drones in the area. I'll contact the Ops Center at Holloman and have them e-mail me the video feed from last night up to three today."

"What do they have on board, infrared surveillance?" Johnny was hopeful this was the case.

"You bet. We can spot vehicles day or night and even tell how many people are in the car. We can't promise we'll be able to find which way Penny's kidnappers went, but we can do infrared heat sensing to find humans inside buildings. We might get lucky."

"That's great news," Johnny said. He smiled, realizing that unlike his own office, the Feds were fully equipped with the latest technology. He had always complained about the government overspending, but in this case, he was happy they had done so.

I'll ask the National Geospatial-Intelligence Agency to send me a feed of their satellite images taken in the last twenty-four hours in northern Mexico. We can compare those with the Predator video and see if it helps locate Penny."

Johnny hung up the phone with Marshal Lujan. He had one stop to make before heading back to the jail in search of the sheriff. He was certainly not at the hospital. Johnny would go to ICU and check on Leo. If he had lived through surgery, maybe he would be awake enough to tell him that Penny was missing. He deserved to know.

CHAPTER 51

Juan began the long climb up to the mine's entrance. He was grateful the flashlight was pointing at the wall ahead, allowing him just enough reflection to keep from slipping on a wet spot on the gravel floor. If he fell, even a few feet, he could break a leg or worse and not be able to get back to his truck.

The reach of the flashlight would soon end at the place where the tunnel narrowed and turned left, making him have to crawl the rest of the way to the top in complete darkness. Juan stopped to rest and catch his breath. His fingers were cold and numb from pressing his hands against the damp walls.

Maybe he would be lucky enough to make it back on top without injuring his hands any further. His shooting hand was feeling better, and he didn't want to hurt it any more by slamming it against the wall. As his breathing slowed, Juan studied the place where the light hit the left side of the tunnel and then ricocheted, like a bullet into the opposite wall. Something was off. Juan blinked. He thought his weary eyes were playing tricks on him. Where the light hit the right side of the tunnel, it looked yellow, not gray like almost everywhere else. Was he delirious? Juan promised himself that if he got out of the mine in one piece, he was going home to his wife and children. He would work sweeping floors or stocking grocery store shelves, just to be near them. His Uncle Martín had been right. Crime does not pay.

Juan stepped back a couple of paces and leaned against the wall again so he could get a better look at the yellow spot on the tunnel wall. He leaned forward and rubbed his numb fingers over the wall of yellow but felt nothing unusual. Then he noticed there was a small ledge, an indentation that would never have been noticeable in the dark shaft without this small beam of light pointing right at it.

He placed his right hand on the ledge and felt around with the tips of his fingers, hoping he didn't run into a spider or a scorpion. He discovered a small rock and pulled it off the ledge. In the dimness of the mine, he couldn't tell what it was. Rico raised his arm so that the rock was fully exposed by the flashlight. He couldn't believe his eyes! It was a nugget of gold, as big as the golf balls he used to steal from the country club and sell to a sporting goods store. He stood on his tiptoes and felt farther back on the ledge until his fingertips touched the wall. He found more rocks and rolled them forward, one at a time, until he was able to grab each one and hold it up in the light. He had struck it rich without mining for it!

What was gold worth now? He had read it was worth about a thousand bucks an ounce.

Suddenly, everything Juan had gone through had been worth it. *I'm rich!* To heck with the gun running! He could live off the gold and maybe even find more—it would last him until he got a real job.

Juan shoved the nugget in his pocket and returned the others to the ledge for safekeeping. He was now full of energy and in a hurry to get out of this hole. He crawled without incident to the face of the mine and was making his way out into the sunshine when he heard voices. They sounded like they were coming closer. "Rio told us to pick up the guns from Juan Rico at his cabin at 7:30 Friday night. He wanted us to surprise Rico by arriving early."

Juan shrank back inside the tunnel, crawling on his hands and knees and then lying as flat as possible against the floor.

"Maybe he moved them after his uncle was shot by the sheriff. Wasn't that too funny? One bad guy accidentally shoots the other?" Juan heard one man chuckling.

"I think they call that friendly fire!" Now they were both laughing uncontrollably.

"Flaco, thank God you and I were late for the buy, or the Betas would have killed us like they killed Rio at the hospital."

Rio was Anderson Dean? And now he was dead? Juan was stunned by the news. Just like that, Juan was out of business. And what else were they talking about—one bad guy shooting at the other? His uncle was one of the most respected ranchers in the area. The sheriff was dirty, but not Uncle Martín!

"We've searched all over the property, and found his jacket and his empty gun, but no Juan Rico. His truck is here, so where is he?"

Juan could see the legs of the men, one wearing black jeans and the other blue. He did not dare move for fear they would hear him.

"Could he be in the mine?"

"No, Beto. I don't think anyone would be that stupid, even Rico." Juan watched as the legs in black jeans turned to leave.

"I've never been in a mine. Maybe I'll check it out!" Juan saw Beto's blue jean legs and cowboy boots, squeezing around the cactus that protected the entrance to the mine. "Ouch! It got me!"

"You deserve it!" Flaco was laughing.

"I'm giving it one more try," Beto yelled. "Nothing beats me, not even a cactus!"

Loose gravel from the movement of Beto's feet dropped onto Juan's head. He was trapped! If he moved, Beto would hear him retreating deep into the mine because he would stir up the gravel too. Juan gasped for air as his lungs compressed against the cold, rocky floor. He couldn't hold on much longer.

A cell phone rang, and Juan heard Flaco on the phone. "Sí, jefe. ¡Ahora!"

"Come on, Beto. We missed out. Martín Romero may already have the guns. Rico must have changed his mind and sold them to his uncle. *El Jefe* is pissed. He wants us to search Romero's ranch house."

"But Rico's truck is here!"

"Yeah, apparently he rode with the ambulance to the hospital with his uncle. Probably hasn't had time to come get it. We will deal with Rico later."

CHAPTER 52

Margarita opened the third door on the right in the middle of the hall and motioned for Penny to enter the room. The bedroom was about twenty feet square and nicely furnished with a four-poster bed and antiques that looked like they'd been imported from Europe. She dutifully followed the housekeeper to the closet where there was enough clothing— without ever replicating an outfit—for months on end. She hoped she wouldn't be there that long, but then she considered her alternative accommodations, a forever bed in the desert, and smiled at the housekeeper.

"Gracias, Margarita."

Margarita didn't smile back. Instead, she answered with a low grunt, her small black eyes filled with hate. Or was it fear? Penny wasn't sure. The housekeeper marched over to an antique armoire and showed Penny the big selection of underwear and bras and even negligees. Then Margarita opened another door in the room, which lead to a huge bathroom, which was almost as large as the bedroom. There was a jetted tub and a big selection of creams and cleansers and makeup. It looked like nothing had ever been touched. Had they been expecting her? On the top shelf of the vanity were several French perfumes that Penny recognized from fashion magazines.

"¡A las meras ocho¡" Margarita turned abruptly and headed for the bedroom door, and just in case Penny didn't understand Spanish, she reminded her in broken English. "Dinner sharp at 8!" She slammed the door, and Penny heard a key in the lock and a bolt engage. If she were to be at dinner at 8:00, surely somebody would have to come and get her. She wasn't going anywhere on her own.

Penny searched for a clock and found one on the bedside table. It was porcelain, painted with pink and blue flowers, probably from France. It was 6:30 p.m., which meant she didn't have to get ready for dinner for almost an hour. She walked over to the heavy velvet curtains that covered the windows and looked out. It was twilight, and the sun was sinking quickly behind a massive mountain range to the west. She saw two men hauling wooden boxes into a large metal storage building. The boxes looked a lot like her traveling companions in the dune buggy. They were very heavy, and one of the men was struggling to hold onto his end. Finally, he let go, and the box fell to the ground. Guns of all shapes and sizes lay scattered on the gravel driveway. Penny couldn't believe her eyes! There were many different kinds of firearms and ammo in the boxes. She watched as the men grabbed at the guns and tried to put them back in the box. Penny had seen enough. No wonder his name was Steel.

Penny slipped out of her black sweatshirt and sweatpants and looked down at her feet, which were black with dirt. She didn't care. She pulled back the duvet and crawled between the sheets, which were cool on her skin. She stretched out and laid her head on the down pillow. Wouldn't it be wonderful if she could just hide in the depths of the bed until help came? *Will anyone come for me?* She would do well to get some rest. There was nothing she could do about her circumstances right now, and she would need her strength to fight back.

She turned on her right side and began counting backward, trying to find a way to completely relax. Penny drifted in and out of consciousness. In a dream, she saw a barrage of bullets flying in the air and a patient in a hospital cart being wheeled down the hall. Then an image of Leo appeared. He was shooting at someone! Then he fell to the ground and landed behind some tall bushes. There was blood everywhere! Penny woke up with a start and realized she had been having a nightmare. At least, she hoped it was just a dream and that Leo was okay.

She yawned and fell back asleep. This time, she was in an operating room, but they weren't working on her. Who was on the table? She looked more closely, and to her horror, she saw Leo. The surgeon was cutting on Leo's shoulder and then holding up a bullet for all the rest of the medical team to see. Everyone in the operating room clapped.

Penny was awake again, and this time, she knew what she saw was not a dream. Leo had been shot. She prayed for him. She didn't know what else to do. "Please, God, save Leo!"

Penny rolled out of bed and checked the time. It was 7:30, giving her thirty minutes to bathe and dress. There was no shower, so she drew her bath and turned on the jets. The water pummeled her back, and she leaned against the porcelain tub. She had been avoiding her skills as a remote viewer because she really didn't want to know what was happening, but now she needed to have all the information available to her, if she were going to get out of this alive. Her psychic ability was all she had left. Martín Romero didn't know about her abilities, thank God.

If Penny could foresee anyone coming for her, she could delay her attempt at an escape for as long as possible. She worried about the compromises she might have to make, but it looked as though Romero was in no shape to make any sexual advances toward her. She might have a chance.

She shut her eyes and let the water roll over her in a rhythm of waves that comforted and consoled her. The swirling water drew her mind inside a spiral of dreams and returned her to the old jail. She saw herself shaking and crying as the masked man lifted her up and carried her to a white van where he loaded her in the back like a bag of laundry. The image of her being jostled around in the back of the van faded to black. She awoke and rubbed the bar of chamomile soap over her legs and arms and then rested with her head against the rim of the tub. This time when she closed her eyes, she was surprised to see a vision of Johnny pulling into the driveway of an old jail. Penny knew what this was. She had seen it once before when she waited for Leo in the troopers' headquarters. Penny noticed that Johnny was searching for something. Was he looking for her? She looked in his eyes as he turned and scanned the horizon. Why hadn't she noticed how kind those eyes were before? She saw him lean down and pick up something red from the ground. She recognized it! It was her red cowboy scarf that he had bought her at the western store. It must have fallen from her neck while she was struggling with her captor.

Penny watched Johnny running to his car and roaring out of the driveway. "Please, Johnny. Hurry! I don't have much time."

CHAPTER 53

Penny was awakened from her dream by the knocking on the bathroom door. "Senorita! Dinner now!"

Penny jumped out of the tub and pulled a terry cloth robe around her shoulders and opened the door. Margarita stood there, scowling and wagging her finger. Penny ran to the armoire and pulled on some black silk underwear and bra, then ran to the closet where she found a long, black dress. She ran hair jell through her cropped hair and jammed her bare feet in a pair of black, three-inch heels. Penny staggered out of the closet. She hadn't ever worn such high heels and didn't think she could pull it off. She was no fashion model.

Margarita actually smiled when she saw Penny's dress. "Sí. ¡Muy bellísima!"

Penny could smell the food as she entered the dining room, and her stomach responded with a hunger pain that was way beyond anything she had ever experienced. It almost doubled her over. *When did I last have something to eat—breakfast yesterday?*

Margarita pulled out a dining room chair for Penny. The chair was actually taller than the housekeeper, and in her black dress, white apron, and small cap, her rigid movements reminded Penny of a marionette. She patted the seat and asked Penny to sit down. "Sentarse, por favor." Penny's chair was midway between the head and the foot of the dining table. She noticed a selection of cabernets and pinot grigio wines and a beautiful centerpiece, filled with fresh apples, pomegranates and pears, encircled with the leaves from a live oak tree. It would have been a perfect setting if it weren't for the host, whom Penny saw walking into the dining area from a hallway, on the west side of the great room. Behind him was another man, about forty years old, Penny guessed. He was taller than Martín and walked confidently to the table and sat directly across from Penny. Martín took his place at the head of the table and began taking wine orders. "René will be along shortly. Ricardo, please place a glass of pinot grigio at her place." Ricardo stood and reached for the wine and carried it to the foot of the table. "And for you, Ms. Larkin? Would you like a glass of wine?"

Penny was stymied by the question. If she said she did not want anything, it might appear to be rude, and they would dismiss her from dinner, and right now, nothing was going to stand in the way of her having a chance to eat. "I would like a cabernet, please." She let out an inaudible sigh and placed her hands in her lap so the men would not see her wringing her cloth napkin into a tight wad of despair.

Ricardo did the honors again and this time carried the glass around the table and handed it to Penny. His eyes, a particular kind of gray, were penetrating hers and making her fidgety. She took the glass from him and nodded her appreciation. She wrapped her fingers around the bulb of the stemware, welcoming the coolness of the wine and easing the pain in her bruised fingers. Ricardo remained at her chair. "Please taste the wine, and see if it is to your liking."

Penny hesitated. Had they counted on her ordering a red wine, planning to knock her out or even worse, poison her? If they were up to no good, she had no choice but to take a small drink. She rolled the cabernet around in the base and watched the legs of the wine linger on the sides of the glass. She took a whiff of the oak and cherry overtones and smiled. If she were going to die tonight, it might as well be with a glass of fine red wine in her hands. She took a sip, letting the wine linger in her mouth, before its bite hit the back of her tongue. She swallowed it gratefully and took another drink before placing the stemware on the table. "Perfect!" Penny smiled at Ricardo, who seemed pleased with her response. In reality, the alcohol hit her like a train and unraveled her ability to think logically. There probably wasn't anything in the wine, but she was so starved its effects were overstated. She felt the room spin and held both hands on the edge of the dining room table.

Ricardo returned to his seat, just as René walked in wearing a long, flowing beige evening dress that was cut a little too low for Penny's tastes. Her neck was adorned with larger-than-life diamonds and earrings to match. The lights from the chandelier were drawn to the shape and cut of the stones and danced around René's shapely body. She was a stunning sight and, Penny had to admit, an impressive addition to the dinner table.

"¡Buenas noches!" She practically sang her greeting and smiled broadly. Penny joined the chorus with "Good evening."

Martín stood and made a toast. His left arm was free from his sling, enabling him to lift his glass and still keep his balance. "To this evening and our special guest—Penny Larkin. ¡Salud!"

René and Ricardo joined in with the customary "¡Salud!"

A waiter, wearing a white chef's coat, appeared with plates of prime rib. Penny, feeling the saliva in her mouth, took her napkin and discreetly wiped her lips. Her stomach growled so loudly that Ricardo looked over at her and winked.

Everyone dug into the food. Penny tried to restrain herself from stuffing her face with the meat. It was some of the best beef she had ever tasted. As the steak reached her stomach, she felt the tingling sensation caused by the wine ease a bit.

"I see you like your dinner, Ms. Larkin. I raise my own beef. It is always best to feed your guests well, even if they aren't planning to stay all that long."

Penny stopped chewing and considered his words. "How long do I have?" Her teeth were chattering. She hoped he didn't notice. "That depends on your attitude, my dear. No one likes to lose guests before their time, particularly someone as attractive as you." The reminder that her days were numbered dulled her appetite. She had tried playing along, but betting on her own life was not something she cared to wager. She also knew that during her dream, she had seen Johnny searching for her. She felt if she stalled them long enough, he might come or send help. But then how did he know where she was taken? He was smart. He would figure it out.

He had better arrive with a whole truckload of automatic weapons, Penny feared, or her rescuers would be outgunned. Was it conceivable that El Acero's ranch served as a distribution point for firearms across Mexico to warring drug cartels? Could there be such a thing as a gun cartel?

"Con permiso," Penny said. "May I return to my room?"

"Of course!" El Acero smiled and motioned to Ricardo. "Please escort Ms. Larkin to her room."

A curtain of dread dropped over Penny's shoulders as she stood. She still hadn't shaken the lightheadedness that the wine had caused. Was there something more in the bottle than grapes? Her hands were shaking as she straightened out her black dress and slipped on her high heels, which she had discarded under the table. She had to exit with grace, and it wouldn't be easy. Penny was wobbly as she took her first steps out of the dining room. She wanted to run for her life, screaming, but Ricardo joined her, holding out his arm.

"Buenas noches, señorita," René said, waving good night, as Penny and Ricardo left the dining room and headed down the hall. The brass sconces were so dimly lit that Penny tripped on the thick rug, and Ricardo caught her at the waist. His arms were wrapped tightly around her, and he wasn't letting her go. She looked away from him, hoping to keep his intentions in check.

"Thank you." Penny pushed away from him but did so politely.

"De nada."

When they got to the door of her bedroom, Penny turned to shake Ricardo's hand and send him on his way.

"Please, I will come in and make sure you are comfortable for the evening," he said. He was even taller than she had first thought. He towered over her, blocking out the meager amount of light that fell on them from the wall lamps.

"Thank you, but that isn't necessary." She turned her back to him.

"I insist!" Ricardo's smile showed two rows of perfect teeth. His gray eyes were now black. He opened the door and used his size and strength to move Penny into the room. She was thankful she had left for dinner so quickly that she had not turned off the lights, which were glaring and unkind to his face.

"Please leave now!" Penny protested again, but Ricardo placed his hand over her mouth and nose and scooped her up in his arms. He was breathing heavily, and she felt his heart thumping against her chest and his hot breath against her cheek. She tried shoving his hand away from her face, but he compressed her arms against her breasts, depriving her lungs of air. Only her eyes were free of his grasp. She watched as he grunted and heaved her onto the bed. Through some sort of miracle or answered prayer, Penny rolled out of his reach and onto the floor. She jumped up, ran to the bathroom, and locked the door.

CHAPTER 54

Juan clawed his way out of the dark mine and into the dark night. He stumbled toward his truck, being careful to avoid the scattered piles of stones he knew were all along the way. His uncle's ranch hands had taken special care to gather the rocks into piles, hoping to make the land more accessible to the cattle, but the project was abandoned as a waste of time.

Juan's hands were sore from pushing against the slabs of volcanic rock to pull his body out of the mine. He started the truck and dropped his right hand onto the knob of the gearshift and jammed the stick into reverse. A stabbing pain hit his chest. He rammed the transmission into neutral and stretched out on the front seat. Now what? Was he having a heart attack? The truck's engine choked on its first taste of fuel in a couple of days. The "check engine" light popped on.

Juan turned the ignition to off when he smelled gas and decided to let the truck rest a few minutes. He stretched out on the truck's bench seat and shut his eyes. Juan noticed that as his breathing and heartbeat slowed, he felt better. His pain was subsiding. Maybe it was just his stress level. He would rest for a while, at least until the fuel system cooled down.

Juan must have dozed off because he heard the voices of Flaco and Beto. They had returned to look for him again! Juan dropped to the floor. He had an old blanket on the seat for times when he slept in his truck. He pulled it over his body and hoped they couldn't see him. One of them had climbed into the bed of his truck. He was jumping up and down, causing the truck to rock back and forth. "Hey, Flaco, I like this truck. Maybe we should take it off Rico's hands!"

Juan remembered that his keys were still in the ignition. *I have to get them out of there!* He reached up with his left hand—the one with the badly bruised fingers and yanked the keys out. They fell onto the blanket and thankfully didn't make much noise.

"I don't want to be caught with this guy's truck," Flaco said. "That's like wearing a neon sign on your back—that you're a thief." "Yeah, you'd be right on that. Since we didn't find them in Romero's house, our orders are not to return until we to find Rico and get those guns back. El Jefé didn't believe me when I insisted the guns were gone."

Juan felt the truck rock again as Beto jumped out of the bed. "You goofball!" Flaco was laughing at Beto. "You got dust all over your ass!"

"Come on. We're supposed to check out the mine. Let's get it out of the way."

"Yeah, let's go. I got the flashlight."

Juan lay very still on the floor of the truck, giving the men time to reach the mine. He could smell the rubber floor mats, and the dried coffee he had spilled last week. Was this any way to live—in constant fear for his life? He fingered his keys and crouched on his knees. He peeked over the dashboard. He couldn't see any signs of the men or their flashlight, but they should be at the mine by now.

Juan took a few deep breaths. As anxious as he was to get out of there, he needed to wait a little longer. He wanted to make sure the men were inside the mineshaft before starting his truck. They might hear the engine fire up, but they wouldn't be able to get out fast enough to chase him down.

The time seemed to drag on, but Juan knew it would take ten minutes to get past the prickly pear and reach the face of the mine. The longer he waited, the better were his chances of a clean getaway.

Finally, he pulled himself onto the bench seat and started the truck without any more trouble. Juan shoved the truck into first gear and inched his way down the driveway. He saw their open-air jeep parked on the side of the main road leading out of the park and was tempted to pull a few wires. Having the Chihuahua cartel on your tail was bad enough. He didn't need to tempt fate and make them angry.

Before returning to Lordsburg and his family, Juan felt compelled to stop at the hospital to check on his Uncle Martín. Certainly what he overheard from Beto and Flaco was a lie. His uncle was one of the most honorable men he knew, but he had to hear the truth from his uncle's own lips.

Juan still had a twenty-dollar bill in his wallet and decided to buy some new clothes at Walmart. He could create a disguise with khaki pants, a button-down shirt, and a baseball cap to cover his curly hair. No one he knew would ever expect him to wear such a getup. What he couldn't hide were his bruised hands and his gun, which he dropped into his right hand pocket. It was heavy, but he had no other choice.

After creating what Juan considered an excellent new look, he drove into the hospital parking lot. The Luna County Volunteer Fire Department was still there! Several of the firemen were gathered around a light pole talking. Juan had been hauled off to jail by the sheriff several hours ago. Did the fire department have nothing better to do than hang around making small talk?

Juan pulled around to the front of the hospital and parked as close as he could to the entrance, just in case he needed to make a fast exit. When he got out of his truck and approached the front door, he noticed that a Deming City policeman was standing guard. What sort of excuse could he give to get inside the hospital? Would he have to show his ID? By now his name would have been plastered all over the news as having escaped from the jail.

Juan remembered the side door where employees took smoke breaks. He headed for that door instead. Two people were smoking there, and he thought by making some small talk, he might be able to get inside the door, which required card-activated access. A nurse in green scrubs and white tennis shoes dropped her cigarette on the asphalt and snuffed it out with her shoe. She turned around, hit the electronic eye at the door with her plastic card, and entered the hospital. The man, who appeared to be an orderly or hospital aide, was dressed in brown scrubs and brown work shoes. He was still puffing on his cig and blowing smoke rings in the air.

"Hi there," Juan said. "You got another smoke I can borrow?" "Sure, why not?" The man pulled a pack of Camels out of his shirt pocket. He hit the pack with his hand and a cig popped up. "Thanks. I'm a temp in the intake department, and my agency never did give me a pass into the hospital. Mind if I go in with you after we're done?"

The man, who was even younger than Juan, looked him over carefully. "We just had so much excitement, I'm not sure I should." "What happened?" Juan was hoping he wasn't going to say somebody went bonkers in the emergency room and had to be arrested and hauled off to jail.

"Everybody on staff kept complaining that two El Paso County Sheriff's officers were guarding the public entrances, saying it was a waste of time and a real inconvenience to us. We had to keep showing our hospital credentials every time we left, even for lunch."

"Something bad happen?" Juan braced himself for the news that might implicate him. What if the hospital was circulating his photo?

"Yeah. Some jerks dressed in black broke into the hospital and stole one of our patients—rolled him right out the front door and loaded him into a black SUV. Sheriff Tellez blew one of the guys away though, and he died right in the parking lot but not before one of the sheriff's own deputies died, and the sheriff got hit by gunfire too. Sheriff Tellez just got out of surgery. I was in the operating room, and the sheriff is lucky to be alive. The fire department is still hosing off the blood."

"Who was the patient?"

"His name is Martín Romero. He owns the Double R near the City of Rocks State Park. If you're from around here, you'd recognize him."

Juan inhaled and let the smoke settle into his lungs before blowing it into the starless sky. He wanted to cry out. He was so angry. Juan's whole world was falling apart. What he had heard in the mine was probably true. His uncle had been working against him all along. It explained why Uncle Martín turned up at the cabin right when he had scheduled the gun buy. It didn't take a genius to figure that out.

Juan could feel the sweat rolling down his sides and pooling at his waist. He still had his holster and gun without a clip stuffed in the pocket of his khakis. The right side of his pants sagged a bit, carrying the weight of the heavy pistol. He wished that the lights outside the side door weren't so bright. He felt exposed.

"Hey, what did you do to your hands?" The orderly showed genuine concern for Juan's fingers, which were multiple shades of purple. "You need to go to the emergency room and have those puppies looked at."

"Sure, I'll do that right after my shift ends. Thanks." Juan couldn't think of anything but his uncle right now. His hands would have to wait. His Uncle Martín had loved him like a son. *Do you double-cross a son?*

The orderly dropped his cigarette onto the pavement. "Well, my break's over. Come on, I'll walk in with you."

Juan threw his cigarette into a pile of decorative stones lining some bushes and entered the hospital, following the orderly down the hall. He would check to see if it were really his uncle who had been snatched by the cartel. If he didn't find Uncle Martín in his room, he would get the hell out of there and drive straight to Lordsburg.

The orderly noticed that Juan was not headed to the adminis- trative offices and called out to him. "You're going the wrong way. The intake offices are to you left."

"Thanks. This place sure is confusing."

"No problem, buddy. Take care." The orderly waved to Juan and disappeared into the cardiac unit.

Juan made a U-turn and headed to room number 220 to check on his uncle. When he rounded the corner, Juan found himself near the restroom where Officer Jackman had thanked him for saving his life. He thought about heading in there but noticed two Deming police officers standing in the hall. Juan thought he had better stay focused on his one goal—to take a quick look in his uncle's room and get out of the hospital.

"Yeah, I got called in from my vacation!" Juan heard one of the officers complaining about having to be there. Both men were so deep in conversation that they paid little attention to Juan, which was good. He passed his uncle's room without any problems and caught a quick look in the room. The bed was empty. Juan walked a bit faster and made a quick right turn into the ICU waiting room, out of the view of the officers. He smelled fresh coffee and took a chance and poured himself a cup. When he turned to leave, he spilled his coffee on the boots of the New Mexico State Trooper who had convinced Penny Larkin to let Sheriff Pritchard hail Juan off to jail.

"Excuse me, sir." Juan turned back to the coffee bar, grabbing some napkins and hoping the trooper didn't recognize him. But he did.

"Aren't you Juan Rico?" Juan wanted to lie, but he was so exhausted and so discouraged, he nodded his head.

"You're under arrest, and this time, you won't get out of my sight."

The trooper cuffed his left hand to the arm of a metal chair. The trooper poured Juan another cup of coffee. "You drink this while I call for backup." Juan was so upset with himself that he threw the cup of coffee into the wastebasket next to the chair. It splattered against the creamy plastered wall and dripped slowly down to the floor. *I did all this work for nothing.*

CHAPTER 55

It was a few minutes before 9:00 p.m., and Johnny had about an hour and a half before meeting up with Marshal Lujan and the ATF agent, both of whom agreed to help him carry out a bold plan to pursue Penny's kidnappers into Mexico. The marshal had received a report at 8:03 p.m. from his IT department that Penny's cell phone had just died about fifteen miles due south of Palomas.

Johnny was anxious to get going, knowing that every minute was precious. Now his fear of being too late to save Penny became even more of a concern with the arrest of Juan Rico. What could he do with him? Leaving him at the Luna County Correctional Facility was out of the question, and in this isolated part of the state, there was no other viable place within a hundred miles to lock him up. Johnny made a couple of phone calls and learned that the Federal agents who were assigned to question Rico had headed back to El Paso two hours earlier. Getting anyone to turn around and return for him tonight wasn't an option, and Johnny knew finding Penny was something that had to happen now.

But before leaving Deming, Johnny wanted to check on Leo. Luckily, Johnny bumped into Leo's surgeon, Dr. Jayant Patel, coming out of the ICU, where Leo had now been moved. The surgeon reported that Leo had lost a lot of blood from the bullet to his shoulder and had consequently suffered from hypovolemic shock, which caused his blood pressure to fall dangerously low while on the operating table.

"It was touch and go, but we were able to stabilize his pressure and remove the bullet, which had lodged in his scapula," Dr. Patel reported. "When he awoke from the anesthesia about an hour ago, he was quite agitated and kept asking for someone named Penny. Do you know who that is?"

"Yes, I know her." Johnny anticipated the surgeon's next question. "But she's not available to come to the hospital right now."

"That's just as well. We've sedated him, and we won't know for twenty-four hours how Leo will respond to forced rest. But our plan is to keep him as quiet as possible, and that means no visitors."

Johnny thanked the surgeon for updating him on Leo's condition and left the doctor his cell phone number with instructions to call him if anything should change. "If my phone goes to voice mail, please leave me a message. I may be out of range for the next twenty-four hours myself."

"Yes, of course. And will you notify Leo's friend, Penny, about his condition and our request for no visitors? I think this approach is the best chance the sheriff has for a full recovery."

"As soon as I see her, I'll give her the message and also pass the information onto the sheriff's department in El Paso." Johnny was full of wishful thinking that he would see Penny again. It was a risky maneuver to enter Mexico, especially armed, but the ATF had assured the marshal that the Mexican Federal Police would be notified and served as cover for the operation.

Johnny knew the ATF moved in and out of Mexico on a regular basis, and the Mexican government would probably go along with it, although it frowned on US agents carrying guns. Mexico's president, Enrique Peña Nieto, had just been elected and wanted to weaken the cartels' stranglehold on his country, so he too had reluctantly agreed to help the Americans find Penny. Johnny knew it was a gracious act on his part, and he wouldn't forget it.

Still, it would be a crapshoot to find Penny and then rescue her, but Johnny was determined to try. He returned to the coffee bar and uncuffed Juan and led him to his car where he recuffed his suspect inside the caged backseat. "Buckle up! It's 9:45, and we've got to make it to Columbus in thirty minutes!"

CHAPTER 56

Johnny raced down State Highway 11, making the thirty-two miles from Deming to Columbus in twenty minutes. Plans were to meet ATF Special Agent Paul Rockney at 10:15 p.m. at the Rio Rancho Hotel, which had a small café and coffee shop. The hotel was the only place to stay in Columbus and had become a catchall of tourists, aging widowers, and young unemployed men who hung around the hotel recreation room, drinking coffee and playing pool. Johnny had picked the hotel because it was close to the town's Gas N Go convenience store and was two doors from the city hall, the Luna County Sheriff's Columbus office, and the mayor's office.

From their central location, it would be easy to buy bottled water, sodas, and a Styrofoam cooler from the convenience store, as well as sandwiches and a Thermos of coffee from the hotel café. Marshal Lujan had arranged to pick up an armored High- Mobility Multipurpose Wheeled Vehicle or Humvee from the Santa Teresa Border Security Station. He was planning to drive the Humvee to Columbus and wait for the team at the Pancho Villa State Park on the outskirts of town. The trip was less than seventy miles and should take the marshal only a couple of hours, accounting for his drive from his office in downtown El Paso to the Border Station.

The Humvee, a four-man vehicle, had been shipped back from Iraq and was mine-resistant and had a range of 250 miles on diesel fuel. Upon arriving in Columbus, Lujan would have to fill up the Humvee with more diesel at the FINA station a few blocks away. Johnny had everything timed out well, and so far, they were on schedule. The only snafu was Juan Rico's presence. He had seen Rico's file when he was working with Penny, and noted his expert marksmanship. He had a wild thought. Could they use this skill on this rescue effort? You bet! But would the marshal agree to such a crazy idea? Johnny didn't know Lujan all that well, but what choice would he have but to bring Rico along? If he couldn't convince the marshal, then Johnny would be the odd man out and have to stay behind and take Rico to jail in Las Cruces. There was no way he was going to let that happen.

Lujan was also bringing the information he had available on Predator B drone cameras in the area during the time of Penny's abduction, which as far as they could ascertain was about six hours ago. The marshal was supplying a self-contained, secured hotspot to download the video from the predator drones and GPS tracking software because there were few roads marked on a Mexico map in that region.

The marshal also promised to pack a satellite phone in case they needed it to call for an airlift for Penny. The chances of finding Penny alive were slim, but he was grateful the marshal and the ATF were willing to try. Besides convincing the marshal that bringing Juan Rico would be a good idea, Johnny also had to convince Rico to help out, possibly in exchange for some leniency with the law, if the marshal agreed. But even if the marshal said yes and Rico said no, Johnny was out of options.

Johnny pulled up in front of the Rio Rancho, which was a two-story colonial-looking structure that had been added onto over the years until the original intention of the architect was lost on its guests. They would wait here for Agent Rockney to arrive. He was being ferried there by another agent who planned to drop Rockney off and head back to Tucson. Johnny rolled down the window and inhaled the dry air into his lungs, stinging the inside of his throat. He was grateful that the moon hung like a boulder over the Little Florida Mountains. It would be easier to see as they crawled across the desert floor.

"I've got to use the head," Juan said.

Johnny looked back at his prisoner and shook his head no. "I'm telling you, I need to pee!" Rico was squirming in his seat.

Should Johnny drive Juan out in the desert to let him do his business or walk him, handcuffed, into the hotel?

Before he could make that executive decision, a black SUV with federal plates pulled alongside Johnny's car. The ominous looking vehicle with its darkened windows was a clue that the ATF had arrived. Now all they had to do was wait on the marshal. Johnny decided to take Juan to the Gas N Go for the restroom break. They would have to go in the bathroom together, but it would draw fewer stares than him walking into the Rio Rancho cuffed to a fugitive. He could also pick up the bottled water and sodas and ice and a cooler and then load them into the trunk of the Charger.

Johnny was pleased with his plan and got out of the car and tapped on window of the SUV. He motioned that he was headed to the Gas N Go and would be right back. Then he returned to his car and drove away.

When they got to the store, he cuffed Juan to his own wrist and walked inside the store. The manager pointed out the men's restroom. Johnny walked with his prisoner to the bathroom, which was only about four feet square, making the tasks at hand more difficult but not impossible. Why did every gas station bathroom have to be grungy? Johnny thought maybe there was some law that required them to be as filthy as possible, perhaps so the user wouldn't stay long. Not much chance of that! Even Juan appeared to be grossed out by the smell.

Ten minutes later, Johnny and Juan were roaming the aisles of the store, looking for salty snacks, Slim Jims, and a few bags of hard candy. Then they headed to the back of the store where they picked up a cooler, a case of water, bottled teas, and sodas. Johnny dropped his purchases on the counter. "I'd also like two bags of ice, please."

"We got a sale on Slim Jims. You buy one, get one free—want to get three more?" The store clerk was a pleasant guy, about sixty years old, Johnny guessed. When he smiled, his teeth became the centerpiece of his long, black beard.

"Sure," Johnny said. "Why not?" He and Juan had just turned around and headed down the aisle where they had found the Slim Jims when the plate glass window at the front of the store exploded. Shards of glass flew across the room. The store clerk dropped behind the counter, and Johnny pulled Juan with him to the floor. A follow-up volley from an automatic weapon peppered the store with bullets. Johnny threw one leg over Juan, forcing the fugitive's body against the cement floor. Johnny could smell the sweat emanating from both men and mixing with their breathing, punctuated by fear.

"I've been hit!" The store clerk shouted from behind the counter. "Help me!"

Johnny pulled his pistol out of his holster, fully expecting the shooter to come barging into the store to kill everyone, but no one came. He asked Juan to stand, and he cuffed him to the door of the cooler that held the sodas and crawled toward the shattered front window.

"Hey, don't leave me here to get gunned down!" Juan yelled at Johnny.

Under the gauze of streetlights, Johnny thought he saw ATF Agent Rockney cuffing a tall man in a suit. "What in the world is going on?" He asked this out loud to no one in particular and ran back to check on the store clerk, who was upright but leaning against the lower cabinets. His face was damp, and his eyes looked like someone had circled them with a red marker. Johnny got on his cell phone to call for an ambulance. The dispatcher told him they could have one to Columbus in forty-five minutes. Johnny thought that might be too long to wait.

"I'm freezing." The clerk was shaking uncontrollably, and his nose was running and catching in his mustache.

Johnny knew he was going into shock. He had seen it before with gunshot victims. He searched the store for something to keep the man warm. He found a rack of Mexican Ponchos and yanked one from the hanger. He covered the clerk with it and examined his arm for any exit wounds. The bullet had gone clear through his upper arm, which in many cases is a good thing. A hollow point bullet lodged there could do additional arterial damage, and the clerk could bleed to death before help came.

Johnny opened a travel size package of tissues and pressed them against the wound, trying to stall the bleeding. He felt the clerk's neck for a pulse. It was racing, but then whose wouldn't be?

"Is there a doctor in Columbus?"

"Yea, Dr. Archer. He's on Taft Street. His emergency number is by the telephone. We keep it in case we—in case we have a customer get sick."

He asked the clerk to use his other hand to apply pressure to the wound while Johnny left long enough to dial Dr. Archer's emergency number. He answered!

"I'm only three blocks away!" He was treating an elderly diabetic man at a private nursing care center. "I will be there in ten minutes!"

Relieved, Johnny raced back to the clerk and resumed his compression with the tissues, opening a new package, as the blood soaked through the used one. He knew it was important to keep the man talking. "How are you doing?"

"I'm a Vietnam vet. I've seen worse." "What's your name?"

"Pete. Pete Drury."

"Dr. Archer is on his way, and the ambulance is not that far behind him." "Thanks, man."

Johnny was amazed at how tough Pete appeared. Certainly Johnny would not be putting on such a brave face, with a hole in his arm. "You're a courageous man, Pete."

"Just lucky I never caught a bullet in 'Nam. My best buddy, Joe, didn't come back home. Never forgot the look on his face when he died." The look on Pete's face changed from courageous to sorrowful in a split second. Johnny could tell that the memories of the war were as fresh as yesterday.

"I'm sorry for what happened to Joe, but now we've got to make sure you don't lose too much blood. I've got to make another call. Can you hold the tissues on your wound as hard as possible?"

"Sure." Pete offered a weak smile, but his eyelids were heavy. Johnny knew he had to get help investigating the shooting, and the Luna County Sheriff's Office was useless. He dialed his headquarters in Las Cruces and asked for Trooper Robertson. "Rob, I need you to come to Columbus ASAP and oversee the investigation of a shooting at the Gas N Go. The manager was hit, and he's on his way to the Luna County Medical Center. I'll be gone by the time you get here too, so I'll leave the key to the convenience store with the hotel concierge at the Rio Rancho. And don't trust anyone in law enforcement except fellow troopers."

"Sure, Captain. But what's going on there?" "We've got dirty cops littering the whole county!"

Satisfied that Officer Robertson could handle the post op, Johnny closed his cell phone and took another look at the gunshot victim. He appeared to be sleeping, but when Johnny leaned down to replace the tissues with some fresh ones, Pete opened his eyes. "I can't tell you how glad I am that you were here." He shut his eyes again, but tears were seeping from under his lids.

Dr. Randall Archer arrived as promised and Johnny exhaled in relief. The doctor glanced at the man handcuffed to the cooler and rushed to the back of the store. "Pete, what in the hell happened? There's two federal agents out in the street, and they've got the mayor thrown up against the wall of city hall!"

"Damned if I know." Pete coughed and spit on the floor.

Johnny was curious as to what the mayor had done that warranted him being detained by the Feds, but he didn't want to leave the store for fear the crime scene might be compromised. *Certainly he couldn't have shot at us?*

It was Johnny's training to stay the course, and he just couldn't break the rules and leave the store, even though he was growing increasingly worried that he was wasting everyone's time, trying to get Penny back from the cartel.

Johnny began a search for the bullet and found the 9 mm wedged in a crevice of the windowsill, which was about level with Pete's shoulders when he was standing behind the counter. Johnny began taking notes for Trooper Robertson, and this included having him search for the bullet casing in the parking lot of the Gas N Go. He looked on as the doctor examined Pete and noticed that his cheeks were now ashen, and his lips were pale; Pete's hand trembled as the doctor examined his arm. "An ambulance should be here in twenty minutes or less," Johnny told Dr. Archer, who was wiping the perspiration off Pete's face. Even so, Pete's teeth began to chatter.

"Hang in there, Pete." The doctor wrapped a blood pressure cuff around Pete's good arm and gave Johnny thumbs-up on the reading. "You haven't lost that much blood, thanks to the quick work of Captain Trejo."

"If it's okay with you, Dr. Archer, I need to take care of my prisoner." Johnny pointed to Juan, who was leaning against the cooler, with his head resting against the glass.

"Certainly, Captain. I can take it from here."

"After we load Pete in the ambulance, I will need to lock up the store," Johnny said. "Anyone needing something will just have to be inconvenienced until the owner can get here from El Paso." Johnny looked over at Pete, who was breathing rapidly, the sweating pouring down his face and then asked the doctor's help. "Will you please leave the key with the concierge at the hotel?"

"Sure will. Don't worry about anything, Captain. I've got this covered."

Johnny was grateful that Dr. Archer was so capable and committed to helping him out.

He called Trooper Robertson again. "Rob, I'm leaving you some notes on the store counter on what happened and some suggested follow-up procedures."

"Where will you be, Captain?"

"That's classified for right now. I need you to be my eyes and ears down here. We've got a little town with big problems."

CHAPTER 57

Juan was still suffering the effects of the bullet that had broken the plate glass window. He knew that had he and Johnny not gone back for more Slim Jims, one of them would have been shot in the back. Was someone gunning for him? Probably so, and he deserved it. He was a lousy thief, and a stupid one, at that. Everything was coming down on him now, and he deserved what he got. Juan was shaking so hard he was afraid he would black out. He was cuffed on the hand with bruised fingers and had to hang onto the door handle with his right hand—his only good hand now. Juan leaned against the cool glass door. He found the humming of the cooler's motor soothing, in contrast to his heartbeat, which bounced against his chest like a rubber mallet. The possibility of losing his wife and children made the pain in his chest unbearable. His heart hurt so much. Even Uncle Martín didn't seem to have any use for him. What had he ever done to his uncle but love him?

Juan tried to hear what was going on in the back of the store, but he caught very little of it. There was something about an ambulance, and he swore he heard Federico's name. Was he somehow involved in the shooting? Why would the mayor want to kill him? Wasn't he expecting Juan to pay him for those automatic weapons? Juan had so many questions, but his brain was on fire. One answer jutted out of his skull like a dagger. His family would be better off if he did die. Juan had totally ruined his life, and if he kept going, he was going to ruin theirs.

Another round of gunfire erupted outside the store. Juan was petrified. He was hanging out like a goose in the Chinese market he had seen on the Discovery Channel. If the gunman came in the store, he was a goner. *Maybe that is a good thing.*

He watched as Captain Trejo charged toward the front of the store and crouched before the broken window. "They've shot the mayor! What in the heck is up with this town?" He left the store, gun drawn.

Juan heard the siren from the ambulance from several blocks away. It shook the wall of coolers, as it pulled up in front of the store, red lights flashing. Two EMTs rushed in with a cart. He observed the care that the EMTs took with clerk as they wheeled him out of the store. He wished someone would care for him like that.

Captain Trejo returned and unlocked Juan's handcuffs. His hands fell to his waist. The blood had run from them, and they looked white as the frost on the freezer's windows.

"Hey, Doc. Before you go, can you take a look at this man's hands?" The Captain surprised Juan with his kindness.

"Sure will," the doctor said. "Let's take a look, young man."

Juan held out his hands. They were shaking, which embarrassed him a little. He should be strong.

"Your right hand is bruised but on the mend. Your left hand looks like the digitus annularis—your ring finger is broken. I'll secure it with tape to your pinky, and that should help it heal." He dug inside his medical bag. "Here are some 800 mg tablets of ibuprofen. Take one twice a day, and keep ice on it when you can." He handed Juan a small white envelope of pills.

"Thanks, Doctor. I really mean it." Juan was overcome with the doctor's concern. Tears fell from his eyes and rolled down his cheeks.

The doctor took a clean white handkerchief out of his pocket and wiped Juan's eyes.

"Young man, you've got a whole life ahead of you. Take my advice and clear up whatever you did wrong, and get some training for a good job."

Juan turned his face away from the doctor, ashamed that he would never have the chance to turn his life around.

Captain Trejo returned from collecting their purchases. He shoved the Styrofoam cooler in Juan's arms. It was filled with sodas and bottled tea, and the weight caused Juan's knees to bend.

"Too much for you?"

Juan got a better grasp of the load and shook his head. "No, I'm okay." Since he was free from his handcuffs, he wrapped his arms fully around the cooler so that there was little pressure on his hands.

"We'll pick up the ice outside. You can use it on your hands once we get going." The Captain shook the doctor's hand, and they exchanged a few words that Juan couldn't hear. The doctor walked back inside the store to pack up his bag.

Johnny opened the trunk and unloaded his arms and got out of the way so Juan could place the cooler inside too.

"What was all the shooting about?" Juan asked. If the mayor was dead, there was no one to implicate him in the last sale of guns, unless of course Sheriff Pritchard was involved.

The captain moved Juan slowly toward the passenger door. "Don't worry. I'm sure the Feds have everything in hand."

The presence of the Feds would play perfectly into Juan's plan. He could run, and they would have no choice but to shoot him. This would end his misery and give his family permission to move on. He just had to figure out the right time to make his getaway. He didn't want anyone else getting hurt.

Once Juan had made up his mind, he felt much calmer. He would do this for Alicia, Nancy, and Paula. They deserved better than he could deliver, and it would be his parting gift to them.

CHAPTER 58

Juan and Johnny were loaded and in the car when a man knocked on Johnny's door. Johnny lowered the window. "I'm Paul Rockney. I'll be heading across the border with you. You need some assistance inside the store?"

"Not necessary," Johnny said as he reached out and shook the agent's hand. "I've got a trooper on his way to do the investigation. Dr. Archer is just cleaning himself up and will take the key to the hotel when he's finished." Johnny looked around the parking lot and saw the mayor lying on the ground, his body riddled with bullets. "What happened with the mayor?"

"My partner and I had the mayor under arrest for shooting up the Gas N Go, and we no sooner got him cuffed, when someone drove by in a black SUV and shot him too."

"I'll have Trooper Robertson arrange an ambulance to move the mayor to the funeral home in Deming. By now, they've really got a pile of bodies." He turned and looked at Juan, who was standing in the shadows of the building." Johnny said. "This is…" Johnny hesitated, not wanting to set Juan up for failure. "This is Juan Rico, a crack shot with a rifle. He's coming along too, if the marshal approves." Johnny saw Juan's eyes widen and nod. If he were shocked by this turn of events, he did not show it.

Agent Rockney reached in the car and extended his hand to Juan Rico. Rico shook the agent's hand. "It's nice to meet you," he said. Johnny watched as Juan handled himself in a professional manner, which greatly relieved him.

"I'll just follow you," Rockney said.

"I've got to make a couple of stops at the hotel," Johnny said. "Do you want to join us or wait in your vehicle?"

"Gives me time to take a smoke!" Rockney laughed and pulled out a pack of cigarettes from his jacket pocket.

"We should only be about fifteen minutes," Johnny said. "And with the marshal pulling into town any minute, we're right on schedule."

The team had agreed to meet the marshal at the Pancho Villa State Park after it closed for the night. They could load the Humvee away from prying eyes.

Johnny parked in front of the Rio Rancho Hotel again and led Juan inside. He wanted to tell the concierge that the key to the Gas N Go would be delivered by Dr. Archer. The concierge was gone for the day, so Johnny headed to the front desk.

The young man behind the desk lifted his head out of his high school chemistry book, pulled the long bangs draping over his forehead out of his eyes, and stood. Johnny introduced himself and then gave the man specific instructions.

"Dr. Randall Archer will be delivering you a key to the Gas N Go soon. Please don't release the key to anyone except the New Mexico State Trooper Michael Robertson."

"When do you expect the trooper, and what does he look like?" The desk clerk, in spite of the late hour, was courteous, not something Johnny expected out of someone so young. Johnny liked that about him and gave him props for asking an obvious question.

"Thanks for asking!" Johnny got out his cell phone and pulled up the New Mexico State Troopers website and showed the clerk a photo of Trooper Michael Robertson.

"I appreciate that you're cautious. We've had a shooting at the convenience store and need to keep it contained until Trooper Robertson can get here."

"I plan to study criminal justice when I get to college," the young man said. Upon this pronouncement, he straightened his shoulders and stood erect.

Johnny noticed his nametag. "Roberto, you've just passed your first exam! What you're doing for us is very important in solving a big case. Thank you!"

"Here's my cell phone number," Roberto said, with great seriousness, "in case you need to follow up with me about the key." He handed Johnny a piece of paper, which Johnny tucked in his slacks, and shook Roberto's hand, which was ink-stained from lots of studying, no doubt.

"Don't forget to look me up when you graduate. We need more young men and women like you in law enforcement." Johnny smiled and turned around, pulling Juan along by the arm.

Johnny, with Juan in tow, arrived at the hotel coffee shop where he ordered cold sandwiches and filled his mother's Thermos with coffee for the road. As they waited for the food, Johnny asked Juan to sit with him at a table. The small round metal tables and curved wire chairs reminded Johnny of trips as a kid with his dad to the ice cream shop in Las Cruces. Little did he realize how innocent those days had been until now, when it felt like his future was in question.

He leaned in close to Juan and whispered, "You were probably surprised by what I told the agent. I do have a proposition for you. What if I could make those gun trafficking charges go away?"

"Why would you do that?" "You remember Penny Larkin?"

"Yeah, why wouldn't I? She's ruthless."

"Well, she had her orders to bring you in by the US Marshals Service. There's a warrant for your arrest on suspicion of gun trafficking. Did you realize that?"

"No. What made the marshal think I'd do something like that?" There was no way Johnny was going to let Juan know there had been a mole among gun traffickers. "I can't tell you that, but what I can do is ask for your cooperation in bringing down the major players in the gun trafficking ring. We think it's real big." "How can I help? And if I do, can I go home? I'll stay out of trouble."

"We're getting ready to head across the border to rescue Penny, if that's possible. We suspect—if she is still alive—that the gun traffickers are holding her. We've heard rumors that they are willing to trade Penny for Arturo Armando, a major player in Mexico's gun trafficking operation. He's cooling his heels in the El Paso County Jail, awaiting trial in December for killing a border patrol agent. If Penny's kidnappers want to trade her for Armando, then that gives us hope she's still alive. We just aren't sure. But if you agree to go with us and be willing to shoot your way out of the trouble that may come, I'm going to ask the marshal to drop your charges. If we get Penny out of Mexico alive, you will be free to return to your family in Lordsburg."

Johnny watched Juan's face as he processed the news. He leaned into his knees and wiped tears from his face with his bruised right hand. *What hardened criminal cries?* Johnny wondered. He knew the world would be better served if he could save one young man from a life behind bars. "So what do you think?"

"Okay. I'll try and help the best I can."

"That's terrific. As soon as we leave the hotel, I'm going to ask the marshal to honor this deal. If he agrees, we'll go through the formality of releasing you from the bond, and you will be sworn in as a member of our team."

Juan Rico looked at Johnny in disbelief. "Nobody has ever taken a chance on me. I won't let you down." Johnny noticed that Juan's eyes were clear and dry now. He even managed a smile— something Johnny had never seen on his twenty-year-old face.

CHAPTER 59

Penny threw her weight against the substantial bathroom door as Ricardo pounded on it. The only way Ricardo was going to get in was to get El Acero to unlock the door, and Penny was pretty sure his pride would keep him from asking. Besides, he had had more alcohol than the wine at dinner because she could hear him slurring his words.

After several minutes, Ricardo gave up. Penny took a deep breath and moved away from the door. She splashed water on her face in the marble basin and looked at herself in the oval, gilt-edged mirror. Her green eyes were lost in a sea of dark circles, and her lips looked purple. *I have to get out of here!*

XXX

Was Ricardo just pretending to leave, or was he waiting for Penny to open the door so he could pounce on her again? She decided to take her chances and if necessary fight him off once more. There probably wasn't much time before Margarita came by to check the lock on the bedroom door. She had to move out now! The heavy bathroom door groaned on its hinges as she pulled it open. She scanned the inside of the bedroom, waiting a couple of beats before stepping back in the bedroom. All was quiet. *He is gone!*

There was no time to waste. Penny ran to the closet and threw off her black dress and heels and yanked on a T-shirt and then the heavy black sweatpants and sweatshirt. She found a pair of black flats that felt cold on her bare feet. They would have to do because a quick search of the closet did not reveal any tennis shoes. She also grabbed an extra pillow, and much to her delight, she discovered a shelf of wigs in various colors. She chose a blonde one, closest to her hair color, and headed to the bed, where she made the pillow into a body and covered it, letting the lengths of the blonde wig peek out under the blanket. She looked at her handiwork and decided a quick glance in the room would convince Margarita that she was fast asleep.

Penny was panting, and her adrenalin was pumping through her veins, providing her with a natural high and unwarranted courage. She ventured into the hall and walked quickly in the opposite direction from the dining area. From there, she turned left at the corner, leading her to an equally long hallway with four doors, two on each side. She heard voices. She moved to each door, hoping that at least one was unlocked. After three unsuccessful tries, she found an open door to the left and darted inside the room, closing the door behind her.

By all appearances, the room was used for meetings. The long, rectangular oak table matched the rest of the woodwork in the hacienda. Ten leather chairs, each with circular designs of silver studs, reminded Penny of a cowboy's saddle. Penny took a moment to catch her breath. She laid her hand upon her chest, questioning her endurance as her heartbeat pulverized her ribs. She leaned against the wall, determined to regroup and figure out how she could escape. She heard the murmur of male voices outside the door even before she saw the large brass doorknob turning. She slipped into a closet designed for office supplies, closed the door, and laid her body flat against the floor. She hoped her gasps for air didn't give her away because her fear and exhaustion made it hard to breathe at all.

Penny heard a flurry of Spanish as leather boots shuffled across the floor. They were spitting out their words so fast, she couldn't translate everything, but there was one phrase they repeated throughout their conversation that she did understand—*la venta de las armas. They are selling guns!*

What had she gotten herself into by tracking Juan Rico? And why was she being targeted? Certainly Federico Castañón wasn't that afraid of a five-foot, four-inch blonde?

Penny could hear El Acero's voice above the din, and thankfully, he spoke in English. "We have a decision to make about Ms. Larkin. Do we offer her in trade for Armando?"

Penny was rattled by the news. So this is the reason they had let her live! She was a hostage in what sounded like a very dangerous game. The United States didn't negotiate in hostage situations. But maybe they didn't know that!

The side of her face was resting against the wood floor, and small granules of sand, courtesy of windy days in the desert, scratched her cheek whenever she moved, even slightly, but she could still hear as the voices lowered to a whisper.

"Is this wise," a deep voice asked, "to deal with the Americans?"
"Do you want Armando back or not? This is the best chance we have to bring him home," El Acero said.

"Do we need him now?" Still another man wondered.

"He has everything in his head. He knows the deals we have in place with El Chino and the Guatemalans, as well as all the cartels. Everyone knows Arturo Armando. And he is so paranoid he never kept records."

Penny heard a round of "Sí. Okay. We trade her for Armando!" Penny felt the movement of the heavy chairs vibrating the floor as the men shoved them away from the table; the clanking of glasses, and a chorus of "¡Salud!" followed this.

They were no doubt downing shots of tequila, the Mexican national pastime. But she was confused. *What did the El Chino, or the Chinese, have to do with gun trafficking—or Guatemala, for that matter? I thought the United States was the main source of Mexico's guns.* Nothing would surprise Penny these days—especially after helping Leo break up a Russian child trafficking ring along the border.

While she waited for the men to finish discussing their business, Penny made a plan. Her first move was to get out of the house. Her second would be to try and scale the tall chain link fence with concertina wire and run like hell. She tried to remember how the hacienda was laid out in relation to the rest of the property.

Within ten minutes, the men left the conference room, freeing her to crawl out of the closet. Her arms and legs felt numb from lying on the floor, and it was difficult to stand. She pulled herself up with the help of one of the chairs and stretched her arms and legs. They were stiff and achy. Penny opened the door to the hall but just as quickly closed it part way when she heard the rattling of keys. Through a small crack in the door, she watched Margarita locking her bedroom door. Hopefully, she didn't have plans to lock this door as well! Penny moved away from the opening and flattened her body against the backside of the door, should it swing open. Instead of moving toward the conference room, Margarita had apparently returned to another part of the house because she never came by to lock it up.

It was time to go! Penny opened the door just wide enough to slip through, ran to the end of the hall, and turned left, taking her, she was sure, to the rear of the house. She figured there must be an exit just beyond this last hallway or, at the very least, some servants' quarters. She would have to take the chance that the servants were still at work and not resting in their rooms. She saw an alarm at the top of a doorway, which indicated an exit to the outside. She hoped El Acero had not yet set the alarm with so many houseguests.

She shoved the door open and stepped into a glassed-in porch. She glanced at the bodies of old cigars, three with burning embers, lying in the ashtrays scattered around the room. The men had come in here before heading to the conference room, no doubt. Penny's lungs filled with the rancid smell of cigar smoke that had settled on everything, even with the jalousie windows open. She was choking on the odor but didn't dare make a sound. The aluminum door out of the porch creaked open as she stepped outside, gasping for fresh air. A stunning display of stars dominated the night sky. It made her feel small and insignificant.

Would Leo or Johnny, or anyone for that matter, care if she never came home?

The back of the house was dark, except for the light from two windows. Penny was grateful that no motion sensor had kicked on the safety lights, warning guards of an intruder or, in this case, an escapee. She was on her own. This thought invigorated her and gave her the courage to keep going. She traipsed carefully over the uncertain ground, occasionally having to use the side of the stucco house to maintain her balance. As she passed the first lighted window, she saw Ricardo, lounging in a leather chair and reading a newspaper. The pistol lying on the side table startled Penny and caused her to step on a rock. She fell backward, landing on her rear end. She had no time to worry about bruised hips. She ignored the pain and quickly jumped up and brushed the sand from her clothes. Her right hip throbbed, and she placed her hand over her mouth, blunting the urge to cry out.

The noise had apparently drawn Ricardo's attention because Penny could see his looming frame standing in the window, holding a curtain, to gain a better view. Penny leaned as far into the wall as she could to avoid being seen. Her breath was rapid, and her heart followed suit. If he didn't leave the window soon, she'd lose her nerve to continue. Thankfully, Ricardo lost interest after several minutes because the curtain was now closed, leaving only a brush of light painting the dark yard.

Penny ducked beneath Ricardo's windowsill on her way to the front of the house, not sure what she to expect when she got there. The second lighted window revealed an empty room, which didn't make Penny feel any better because if the guest wasn't in his room, where was he?

The black-bearded Paco had been on guard earlier, and she wondered if he or someone else was still standing on the front porch with an AK 47. She took a quick look around the corner. *Darn it!* Two men were leaving the house and heading in her direction. *There is no place to hide!* She dropped to the ground and rolled against the wall, just beneath Ricardo's window. She hoped the noise did not disturb him again. Thankfully, she was dressed in all black, which helped some.

Penny could not see their faces as the men walked away from the house, but she could see their camouflage pants and their combat boots from her view on the ground. They were speaking in low tones, making it impossible for Penny to hear what they were saying. As they approached the large metal shed, floodlights, as bright as flashbulbs at a Hollywood Premiere, illuminated the area. Fractures of light rested on her face and made her squirm. *If they look over here, they will see me.* She could do nothing but remain still and hope they had other things on their minds.

Penny watched as an electric garage door strained on its chains to lift off the ground. Both men were laughing and shouting above the noise in a smut kind of Spanish that Penny tried to keep out of her head. She put her hands over her nose and mouth. She felt like screaming. She was falling apart, and she couldn't afford to. The men entered the building, which she recognized as the very same one that held the guns that had arrived from the states, along with Penny. She took advantage of the moment, jumped to her feet, and ran through the field of bright lights. Penny felt vulnerable and reckless as she tried to outrun her shadow into the back of the warehouse and into the cover of darkness. When she arrived, she looked up at a twelve-foot high fence and shook her head. What had she been thinking? And what was the use? She was trapped.

Penny bent over and rested her hands on her thighs. She was wheezing from the sprint, and her legs were aching. How could she climb such high fencing that was also crested with concertina wire? She would be ripped to shreds, if she tried. She would have to wait here overnight, and when El Acero discovered she was missing in the morning, he would send people to search for her. They would find her right here, shaking from the cold and at their mercy. El Acero would be angry and perhaps give up on the idea of trading her.

A cold wind was shifting the sand around her feet, and Penny began to shiver. It had to be after midnight. She wrapped her arms around her shoulders, but that didn't help. Why hadn't she grabbed a coat? Penny had underestimated the chill of an August night in the desert, but being cold was way better than being dead.

CHAPTER 60

Leo was in excruciating pain. Every time he tried to take a breath, his lungs felt like the bellows of an accordion pushing out the air in a sorrowful tune. His left shoulder was contained against his body in a tight dressing. He pulled the oxygen tube out of his nose with his free hand so that he could lift his head and look around. The hospital room was freezing, and the stark white walls served as a direct contrast to his badly wounded body, which was warm to his touch. *God, I survived!* The realization surprised him as he recalled being outgunned in the hospital parking lot. Leo could still see flashes of the gun battle in raging color—much like the comic books he used to read as a kid. The garish greens, yellows, and reds of the cartoon world morphed into bursts of gunfire aiming for his body and causing his adrenalin to push his heart to capacity. The lights on the ceiling burned little blisters into his skin, at least he imagined that, as he moved in and out of consciousness. He was sweating profusely, and the damp sheets made him shiver and shake. He needed someone to help him get warm, but how could he do that? He was alone.

He could smell the gunpowder. It stung the insides of his nose and brought tears to his eyes. They were shouting insults now—in Spanish—taunting him to come out from behind the hedge. He steadied his hands and looked through the sights of his pistol—old devil eye, he fondly called his favorite gun.

Two men were dancing in front of him. They were cowards covered with black ski masks and black Kevlar vests. He would have to aim for the head—a tough shot even for him. He squeezed the trigger anyway. He saw one man laugh and then fall to the pavement. But someone returned the favor, and Leo felt a hot spear of lead pierce his shoulder. A black cloud hovered over him, making it impossible to catch his breath.

Leo's own moaning woke him again. The room was spinning and making him want to vomit. To prevent it, he shut his eyes. Every time he opened them back up, the room twirled, and the circular light above his head became a missile primed to spin across the room and explode. He took refuge in counting the beats coming from his heart monitor. As long as he could hear them, steady as they go, he was still present and accounted for— like an army private in the barracks of life.

He didn't know how long he had wandered through the outskirts of the barely living, where the air was thinner and the breathing shallow and short, but when he opened his eyes this time, the room was not spinning, and he could inhale without pain. The sun was spreading its warm fingers across the linoleum floor. He used his legs to kick off the blanket, which was now stifling. At first, he thought he was dreaming again when he saw Alejandra standing beside his bed—her arms reaching for him. Her smile melted his soul. This was real because he could hear his heart monitor, his sign of life, speeding up. He wanted to ask her a big question. "Why did you die and leave me alone?"

"It's going to be okay, Leo," she said as she brushed a cool cloth across his forehead. The doctor says you'll fully recover."

"Alejandra?" He tried to sit up so he could hold onto her with his one good arm. "I'm so happy you are here."

"No, Leo. It's Adriana. I've come to take care of you. Everything's going to be just fine."

CHAPTER 61

Johnny pulled his Dodge Charger down the long driveway that led to the state park. The chains that blocked off the entrance after hours had been removed, allowing their vehicles access to the parking area in front of the visitors' center. Agent Rockney and another unnamed agent followed closely in their black Tahoe. Little buttons of light from their vehicle bounced around inside Johnny's car, giving both him and Juan a pox-like appearance, and accentuated the gravity of the task at hand. Across the lot, Johnny saw the Humvee parked under a mercury vapor lamp, set on a towering pole. The Humvee was a huge rectangular box, painted in camouflage colors, and sporting big balloon tires. It reminded Johnny of a desert beetle on the hunt for smaller prey. Eugene Lujan stood alongside the Humvee, dwarfed by its size. Johnny took comfort in its hugeness, realizing that if they caught up with the kidnappers, the armor-clad vehicle would help protect the team from the arsenal the Mexicans were bound to possess.

Johnny parked about fifty feet from the visitors' center and waited as the Tahoe pulled alongside. "Juan, please stay here until I call you, okay?"

Juan didn't speak but nodded as he rested his wounded left hand in between two plastic bags of ice cubes.

Paul Rockney jumped out of the Tahoe and joined Johnny. "Need some help loading up the Humvee?"

"Sure, but can you wait a minute or two? I need to speak with the marshal alone."

"No problem. I'll just unload my gear, send Agent Valle on his way, and wait for you here."

Johnny joined Marshal Lujan at the Humvee, where he was loading his MPI AR-15 with ammunition.

"Marshal, I've got an idea, and before you reject it out of hand, I would like you to hear me out."

"Do I have a choice?" Lujan got out the flashlight clipped to his belt and shined it on the ground. "I dropped a NATO magazine around here somewhere." The beam darted across the rocky terrain and landed beneath the Humvee.

Johnny spotted the magazine in front of the left rear wheel. It was packed with hollow points. He hoped they wouldn't have to use tracer bullets because that would mean the team would be in a full-out assault. He brushed the sand from the cartridge and then noticed the webbed-rubber tires on the Humvee. He'd only heard about them but never seen them in real time. He handed the magazine to Lujan. "I see you've got us a high mobility vehicle with airless tires. How'd you pull that off?" Johnny was encouraged by Lujan's preparedness.

"I'm not going into Mexico without taking every precaution. Those babies will keep us from having a flat tire in the middle of nowhere." Lujan shoved the NATO magazine into a case and snapped it onto his black leather belt. "So what do you want to ask me?"

"I've got Juan Rico in the car. I want to take him with us. We need the firepower, and from what I've been able to see, he's a good kid, who, with some male mentoring, could turn his life completely around."

The marshal adjusted the ammunition clips on his belt, cleared his throat and spit on the ground. "I don't have the authority to ignore a federal warrant."

"Juan Rico is small potatoes. You said so. And if you read his file, he was the New Mexico State Rifle Champion while in high school. He beat out men twice his age."

"What's this really about—saving a kid or saving Penny Larkin?" "Both. With Rico, we've got a better chance of bringing her back alive—if she is still breathing. And I am going to do whatever it takes to bring her back dead or alive. You know what cartels do to women—they rape, dismember, and bury them in the desert. We'll never find her, if she's dead, without grabbing one of the kidnappers and forcing him to tell us where she is."

Lujan rubbed his chin with his fingers and looked at Johnny with doubtful eyes.

Johnny widened his stance and dug his boots into the gravel driveway. "Look, you wanted Rico, and I've got him, but we don't have any place to lock him up. This whole place is dirty. Rico told me that Sheriff Pritchard turned him loose after Penny apprehended him. I ran into him at the hospital when I went to check on Leo before heading over here."

"I can't make that kind of decision without a judge."

"This is a good kid. I can read people, and we've got a chance here to save a young man from a life of crime."

Lujan pulled out his cell phone. "Give me some time."

Johnny returned to his car where Juan and Agent Rockney and Agent Alan Valle were unloading the back of the black Tahoe and stacking gear and grub behind the Charger. Johnny opened the trunk, and everyone helped pull out the cooler, the sandwiches, and the drinks. He looked over at the marshal, who was talking on the phone and waving his left arm, as if trying to make a point.

"Juan, grab the two flashlights strapped to the sidewall." "Should we walk over to the Humvee with this stuff?" Juan asked.

"Hold on."

It was time for Agent Valle to hit the road. He shook hands with Paul, Johnny, and Juan, and climbed back in the Tahoe, ready for the trip back to Tucson. He waved good-bye and left the men standing next to one another, watching and waiting for the signal that they could go forward with the mission. Johnny felt a chill in the air. The temperature was falling rapidly.

Johnny left the group and checked the Charger's doors, to make sure they were secured, and decided he had better call his mother. She answered on the first ring. "Mom, I'm going to be gone for a couple of days on a special assignment. I'll call you when I'm on my way home."

"Are you still working with that lovely girl, Penny? I like her!" "Yes, Mom, my assignment involves Penny. Don't worry. Love you."

By the time Johnny had disconnected from his phone call, he saw that the marshal was also off the phone and motioning to his team that it was time to go.

The men grabbed their gear and hauled it to the Humvee. The marshal placed his hand on Juan's shoulder. "Son, can I speak with you?"

XXX

Juan shivered from fear as well as the cold air as he and the marshal walked a few feet away from the Humvee. The wind had picked up and tossed the sand in the air, blasting the sides of their faces. He wanted so much to believe Captain Trejo—that he could have a second chance. He would do whatever it took to get back on the right side of the law.

"Juan, I have great respect for Captain Trejo, and he believes in you. He thinks you are worth the investment. I've called a federal judge in El Paso. I actually got him out of bed, and he has voided the warrant the US Marshals Service had issued for your arrest." Juan brought his hands up to his face. He did not want the marshal to think he would cry over this news. He dropped his hands and looked directly into the marshal's eyes, his own eyes filled with tears anyway. "I'll do anything to get back with my family. I shouldn't have got in with the Chihuahua cartel, but the money was too tempting."

The marshal placed his arm around Juan, hugging him like a father—the father Juan never knew. "We've got to get going, but I'll take the time along the way to ask you some questions about your contacts. We've got to stop these guys in their tracks. Dead bodies are piling up in Mexico, and it's starting to spill over into the US."

CHAPTER 62

Penny was huddled against the wall of the metal shed, her arm shielding her face from the dust storm that blew furiously around her. The chill from the shed's wall permeated her body, and caused her to shake uncontrollably. She leaned her head closer to the wall, trying to hear what was happening inside.

The two men, who had entered the gun storage area fifteen minutes ago, were still in there. She thought she heard heavy boxes scraping against the cement floor—boxes like those that had accompanied her from Columbus to the middle of nowhere. The conversations between the two were growing in intensity. *Are they arguing?*

"To hell with all this inventory! El Arcero won't miss a few."

"¿Cómo ova a lograr eso?"

"We can take a few out of each box and rearrange what's left so that it looks nothing's gone. Podemos esconder las armas detrás del cobertizo."

Hide guns behind the shed? This was frightening news to Penny! If they brought the firearms around the back of the shed, they would find her. Then they would take her back to El Acero and be heroes for doing so. And no doubt, she would be murdered on the spot. She felt the sweat under her arms, even in the chill of the night. She sniffed and wiped her nose on the arm of her sweatshirt and tried to stop shaking. As soon as she heard them walking her way, she would have to move to the opposite side of the shed. It was her only option because of the chain-link fence behind her.

Penny heard even more commotion and agitated words that she understood in her broken Spanish, as cussing. "En la mañana *güey*, we put the guns in the cattle truck."

She stood and prepared to shift to the right or the left side of the shed, but it was impossible to shield her body from the steady blast of sand, and with no coat, it chafed her skin. She endured the grit between her teeth and in her nose, as she waited, hoping they would finish soon. But the men, finding greed and opportunity all in one place, continued to pry open the boxes. Penny leaned her head against the wall and tried to calm her mind, which was running wild. Tears dropped down her cheeks, and when she wiped them, the sand on her fingers scratched her face.

"!Bueno!" One of the men laughed. "!Vamos!" "Hey, Ciero. What's taking you hombres so long?"

A new voice brought Penny alert. She heard the men inside the shed mumbling. She peeked around the corner of the shed and noticed a man standing in the shadows of the front porch. Penny could hear the two men inside the shed scrambling to cover their crime against criminals. "Give us more time!"

"Just drop the inventory, and come inside and help me move the piano. It won't take ten minutes. El Acero is having a concert tomorrow night. Got to set up so the vocalist can practice."

Penny peeked around the corner again as the motion sensors kicked on the lights. She saw the men's long shadows reach the porch before they did. She waited a few moments to see if anyone would stand watch at the front door, but five minutes passed, and the front door remained unmanned. Penny had maybe another five minutes to act. She slipped around the side of the building and, to her relief, found the shed door open. The lights on the side of the house would go off soon, and she had to act fast. She saw a box with a splintered lid and grabbed a pistol. Penny hoped she could figure out how to use it. Then she tore through several open boxes until she found a container with ammunition. She dumped a box of 9 mm shells on the floor and shoved as many as she could in the pocket of her sweatpants. The motion-controlled lights went off just as she finished. It was time to get out of there. Penny had reached the corner of the building when the front door of the hacienda opened. The two men were on their way back! She could hear them scuffing their boots on the porch's wooden floor. She ran back behind the shed and crouched on the rock hard ground. It would have been pitch-dark, but the moon was nearly full, with pinpoints of stars hanging in the broad expanse of sky. She ran her fingertips over the pistol, acquainting herself with it, as best she could in the moonlight. She found the release button for the magazine, and it dropped into her hands. She opened a box of ammunition and tried to load the bullets, but it was almost impossible! On her first try, she pinched her index finger. She shoved her fingers in her mouth, trying to ease the pain. *I've got to do this!*

She was freezing, and her hands would not stop shaking. The gun was new, and the spring was stiff. Regardless, she had to load the gun with as many bullets as she could bear to push inside the magazine. Through sheer willpower, Penny jammed six bullets inside the mag and shoved it inside the handle. She heard the click, indicating the bullets were loaded.

The men had returned. They were shoving things around in the shed again, still laughing and cussing.

Penny had taken a gun safety class at the marshal's service, and the instructor had shown her the location of a safety on many semiautomatics. *Where is it? There is no safety! What does that mean? Think, Penny. Think!*

She exhaled in relief when she remembered that some pistols have a grip sensitive safety. She squeezed the handle, and it gave a little, which would permit her to fire when she needed to. She crouched down, balancing the gun between her knees, and waited for the men to show their faces. She had to drop them both. With any luck, one of the men had the electronic key card that opened the front gate. What if they don't have it? *Calm down! If not, I'll do what I have to do to survive.*

The sound of piano music was floating out of the house, carried by wind, and whipping the dust and the music into an unlikely symphony. Someone was practicing for the concert and singing. Would the music block out the crack of her gun? Twice? She could only hope.

When Penny heard the men roll the shed's door closed, she racked the slide and chambered a round. She measured each of their steps as their boots crushed the gravel under their feet. With any luck, they were carrying a load of weapons and would not see what hit them.

CHAPTER 63

Marshal Lujan directed the loading of the Humvee, and when all four men were situated inside, he turned on his laptop and showed the video that the Predator B drone had shot about the time that Penny was probably moved across the border. Johnny was mesmerized as the marshal pointed to the fancy dune buggy, in which Penny bumped along in the front seat. One man was driving and another huddled between the two seats. They tracked the trio twelve miles south until they reached a small village with a handful of wild dogs and a chicken ranch or two. They had stopped so one of the men could relieve himself, which he did behind a shed. They moved on, this time heading east. The vehicle kicked up so much dust that it was difficult to see anything at all. Johnny feared they were taking Penny deep into the Mexican desert to kill her. He felt his fingernails tearing into the flesh in the palms of his hands.

When the filter of dust finally cleared the camera's lens, the officers were surprised to see a sprawling compound, with a large house, jutting out of the rocky soil, and protected with concertina wire strung in all directions. In the distance, herds of cattle roamed the surrounding land.

"It's a working ranch!" Johnny shouted, and his voice bounced off the walls of the inside of the Humvee.

Johnny recognized the cattle by their distinctive, flea-bitten coats and turned-up horns. In his teens, he had dreamed of joining the rodeo circuit, and the Corrientes were the steers of choice for American ropers and doggers.

"Look at that!" Johnny pointed to a truck, bulging with cows, as it passed the dune buggy, churning up the sand, on its way out of the ranch. "It is headed for the border!"

"I'm going to call the Columbus border crossing station," Marshal Lujan said. "They can tell us who shipped those animals into the states. Paul, while I'm doing that, why don't you show us what you found through the DEA's GPS tracking system?"

"Sure. I was able to get a warrant from a district judge in Arizona to track Penny's cell phone into Mexico." Paul plugged a jump drive into the computer and pulled up a screen with a single fluorescent green circle. "The green circle is the closest cell tower to the location where Penny crossed the border," Paul explained. "As you can see the GPS tracked her about fifteen miles south, and then the signal just snapped in two, like the phone was destroyed."

"That corresponds somewhat with the drone video," Johnny said. "Maybe somebody found her phone and killed it." As Johnny spoke, a gnawing pain ground into his gut. Without realizing it, he placed his hand over his belly. He hoped they weren't too late. The marshal was just ending his cell call when Paul pulled the jump drive out of the marshal's laptop. "We're in agreement. The GPS aligns with the drone data."

"You won't believe what I learned from the border station. Romero Rancho de Mexico owns the cattle truck. Martín Romero apparently has twin ranches, one on each side of the border."

Johnny looked at Juan whose eyes widened at the news. Would this information compromise Juan's ability to handle a gun in a firefight? Johnny watched Juan rubbing his hands against his face.

"You okay, Juan?" Juan didn't answer but instead stared at the instrument panel of the Humvee.

"We have to get going," the marshal ordered. "Do we have an issue with Juan Rico, or are we cool?"

CHAPTER 64

Juan shoved his tongue against his teeth, cutting into his skin until he tasted blood. His entire world had crumbled. It was hard enough to come to grips with his uncle's betrayal, but now it appeared he also had a secret ranch in Mexico that Juan knew nothing about.

Juan could feel the warmth of the marshal's hand on his shoulder. He was saying something to Juan, but Juan could not hear him. His anger was shouting down any surrounding voices. The very person who had raised him as a son had played him for a fool. Should he leave the team and head back to Lordsburg? He still had his dignity left with his wife and girls. But if he didn't step up soon to care for them, then that was finished too.

"Juan, are you with me, son?" The marshal turned Juan's head toward him.

He was surprised that the marshal did not look angry. He had a kind look in his eyes. Juan was not too familiar with kindness, and he wasn't sure just how to take all of this in.

"Son, we've got to know if you can still be a solid team member. We may have to take on your uncle. Can you do it? We understand if you can't."

The image of the merry-go-round reappeared in Juan's mind, and he closed his eyes trying to rid himself of the view.

The carnival had good and bad memories, and he wasn't ready to confront them today. The brightly painted horses refused to go away. They were spinning faster and faster until one by one the centrifugal force ripped them from their posts and flung them into the air. Juan watched as the horses landed in a pile— splintered and crushed—a burial ground of legs and heads and leather reins. But there was still one horse on the carousel, refusing to be thrown away. His jewels sparkled against the lights of the carnival. He was painted in handsome tones of brown and turquoise. Juan realized that he was that horse, and though he felt the wrenching pain as the pegs in the carousel's wooden floor pulled against his hooves, he held his ground. He still had a right to dream of becoming something better, and he would not let his outward circumstances destroy him. If he let the forces fling him into nothingness, he would never recover.

Juan opened his eyes and looked at Marshal Lujan who was still patiently waiting for his answer. "Can we count on you?"

He and Captain Trejo were giving him a chance at a do-over. He could hardly conceive of it. These men had believed in him, when no one else in his family had. He smiled and flipped on his flashlight, pointing it at his face until the marshal could see how his eyes sparkled like the jewels of the carousel horse. "Yes, I can do it. I have no issue taking on my uncle. He has betrayed me. Count me in."

CHAPTER 65

A single stone flew past the corner of the steel shed, kicked into the air by one of the men closing in on Penny's hiding place. She heard their heavy breathing, both gasping for air, as they labored under the heavy weight of the wood boxes filled with weapons. They were upon her now, and Penny, crouched in a tripod stance, was ready for them. But just as the first man cornered the building, a gust of wind slammed her against the wall of the building. Stunned, he watched her try to regain her balance and then fumble for the trigger of her gun. The man dropped the heavy box, scattering guns across the ground. He was not quick enough. Even though sweat trickled into the crevices of Penny's fingers, she fired the gun. The bullet seared his midsection, blowing blood all over Penny's face and sweatshirt. The brass casing burned her cheek as it sailed past her face. He fell forward, knocking her to the ground. He groaned and gurgled but didn't fight back. His dead weight was lying across Penny's legs.

The music of the piano was reaching a crescendo as the second man drove his right hand deep into his holster. Penny aimed high. Her shot drove a hole into his flannel shirt, popping the buttons off his chest. A trickle of blood soaked into the green and brown plaid, but he was still gripping his pistol. His watery eyes were wide with anger, and his hand shook as he aimed his gun at Penny. She dragged her legs out from under the dead man and threw herself against the wall of the shed. A bullet soared above her head. The man was still standing. Penny rolled into a sitting position where she got off another shot. This one hit the man just above his left ear, blowing him back against the shed with such a force that she could hear the crack of his head against the variegated metal.

The music had stopped. Did anyone hear the gun battle? Both men were dead, and Penny had to act quickly. She searched the pockets of both men trying to find the key card that opened the front gate. *It isn't here!*

She had taken a big chance, figuring they had one. *Now what are my options?* Her adrenaline was raging, and she felt her heart contracting under her breastbone. Lights on the front porch flashed on. Penny could hear the scraping of heavy boots on the porch's wood floor and the front door slamming shut. She stuck the toes of her black flats into the chain-link fence and climbed to the top. She had been breathing so fast, her chest hurt, and when she inhaled the cold air, her lungs rattled. Penny swore the wind had picked up speed because it was hard to maintain her balance as she tucked her gun inside her waistband. She pulled her sweatshirt off and threw it over the razor wire to protect her body. As she climbed over the fence, Penny kept a tight grip on her sweatshirt, hoping to take it with her as she dropped to the other side, but it remained impaled on the concertina wire. Her sweatpants were torn, but she managed to save them from complete ruin as she fell to the ground. She landed on a sharp rock, bruising her hips. Penny jammed her fist in her mouth to keep from crying out.

She heard the cocking of automatic weapons and the movement of men marching toward the steel shed. Blood was running from her wrists and her thighs.

The pain was excruciating, but Penny had to get out of there. She got on her knees and crawled as far away from the fence as she could manage, hiding behind a prickly pear cactus, which wasn't much help. Then she realized that her pistol must have fallen out of her sweatpants when she jumped over the fence. She looked back and saw nothing. Hopefully, her gun was on the right side. She would have to go back to find her gun. It was black and impossible to see from where she was hiding.

A laser storm of flashlights was whipping around the front of the hacienda as El Acero's henchmen searched the dark areas missed by the motion sensors. Penny saw three men walking toward the shed.

I have to get my gun! She inched her way back toward the fence, hoping she could find her pistol before the men discovered the dead guys lying behind the storage shed. She could hear angry voices coming from inside the building, just a few feet from her. "¡Se robaron nuestras armas!"

Penny crawled to the edge of fence where the remnants of her sweatshirt now hung. Thank goodness she had pulled on that T-shirt for extra warmth because now that was all she had to wear on top.

She ran her hands through the sand groping for her gun. The flashlights were now covering every inch of the yard. Soon, Penny figured, they would be pointing their lights beyond the fence, figuring the men had escaped that way. Finally, her fingers touched the barrel of the gun, and she grabbed it. She looked up and saw her sweatshirt hanging on top of the fence. It was like a flag pointing the way to her escape route.

She could hear the men wrestling with the wood boxes inside the shed, and she caught a cuss word or two reverberating against the walls of the steel shed. She had no choice but to crawl back up the fence and try to pull the shirt out of the snare of wires.

She was at the mercy of the wind, which buffeted around her and slowed her progress. But Penny was driven by pure fear. She straddled the pockets of chain link with her hands and feet and lunged her body into the air, grabbing hold of the shirt, which gave way under her weight. She dropped to the ground and rolled.

Every bone in her body was crying out in pain but she had to move as far away from the fence as she could. Penny saw a small hill and possibly safety just a few yards ahead. It made her almost giddy with relief. If she could reach the top, she could hide on the other side and maybe even rest for a while. Penny's body felt as heavy and dead as the men she'd left behind, making even this tiny rise in the desert floor looked insurmountable. She dare not stand and run toward it! She struggled to pull herself toward the crest while keeping a low profile. The rocks bruised her fingers as she tried to pull herself forward. The deep cuts from the concertina wire stung her wrists, but thankfully, she was getting closer to the top of the hill. The men were checking the sides of the house, and she saw the curtains of Ricardo's window open and his silhouette in the glass.

Penny had to stop and catch her breath. Her throat was raw from panting. She brushed the gravel out of her wounds and thrust her hands back onto the ground, inching closer to her goal. Now the men were yelling at each other in broken border Spanish, and having found nothing, they ran back toward the shed. Their flashlights were zigzagging across the sky as their boots pounded the ground.

At the base of the hill, instead of rocks, Penny's fingers found a pocket of loose sand, making it tougher to gain any traction. She still managed to crawl halfway up the hill. In a few more feet, she would be at the top and could hide on the other side. She shoved both hands into the depths of the sand but lost her balance and slid back down the hill, landing in a clump of cactus. She felt the thorns ripping the skin around her ankles, but she could not stop to pull them out. The flashlights had reached the fence line, which meant the men were probably checking around the outside of the shed, and would soon discover the dead men lying behind it. She clawed her way back up the hill by shoving her hands still deeper into the sand. She had to find something substantial, like the root of a tree to grab onto or she would keep sliding back down the incline. Her knuckles smashed into a piece of wood buried in the soil. Penny couldn't believe her good fortune! She gripped the board and wrenched her body over it. In the starlight, she saw a rock jutting out of the earth and grabbed for it. It was hard and cold but didn't feel like stone.

My God, it's a human hand!

Penny muffled a scream. A flicker of a flashlight bounced off the side of the building and landed on the gravesite, illuminating Penny's prostrate body, clinging to the side of the hill. *Does anyone see me?* Tears dripped from her eyes and over her cheeks. She didn't dare move and draw attention to herself. Luckily, the men weren't looking her way.

Penny lifted the left hand of the lifeless body out of the mound of dirt. It was small, frigid, and stiff. In the dimness of the starlight, Penny felt the wedding band that still encircled the ring finger. *Is this El Acero's wife?* The horror of that thought made her predicament come crashing down on her. She was as good as dead too. In the morning, El Acero would search until he found Penny all alone in the desert, limping toward the US border. Her fate would be the same as his wife's.

Penny inched her way over the gravesite and managed to hide as the beams of light circled the yard and then shot out past the fence toward her hiding place again. The lights ricocheted off the sand dune that protected her from view, then faded into the vastness of the desert.

"¡Aquí están!" One of the men was shouting that he had found the dead men. She had reached a hiding place in the nick of time. Fear sizzled through Penny's veins, making her forget how cold the air was. Wearing only a T-shirt, her lungs rattled, but she refused to give into the terror that felt like it was burning her alive.

Penny listened intently, hoping they would conclude that the two men had killed each other. Why else would they be carrying a load of weapons and hiding them behind the shed?

She watched the men pick up the guns, which had spilled out of the boxes when the thieves fell to their deaths. The firearms were placed back inside the building, and she heard the sound of the large door clanging against its metal track as it rolled downward and banged against the cement floor.

When the lights near the shed went dark, the men returned to the house. Penny stood, stretched her arms, and tried to walk, but she tripped and fell. Her toes were numb. She took off her shoes and rubbed her feet, trying to get the circulation back. The wind was howling, and she had no place to take shelter. She pulled the neck of her T-shirt over her mouth and nose hoping to keep the sand out, but it still blistered her forehead. She noticed that the bleeding from her wrists had stopped. The blood was clotted and sticky on her skin. She said a prayer of thanks to God.

Hopefully, Penny still had a few hours before El Acero discovered her missing. She would move under the cover of darkness toward the border. It was a dangerous gamble. She might run into a wild animal or fall and break an ankle. She heard the call of a coyote in the distance. Had one already smelled the blood on her clothes? Hopefully, they weren't running in packs, which Penny knew coyotes were prone to do. Her gun could only fend them off for a short time, plus it would draw attention to her location. A rustle in the underbrush startled her. She jumped and aimed her gun at the sound. A large jackrabbit hopped out of the grass and then turned and disappeared. Penny's heart was pounding, and the sweat tumbled onto her T-shirt, making her colder than ever.

The porch lights went dark—a sign that she shouldn't waste any more time. Penny took a few precipitous steps away from the hacienda. She heard the strains of the piano beginning again, joined by a chorus of voices. The singing blended with the breath of the wind and blew a haunting melody over Penny's shoulders, encircling her neck like a scarf. She passed the trucks parked in front of the gate and walked left, away from the house, avoiding the driveway. The soles of her skimpy shoes felt every pebble and thorn along the way, but the pain didn't bother her anymore. She was above ground, and unlike the dead woman, she still had the use of her hands and her eyes. She would use the stars and the circle of the moon to guide her back to New Mexico.

CHAPTER 66

The wheels of the Humvee bounced the four men up and down in their seats.

"You had better strap yourselves in!" the marshal yelled. "No sense breaking a shoulder, trying to stay grounded."

Johnny was relieved that they were finally on their way. It had taken them a couple more hours than he planned. They had wasted so much time, he had all but given up hope of finding Penny alive, but he was determined to locate her body and bring it back to the States. There had been a glimmer of hope several hours before. The marshal had received a phone call earlier in the day, from the ATF saying that someone was offering to trade Penny for Arturo Armando, a notorious gunrunner. But the ATF had not heard a word from the cartel for the past three hours, and that was usually a sign that they had changed their minds. Cartels were deadly and unpredictable partners.

Marshal Lujan had given each man two mags of 9 mm bullets and an AK 47 or AR-15. Johnny watched Juan Rico slip his Kevlar vest over his button-down shirt and then don a sweatshirt and a canvas jacket with pockets to hold his extra clips. He noticed how comfortable Rico was around firearms. Johnny hoped this was a good thing. He was gambling with the lives of his fellow law officers, especially now that he knew Juan's uncle was at the center of the gun trafficking scheme.

Juan noticed Johnny staring at him and smiled. "Don't you worry, Captain. I've got your back." He reached over to Johnny's own military tactical jacket and snapped in a clip that was hanging loose.

"Thanks." Johnny let out a breath. He could feel the temperature building in the tightly contained vehicle and smelled the stench of perspiration. He reached inside a cooler and pulled out bottles of water and passed them around. The Humvee hit a rock and knocked Johnny into the cooler.

"I said strap your body in the seat, Trejo!" The marshal, gripping the steering wheel, looked back at Johnny, grinned, and grabbed a bottle from Johnny's hand. "Thanks!"

Johnny fell into his seat and buckled up. His compact .45 pistol was wedged against the small of his back. It pinched a bit, but that was okay. It would keep Johnny on his toes.

"Is everyone happy with their equipment?" He flicked on his flashlight and moved the beam across the seats. The light fell over Paul, whose day-old beard gave him a look of homelessness.

"How about you, Rockney?" Paul patted his vest. He had a Sig Sauer jammed into a quick draw holster, and pouches on his chest held a flashlight and a .38 Ruger revolver. On both sides of his vest were double mag pouches attached with Velcro.

"I'm all good," Paul said, running his fingers through his hair and adjusting his baseball cap.

The roar of the Humvee made it hard to carry on much of a conversation. And besides, no one seemed to feel like talking. They all knew they might be driving into a trap.

Johnny got out his iPad and brought up a classified map of northern Mexico. It was sparsely annotated. They were within ten miles of the cattle ranch he'd seen on the Predator Drone video. A little blue dot indicated their progress as they drove deeper into Mexico.

"It looks like the property is surrounded by a wire fence and a slinky of concertina wire," Johnny told the group. "Anybody got experience crossing one without ripping your body to shreds?"

Paul leaned over and picked up a short-handled shovel and flipped on his flashlight. "We're gonna go under it! Just how fast can you dig?" Paul's dark-brown eyes twinkled in the beams of his torch. He threw the shovel toward Johnny, too quickly for him to catch it. It landed on the steel floor of the Humvee where it rattled as the vehicle rumbled across the desert.

The shovel, scratching metal against metal, was like Johnny's fears grating against his skull. Memories of his father dying at the hands of gun traffickers were etched into his brain. He knew better than to take on the Mexican gun runners, but the anger of losing his dad, and now possibly losing Penny, was just too much. He reached in his pants pocket for an evidence bag and pulled out the red scarf Penny had been wearing. He tied it around his neck and took a deep breath. The fragrance of lavender and reach his nostrils. *Dear God, please keep Penny alive until we get there!*

CHAPTER 67

Juan took out a tissue from his jacket pocket and blew his nose. Drops of blood fell onto the legs of his khakis. He leaned his head forward and placed two fingers on the bridge of his nose, trying to stop the bleeding. His tissue was fully soaked. The captain noticed his problem, and threw him a cube of ice.

"Try this!"

"I appreciate it, Captain. The dry air does this to me all the time."

"Call me Johnny."

"Sure. Johnny. It feels funny but okay."

"We're all in this together, Juan. We're a band of brothers. You understand?"

Juan looked into Johnny's eyes. They were soft and sincere. The captain closed his eyes, as if in deep thought, and when they reopened, his eyes were full of tears.

"You really like this girl enough to risk your life?" Juan asked in all sincerity. He didn't mean to pry, but so much effort was being made to save her.

"Yeah, I do. Not sure I realized just how much I cared until just awhile ago."

"What can I do to help?"

"I need your eyes, Juan. We're going to face some real firepower, and we will need accuracy rather than a bunch of bullets blowing in the wind."

"You have that much confidence in me?"

"I do. In fact, I'm pretty sure everyone in this Humvee respects your skills."

"No one has ever respected me for anything. Never."

"I do want to give you a heads-up. If your uncle is at the ranch, he might not survive this."

"My Uncle Martín is already dead to me."

"Don't talk like that. I lost my father two weeks ago in a gun battle with these kinds of thugs. I'm sick of the killing and don't want my dad to have died in vain. If we can stop your uncle's gun trafficking operation, we will save many lives on both sides of the border. And we will try to take him alive too."

Juan leaned back in his seat and tried to block out the memories of his aunt and uncle. They had stepped up when his mother had left him to party in Juárez night after night. The times when he had a fever, his aunt would sit by his side, all night, dipping a cloth in cool water and wiping his face and arms.

He wouldn't forget their kindness, but that seemed like light-years ago. His aunt was gone, and since her death, Uncle Martín had grown cold and distant. Juan had attributed it to his time serving as a sniper in Desert Storm, but maybe that wasn't it at all. Maybe he had turned into a mean and angry man with nothing to lose.

Why Uncle Martín had chosen money over family was way beyond Juan's ability to reason it out. Family meant everything to Juan, and now that he was on the brink of losing his own wife and kids, anger welled up in his chest. He would do anything to keep them—even risk his life on a crazy rescue effort.

Juan's hands were as swollen and bruised as ever, but he squeezed the seat in front of him so hard until the pain in his fingers became unbearable. He released his grip and examined his palms. The lines on his hands ran in so many reckless directions, much like his choices in life. Even the lifeline encircling his thumb looked jagged and short. Tears stung Juan's eyes. He wiped his cheeks with his sleeve. He could stop the blood but not the tears. There was a whole lot of crying to be done before this story ended, he was sure, but wanted desperately to straighten out his life and make his wife and children proud of him.

Juan massaged his hands, trying to prepare for the splintering ache that was bound to come when he pulled the trigger on the AK-47, now lying at his side. Juan was glad he had resisted the urge to end his life with a federal agent's bullet in his back. He was no coward. The blowback would be brutal, but he had to hang on. His team was counting on him and so was his family. They just didn't know it yet.

CHAPTER 68

It was midnight, and the sky held just a hint of the moon's halo amid the stars. Marshal Lujan made a left-hand turn, leaving behind the dog-eared mountain range to the north, which had dominated their view for the last ten miles. Ahead, Johnny saw what looked like a massive dagger ripping the curtain of stars in two. They were entering the foothills of the Sierra Madres, an area so inaccessible that even some residents living in the interior of Mexico thought of this northern border region as untamed.

The Humvee was close now. Johnny could feel it in his bones. He fingered his pistol. The trigger was slick. He wiped the sweat from his hands on his jeans and blew out a large breath. "We're almost there!"

Johnny swore he could hear the collective heartbeats of the four men, driving blood into every vein and energizing them for what they might find. Even their breathing was tight and quick, like dogs on the hunt.

The marshal stopped and turned off the Humvee. "I think we should go on foot from here," he said. "My GPS coordinates tell me that the ranch is one hundred yards away—south and east."

The men piled out of the vehicle and stretched their legs. It took several minutes for them to collect all of their gear and suit up with helmets and heavier jackets. The wind was howling and causing Johnny to shiver in spite of all his clothing.

All the commotion reminded Johnny of the first day of skiing on Mt. Baldy. It was always an awkward time each winter, trying to get his arms and legs to cooperate with his skis, poles, and boots—kind of like a robot in training. He searched in all of his pockets until he found a pair of black tactical assault gloves with the fingertips exposed.

"Here, Juan. These are for you. It will protect your fingers, which still look like they've been through a meat grinder!" He threw the gloves at Juan who dropped one.

"Hey, have you no respect for my gift? I paid good money for those." Johnny tried to lighten up Juan's mood. Ever since their talk in the Humvee, Juan hadn't said much.

Johnny thought he saw a flicker of a smile in the shallow light, but of course, Juan had every right to be tense. "Thanks, Cap—I mean Johnny."

"No flashlights," the marshal cautioned. "We will use them only for signaling each other. One burst means take cover. Two means you're in the clear."

The marshal asked Paul Rockney to be the point man. He was an experienced tracker, having been cross-trained with the Border Patrol, as well as with the ATF.

Paul brought the men into a huddle, as if he were a quarterback ready to call a play. "Look, I don't have to tell you to stay away from the jumping cholla. They will definitely ruin your day, almost as bad as a bullet."

For starters, the marshal suggested they follow Paul in single file until it was necessary to fan out. The marshal offered to bring up the rear, with Johnny and Juan in between.

They walked in silence for several minutes until Paul jerked to a stop and held up his hand. Unbelievably, the sound of a piano floated over the dry desert grass and blended with the heavy breathing of the four men, who were carrying more weight than normal.

"Maybe we caught a break," Johnny said. "They might not hear us coming."

The team approached the ranch from the side of the rangy hacienda that seemed to go on forever. Paul took a peek through his night vision goggles and surmised that the place was completely surrounded by wire.

"Anybody for climbing over that stuff?" he asked under his breath.

"I can give it a try," Juan offered.

"Look, guys. I'm just joking. Where's the shovel?"

Johnny passed the shovel up to Paul, who hitched it to his belt. "Before we each lose a pint of blood, let me take a closer look," Paul said.

Johnny watched the agent creep toward the front of the house. He stood behind a large electric pole for some time before returning.

"Just as I expected, they've got motion sensor lights on the front. We'll have to account for that in our attack and storm the front door at the last moment."

Before the men could make any further moves, the front door to the hacienda swung open, and the porch lights flared to life. Two men in fatigues and combat boots stepped into the yard and headed toward a metal building, about one hundred feet away. The motion detectors signaled the lights, which made it easier for the team to keep an eye on the men. Instead of opening the door to the shed, they headed to the back of the building.

Soon, each man came around either side of the building, holding the arms of what looked like dead men and dragging their lifeless legs across the rugged terrain. When they arrived at the entrance to the ranch, one man waved a card across an electronic field, and the gate opened. It took both men to throw each body into the back of a Ford pickup.

Johnny heard the thump and roll as each dead man landed in the metal bed of the truck. The driver took time to light a cigarette before starting the engine and revving it.

Johnny's breathing quickened. How long would that gate be open?

Paul was reading Johnny's mind. "Okay, guys, we got ourselves a lucky break."

The team watched as the men got in the truck and pulled away from the house.

"Headed for the desert to bury them?" Johnny asked.

"Most likely, but I didn't see a shovel," Paul said. "Could be a temporary fix until morning."

Paul waved his own shovel and motioned for the men to move toward the open gate. "Hurry!"

As they ran single file along the fence line, the headlights of the truck hit them smack in the eyes and bounced their shadows against the wall of the hacienda.

"Damn it," the marshal said. "They're back!" "Hit the ground!" Paul yelled.

The four men, dressed in black, faded into the landscape.

The truck pulled back in the drive, apparently unaware of the marshal's team lying along the fence line. The passenger jumped out of the truck and ran into a nearby garage, returning with a shovel.

There was a collective chuckle as the truck roared back down the road. In their haste, they had forgotten to lock the gate, again.

"It's hard to get good help!" Johnny joked. "Let's move!" Paul said.

Johnny's protective glasses fogged up as he raced through the open gate. What would he find inside that house? He was afraid of finding Penny dead or, maybe even worse, not finding her at all.

CHAPTER 69

Penny was threading her way through the cactus and tumbleweeds as carefully as she could, but she already had quite a collection of thorns clustered on the legs of her sweatpants. She could feel them as she reached down to rub her ankles, which were bleeding. She refused to feel sorry for herself. She had only to remember the haunting eyes of El Acero and his plans for her. At first, she had mistaken the sound of an engine and the grinding of gears for piano chords accompanied by male voices singing off key. But Penny soon realized there was a vehicle coming her way. A cloud of dust blew over her, making it difficult to keep her eyes open. She lunged to the left and slid into an arroyo, scrapping the palms of her hands as she fell. The exhaust from what sounded like a truck slipped over her like a tarp, choking her. Penny watched the large wheels of a Humvee cross within a few feet of the edge of the arroyo. Any closer and the vehicle might have fallen in on top of her.

There was nothing unusual about its camouflage paint scheme. It could have come from anywhere and from any country. She knew the drug cartels were so well heeled these days that they had more money than many small nations. The size of their financial dealings had recently been made apparent when the US attorney general called them out for using American banks to keep their investments safe. And what bank would turn down millions of cold, hard cash?

Penny didn't know if the Humvee was help or a hindrance in her escape, but she desperately needed to know who was inside. She'd seen the Humvee up close, and that was a plus. Could she handle a remote viewing after such a brief encounter with the vehicle? She took a long, deep breath. It hurt to inhale. She would have to relax, but how was that possible with El Acero not far behind? She sat down on the cold, brittle desert floor and looked up at the stars, which now appeared muted, with the moon slipping into the western sky. It was late, and if the moon was leaving, then the sun would soon be making an appearance! She would have to do this viewing in a hurry.

At first, Penny resisted the remote viewing protocols, but she knew she couldn't see inside the Humvee without following the exact orders of her mentor, Zarn Richter. She dropped her head toward her lap and placed her hands on her belly. She let the air move gently in and out of her lungs. The benefits of breathing slowly in a deliberate rhythm always impressed her. In the frenzy of her circumstance, she was actually calming down.

The second step was to abandon any hopes she had for the Humvee. If she thought there was someone inside who could save her, the viewing would not work. She had learned this the hard way. The Humvee was not her savior.

The next step was to be in harmony, in perfect balance with the world around her. Penny breathed in deeply. She couldn't let the rattle of her lungs distract her. She could actually smell the desert. It had a dry, white wine kind of aroma. She loved the desert most after it had rained and the sand was wet, but she had never realized that the aridness had a pleasant smell too.

The last and hardest part of viewing was releasing her circumstance to God. That was the fourth and final protocol, but in spite of her hopes, Penny couldn't imagine how God could save her. In a couple of hours, it would be daylight, and El Acero would discover she was missing, and the border was still several hours by foot. Even with a pistol and bullets, she would be no match for a gunrunner. That was the truth, and she needed to come to grips with reality. But she prayed for help anyway. "Please, God. Help me!"

As Penny prayed, a shooting star blazed a trail across the void. She watched in amazement as the Milky Way—a mass of alien planets, stars, gas and dust—shoved its way across the dome of lesser stars and dominated the night sky. Streaks of yellow and gold encircled the moon, but they could not quench one star, which refused to give in to the galaxy's indomitable show of force. Penny was mesmerized by the star's boldness. It grew brighter and brighter, pulsating with hope and pulling her nearer and nearer until she was drawn into the heart of the star. She felt safe here.

Penny saw her own reflection in an angular wall of mirrors and smiled as the people she had loved in her life gathered around her in the looking glass of her mind. The celebration soon faded as a heavy canvas tarp of beige, green, and brown fell over the mirrors and blocked her view of her family and herself. The camouflage shape morphed into a military vehicle with large, webbed wheels. Penny watched as the Humvee bounced through the desert, kicking up dust and decimating the cactus and the dry grass.

There were four men riding inside. Penny tried to look into the eyes of each man. Was Leo among them? The first person she saw was Juan Rico, the man who had started this whole broken play. *What is he doing here?* These are bad guys! Penny groaned. This couldn't be good! Then she saw the big, brown eyes of Johnny Trejo and another man she did not know. The face of the driver was not visible to her, but his tall, angular frame looked familiar. Suddenly, a shiver raced over her bare arms as she recalled the marshal's warning. There was a law enforcement officer involved in gun trafficking. Had she let that slip her mind because she had been so attracted to Johnny Trejo? Had Johnny been double-dealing on both sides of the border?

Penny clenched her fists and pounded her thighs. She was furious and felt like a fool. Was it possible to feel colder or more alone? Now she had to face the possibility that Johnny Trejo was a gunrunner. There was no one left to trust, except Leo, and maybe Marshal Lujan. And she wasn't even sure about him.

As Penny struggled to get to her feet, she heard the sound of gunfire. She wrenched her pistol out of her waistband. She made the decision at that very moment to make a stand—to confront Johnny—even if it were the last thing she ever did.

The bullets in her pants pocket pounded against her legs as she raced back to the very place she had been desperate to escape.

CHAPTER 70

Paul took the first bullet. He had volunteered to blow open the back door of the hacienda with a barrage from his AR-15.

The plan had been to use Paul and Johnny as a diversion so that the marshal and Juan, the better marksmen, could enter the front door undetected.

An armed guard had been lounging in the hall, smoking a cigar. He threw his smoke to the floor and fired his 9 mm pistol, hitting Paul in the leg. Johnny provided backup and brought the guard to his knees with a shot to the chest.

"Get out of the house!" Johnny yelled at Paul. "I'll return for you when this is over."

With his partner down, Johnny would have to cover the back alone. A second man in a black T-shirt and fatigues charged at him, fumbling for his holstered gun as he ran. Johnny aimed his AK-47 at his midsection and dropped him like a rock on to the oak floor. Johnny stepped over the two dead men and looked around the corner, just as the marshal and Juan shot the locks off the substantial front door.

An elderly looking woman, dressed in a black nightshirt and house slippers, came screaming down a side hall! "¡No me dispares! No shoot!"

"Is there a young woman in the house?" Johnny asked. But the old lady knew little English. Desperate, he searched his brain for what little Spanish he knew. "¿Tiene usted una muchacha en la casa?"

The woman's eyes widened and welled up with tears. "Sí." She pointed to the very hallway from which he'd just come. Before the woman could show Johnny exactly where Penny might be, two more men entered the great room with their guns drawn. In a flare of bullets, the marshal slumped behind the sofa with a shot to his thigh, but he still managed to rear up and fire back at his assailant, killing him. Johnny watched as Juan hesitated to shoot the second man.

"Shoot him!" Johnny yelled.

The second man turned his gun on Johnny. The bullet pounded into Johnny's Kevlar vest and knocked the wind out of him. He dropped to the floor, gripped with agonizing pain. He watched helplessly as Juan chased after the second man, who was fleeing down the hall toward the back door.

If he left the house, the man would find Paul lying there, bleeding. Johnny had to help him, but he couldn't move. He couldn't even breathe. The blow to his chest would take several minutes to get over. By then, it might be too late.

CHAPTER 71

Juan sprinted down the hall after his Uncle Martín. The bastard was not going to get away! He was angry with himself for freezing up like that. He should have shot him when he had the chance. He was ten feet behind Martín, who hopped over the two dead guards and managed to make it to the splintered back door.

Juan wasn't as lucky. He tripped and fell in between the two men who were both lying in a pond of blood.

"What the...?" Martín kicked the rest of the broken door out of his way and jumped down the steps. Juan reared up, blood dripping from his clothes, and followed his uncle out the door. The motion sensors flared to life. The yard looked like the set of a Broadway stage, exposing Agent Rockney, who was leaning against the wall of the house.

Martín aimed his pistol at Paul. "Stop where you are!" Juan yelled.

Juan knew he had taken his uncle totally by surprise. He never thought that his nephew had an ounce of courage, and now here he was confronting him. Uncle Martín shot the gun right out of Juan's hand. Juan dropped to his knees. The blow to his hands was excruciating. Martín rushed over to Juan and pointed the pistol at his head.

"I don't know what you think you are doing or who you're fooling trying to get the guns back I stole from you. Nobody runs guns through Mexico but me."

"I'm not running guns. I'm keeping the ones you have away from the cartels."

Juan saw the red laser beam from his uncle's pistol bounce off his cheek. He readied himself for certain death. He didn't beg for mercy because he wasn't the coward his uncle believed him to be.

Juan's silence angered Martín. "You son of a bitch! After all your aunt and I did for you, it has come to this? Beg for forgiveness, and I might let you live."

Juan watched his uncle's legs move into a shooting stance. Martín's arms were shaking, which caused the laser site of the gun to bounce repeatedly off Juan's head and onto the wall of the hacienda. Juan closed his eyes and braced himself for the gun blast. When it came, he was still kneeling on the desert floor, alive and confused.

His uncle was not as lucky. He was lying on the ground, a bullet through his neck. At first Juan was in shock. What just happened? *I'm alive, and Uncle Martín is dead. How can that be?*

A woman came running over to Juan. It was Penny Larkin! "You okay, Juan? What's going on here?"

Juan answered, "We're here to rescue you!"

Penny said, "Then let's go see who needs our help!"

CHAPTER 72

The whirring blades of the Sikorsky HH-60J Jayhawk drowned out the voices of ATF medics who were caring for the injured at the Romero Rancho de Mexico. The medics' faces were covered with scarves, designed to protect them from the multiplex of sand storms being staged by the helicopter blades and the unrelenting wind.

Penny, Johnny, and Juan were vertical and in no need of immediate medical assistance, but Marshal Lujan and Paul Rockney required urgent care for treatment of bullets to the hips and legs. The trio stepped inside the great room of the hacienda to get out of the wind and to weigh the carnage. The three guards were dead, including the black-bearded Paco, for which Penny could not help but be relieved. Johnny was mumbling that a bullet had broken his ribs, but when Penny suggested he have the medics take a look, he shook it off.

"They've got their hands full," he said.

Margarita, the housekeeper, was running up and down the halls crying and pounding on doors. Penny saw Ricardo stagger out of his room, as well as René and a couple of men. Penny could only surmise they were part of the Mexican gun trafficking network that had been discussing her life as a bargaining chip for the Martín Romero's infamous partner, *Armando*.

Penny, Johnny, and Juan moved to the front porch as the medics carried the marshal via a wood pallet, out of the house, and over to the helicopter. A soldier inside the helicopter helped position the stretcher in the aircraft, leaving room for Paul. From the advantage of the porch, Penny noticed there were only two front row seats. The rest of the plane was a blank canvas for the transport of wounded soldiers or supplies.

A large truck marked "Policía Federale" roared through the gate, stirring up even more dust. A half-dozen Mexican Federal police, their faces covered with black ski masks, spilled out onto the driveway. The sunlight bounced off their shiny white helmets as they drew their automatic weapons and charged passed Penny, Juan, and Johnny. It was their country after all.

The ATF medics waved at the soldiers and headed to the back of the house to care for Paul Rockney.

"Maybe we should just stay on the porch and out of everyone's way," Penny said. The ski masks were scary enough without the machine guns. She could only see the eyes of the police officers, and none of them looked kind. She shuddered as a gust of wind blasted them. Penny grabbed a post to steady herself. She had seen these masks on television when the police investigated crimes in Juárez. Apparently, no one could be trusted, even when there were no television cameras.

"Yeah. Good idea. Too much going on." Johnny said.

Juan just nodded and leaned into the wall of the house as the federales carried two of the dead men out and loaded them in the back of the truck.

René, Ricardo, and the two would-be grave diggers came out handcuffed and hobbled by leg irons. Ricardo snorted when he saw Penny. His eyes were a kaleidoscope of colors, reflecting his anger and the injustice of being hauled off like a criminal. To make matters worse, they were forced to sit inside the truck, right alongside their dead comrades.

The pianist, a robust woman with orange hair and too much rouge, came running behind them. One of the federales grabbed her substantial arm.

"¡Yo sólo estoy aquí para tocar el piano!" She yelled at him and tore herself out of his grip. The handcuffs were apparently too small for her gigantic wrists. She shook her hand at the officer but moved forward as she was ordered.

"Do I resist the temptation to joke that the fat lady has sung?" Johnny laughed and put his arm around Penny's shoulders.

"¡Prisa, señora! ¡Prisa!" The officer hurried the woman to the truck and boosted her inside by turning his shoulders to her backside. Penny could hear her screaming as he slammed the tailgate.

The stretcher carrying Agent Rockney passed in front of the porch. He was awake and looked over at his team. Like an injured football player, he held up his right arm and made a fist, indicating victory. Penny, Johnny, and Juan broke into spontaneous applause. The federales offered Martín Romero no such luxuries. Two officers, one holding the arms and the other the legs, carried his dead body past Juan, Penny, and Johnny. His eyes were still open and seemed to follow them as he moved toward eternity, with a temporary stop in the truck's backseat, where they threw him across the bench and shut the door.

Penny saw that Juan's eyes were red, but he wasn't crying. His hands were pulled into tight fists. He slammed one of them down on the porch railing. "Damn it, Uncle Martín! I loved you!"

"It's time to go!" Johnny said. He put his arms around both Juan and Penny, and they stepped off the porch. When they arrived at the helicopter, a US soldier jumped out of the plane and approached them.

"Can you give me the coordinates for the Humvee? I'm here to drive it back to the States."

"The marshal has the info on his cell phone. Can you get it from him before we take off?" Johnny explained.

"Sure. Thanks." The young man climbed back inside the helicopter. Penny could see him talking with a medic, who reached in the marshal's flak jacket and pulled out his satellite phone.

"Our work is done here?" Penny asked.

"We can't do any more. We were lucky enough that the Mexican government allowed us to come in for your rescue, Penny. But we've exposed Mexico's largest gun cartel. Who knew someone could be so powerful that they would have a lock on most of the guns bought and sold even to warring drug cartels? I hope we've delivered a blow to gun smuggling in both the US and Mexico."

Juan crawled into the helicopter, thanking the medic who gave him a hand up. Johnny jumped in next and then pulled Penny into the plane. His hands were warm. Penny's hands tingled at his touch. She looked into his eyes—those same resolute eyes she had first encountered on the interstate in the middle of another sandstorm. It was only then that she noticed the red scarf wrapped around his neck. It had been partially hidden under his bulletproof vest. She touched it lightly with her fingers and fought off the tears. This was no time to cry. She dropped her hands to her side and turned away, afraid of what she was feeling. It confused her. After all, she belonged with Leo.

"It's okay, Penny," Johnny said. He held onto her arm for a few seconds and moved to the back of the plane, where he and Juan huddled beside their wounded colleagues.

The pilot patted the seat beside him and said to Penny, "Have a seat and buckle up. We're in for a bumpy ride."

Penny looked back at the brave men who had risked their lives to save her. It was way beyond anything anyone could ever ask, but they had done it, and she would be forever in their debt.

The roar of the engine, the rumble of the blades, and the smell of the fuel nauseated her, bringing back memories of her journey in the dune buggy. As the aircraft lifted off the ground, it was buffeted by strong winds, which heaved it against the turbulent sky. Penny leaned over and vomited in a barf bag that had been tucked inside a leather pocket of the helicopter door. Getting sick was a small price to pay for the chance to go home alive.

CHAPTER 73

It was 11:15 a.m., and Leo was resisting Adriana's help in eating his first solid meal in seventeen hours. He could do it himself, and it would look weak to be so helpless. He was starved and tried to keep from scarfing down the plate of enchiladas that the nurse's aide had brought into his hospital room.

"Hey, take it easy, Leo. You don't want to make yourself sick!" Adriana took a napkin and wiped a drop of sauce from his chin.

"Please, I don't need your help," Leo pleaded.

"Yes, I saw how you dropped your rice all over the blanket. Just relax and let me help."

Leo's stomach growled, as if to confirm that his need for food was overriding his sense of independence. Adriana carefully gathered a forkful of tortilla, chicken, and cheese and dipped it into the enchilada sauce before offering it to Leo. He gratefully accepted it, glad to be able to eat normally again. The pain in his shoulder had eased enough to keep his hands from shaking so much, but he still was unsteady on his feet. An hour ago, his nurse had helped him to the bathroom and back and had given him strict orders to begin walking the halls after lunch.

When he had had his fill he lay back against his pillow and took a long slow breath. "Thank you."

Adriana cleared away the lunch tray and sat down next to him. Leo noticed that the chair had a hospital blanket and pillow. It was then that he realized, Adriana had been sleeping here.

While he was immensely grateful for her presence, he was wondering about Penny. *Where is she? Why isn't she at the hospital too?* He didn't feel he could ask Adriana. The question felt out of place. Or maybe Adriana thought he should already know what had happened to Penny.

Whatever it was, it wasn't good. Penny wouldn't miss the chance to take care of him. He had been there for her six months ago when she was in the hospital, recovering from a plane crash. It had been the beginning of something special between the two of them—linked by the pain of loss and the celebration of bringing a child trafficking ring to its knees.

Leo's nurse appeared at the hospital room door. "Okay, sir. It's time to get your legs moving." She walked over to his bed and helped him dangle his feet off the side of the bed. The nurse placed house slippers on his feet. Where had they come from?

When his feet hit the floor, Leo felt a wave of dizziness and began to fall backward into the side of the bed. Adriana slipped up beside him and, together with the nurse, helped Leo take his first steps toward the hallway.

They were just passing the nurse's station when Leo saw Penny. His heart churned in his chest. She had come! He watched her walking toward him, her green eyes alive and her arms swinging confidently at her side. Penny stopped in midstride when she saw him.

"Oh, my goodness, Leo!" She reached her hands out to him. Her fingertips were touching his face. Her blonde hair was short as a schoolboy's. She looked fourteen. He wanted to grab her and hold her and never let her go, but he could only stand there like a lummox.

Leo watched Penny's eyes move beyond him to the nurse and then to Adriana. A cold draft encircled them. Penny's body stiffened. She dropped her hands to her side.

"Adriana, how kind of you to be here for Leo," Penny said. Leo saw a man approaching Penny. He put his arm around Penny's shoulder. "Is everything okay?" he asked.

Leo was having trouble focusing his eyes. The dizziness had returned. His hands trembled. "I'm so cold."

"Let's get you back to bed," the nurse said.

As the trio turned back toward to room, Leo stumbled and fell to the floor. It was the last thing he remembered when the lights went out.

CHAPTER 74

Penny had been sitting in Leo's hospital room for an hour, and he had yet to wake up. Adriana had left, much to Penny's relief. She had swept the blanket and pillow piled in the side chair onto the floor. It angered her that Adriana had been sleeping there. Why couldn't Penny just be happy that Leo had had someone with him during his darkest hours of pain?

Johnny walked in the room and handed Penny a cup of coffee. "I thought you could use this," he said.

"How are the marshal and Agent Rockney?" Penny knew Johnny had gone to check on their status.

"Paul is making good progress, but the marshal is being flown via helicopter to University Medical Center for surgery even as we speak."

Penny got up and walked to the window. The sound of thunder clapped against the walls of the hospital as the Lifeline Medical Evacuation helicopter lifted off its pad on the roof.

"Is he going to be okay?" Penny asked.

"I talked with his doctor here, and the surgery is more complicated than Deming can provide. But they expect him to make a full recovery, give or take two months off his feet."

Penny felt the sting of guilt needling her shoulders. She had caused good men a great deal of suffering. How could she ever repay any of them? Johnny walked over to the window and placed his right hand on her back. The energy stimulated by his touch, forced its way through her chest, and dropped into the pit of her stomach like a landmine. One wrong move, and it would explode. She had to admit, she liked Johnny a lot, but she loved Leo, didn't she?

Johnny turned Penny's body until she faced him. A glint of sunshine fell on his face. His black hair looked exceptionally curly today.

He smiled and rubbed her arms, which were dangling at her side. Her hands formed into tight fists as she fought the passion burning inside her stomach. Finally, she lifted her arms and opened her hands, exposing her palms, still scarred from her ordeal. Johnny took both hands in his and ran the tip of his index finger gently over her wounds. She gasped for air as he pulled her into his arms.

"Well, well, well," Adriana said as she closed the hospital room door. "What is going on here anyway?"

Penny bolted from Johnny's grasp and met Adriana at the foot of Leo's bed.

CHAPTER 75

Juan knocked on the door of his in-laws' small cottage in a lower-rent neighborhood of Lordsburg. He could hear his daughters laughing behind the door, playing a game of UNO that he had taught them. The smell of refried beans and homemade tortillas seeped through the poorly insulated front door. It smelled like home!

When his wife, Alicia, opened the door, she cried. "Juan, you're here at last! We missed you so much."

She threw her arms around him and waited as Nancy and Paula ran toward Juan and wrapped their tiny arms around his legs so tightly, he almost buckled under the weight.

"I have a big surprise for you. He pulled out two matching dolls, and the girls screamed with delight. "Thanks, Daddy!" They ran off just as fast as they had arrived to discover just how these dolls would fit into their world of make believe. He held onto Alicia and pulled a badge from his pocket. Marshal Lujan had given it to him. It had belonged to Marshal Lujan's father. She stared at it in wonder. Her eyes reached into his for answers.

"I am not a marshal—not yet—anyway. I am going to get my degree in criminal justice, and then I will enter the US marshal's program. It's all in the works!"

"One day we can have our own home, then, like you promised?"

"Yes, the US Marshals Service is paying for my college tuition—as a way of saying thanks for helping them out."

"Juan, whatever did you do for them that would make them do this for us?"

"Oh, that is a story for another day. Right now, I need to spend time with my family and hear about everything that has happened since I've been gone."

CHAPTER 76

Johnny stood at the window in disbelief as Penny took on Adriana. "What business is it of yours what I do?" Penny asked. "I am Leo's sister-in-law. We are family. It's my job to protect him."

"No, you are not family—at least not any longer!"

Johnny wanted to interfere but thought better of it. He had never seen a picture of Leo's first wife, but Penny had told him Adriana looked strikingly similar. Penny had laughed at such an irony, but Johnny knew it worried her. How can you compete with a man's dead wife reappearing in the form of her twin sister?

The noise awakened Leo. He bolted straight up in bed and looked straight past Penny. "Alejandra! Where have you been?"

Adriana ran over to Leo's bed and leaned down and kissed him on the lips. "It's okay, darling! I'm right here."

Johnny was anxious for Penny as she looked on in horror. He noticed that her hands were twitching and her face was red. He had to stop her from doing anything foolish. He walked over to Penny, put his arm around her waist, and guided her out of the room.

"I know it's a dirty trick, but Adriana's got the upper hand. Maybe she has been masquerading as Alejandra all along."

"But how can that be? Leo knows the difference. He knows Alejandra is dead."

"The surgeon told me that because Leo lost so much blood his body went into shock, and they were going to give him something called haloperidol to keep him calm after surgery. Maybe he's still on the medicine, and it's messing with his mind."

Penny marched over to the nurse's station. "Excuse me, but I was wondering if you could tell me if the medication that Sheriff Tellez is taking could cause some mental confusion?" The nurse looked at Leo's chart and then rolled her chair over to a large medical index in a three-ring binder. Her long brown fingers passed over a long list of medicines before she finally stopped on the one she was looking for and tapped the page.

"I'm not permitted to tell you what he's taking, but yes, it has been known to cause drowsiness, dizziness, and mental confusion. And the effects can last up to twenty-one days after he goes off of it." Penny's hands covered her eyes, and she began to sob. Johnny led her away from the nurse's station and down the hall, away from the curious. He found an empty waiting room and sat her down on a sofa and handed her a tissue from a box on the side table. A muted television was flashing promises of cures for psoriasis, and a voice on the intercom was calling a code blue. Johnny paced around the room for a few minutes, then sat beside her.

"Penny, this isn't a forever situation. Leo will come to his senses soon." He hated to tell her something that might not be true, but wasn't it his role as her friend, to give her hope?

Johnny pulled another tissue from the box and wiped Penny's tears from her face.

"I'm not so sure. Maybe with the medication in his bloodstream, he's acting like he's wanted to ever since Adriana came to town." In the back of Johnny's mind, he suspected the same thing, but he would never share that with Penny. He had grown to care deeply for her, and that meant working harder to keep from doing anything that would force her and Leo apart. He had been wrong to hold Penny in his arms in Leo's hospital room. He would be more professional in the future, if they ever had a chance to work together again.

CHAPTER 77

Leo spent two more weeks in the hospital. He had been weaned off the haloperidol before he was dismissed, but to Penny, Leo still seemed off his game. When Penny visited him at home, he kept looking around like he was expecting someone else. When she tried to sit down and talk to him, he would jump up and pace around the living room. That Leo was distracted was an understatement. He was restless and irritable, and Penny wondered if the meds had caused permanent damage to his mind.

Penny was impatient, and she felt like she had no role to play in his recovery. Once, when she was leaving the house, Penny saw Adriana pull into the driveway. Penny jumped in her car and roared down the road. What good would it do to upset Leo any more than he already was?

Eventually, Penny gave up visiting Leo and went back to work, trying to locate fugitives for the US Marshals Service. Marshal Lujan was still off duty, but he had filled in Deputy Miguel Lara about Penny's capabilities. She was happy to pick up where she had left off because it kept her mind off the hopeless situation with Leo, and it did her heart good to be productive again.

Penny was grateful she had not received any assignments that had taken her back to Columbus. The thought of returning there right now was too painful. But she did get a tremendous rush when the ATF arrested Sheriff Pritchard. His mug shot left something to be desired in the Deming paper. His lockup in the very jail he ran so fiercely gave the locals enough gossip to last the rest of the year.

Penny began to find the tranquility she needed by visiting Johnny's mother, Ollie, and eating heaping plates of her chiles rellenos or chicken enchiladas. Mexican cooking was soul food to Penny, and she couldn't get enough of it, it seemed. Penny even enjoyed hearing about Ollie's sewing projects as they shared a bottle of homemade pear wine.

Two months had passed since Penny had been rescued from Martín Romero's ranch, and fall was closing in on the desert. This meant that the Trejo's front porch became the chosen place of evening refuge. When the air was still and the stars lit the home stage, Johnny would bring over his guitar and sing an old Mexican ballad or two. Penny didn't understand many of the words, but the music soothed a wretched part of her spirit that was full of disharmony.

Those simple nights, sometimes peppered with rain and an occasional shooting star, provided Penny with a chance to forget—at least for a few hours—that she had lost someone she loved to a strange twist of the mind. Maybe Leo would remember his love for her or maybe he would not. Thankfully, Johnny and his mother were helping to fill that big hole in her heart.

www.ingramcontent.com/pod-product-compliance
Lightning Source LLC
LaVergne TN
LVHW091714070526
838199LV00050B/2387